ALSO BY PETE DEXTER

God's Pocket

Deadwood

Paris Trout

BROTHERLY LOVE

BROTHERLY LOVE

LOVE

Pete Dexter

Random House New York

Copyright © 1991 by Pete Dexter
All rights reserved under International and Pan-American Copyright
Conventions.
Published in the United States by Random House, Inc., New York, and
simultaneously in Canada by Random House of Canada Limited, Toronto.
A signed first edition of this book has been
privately printed by The Franklin Library.
Library of Congress Cataloging-in-Publication Data
Dexter, Pete
Brotherly love/Peter Dexter.—1st ed.
p.   cm.
ISBN 0-394-58573-9
I. Title.
PS3554.E95B76   1991
813′.54—dc20   91-52666

Manufactured in the United States of America
2 3 4 5 6 7 8 9

First Trade Edition

BOOK DESIGN BY LILLY LANGOTSKY

For

Dian and Casey

June 11, 1986

UNION BROTHERS "HIT" 100 MILES APART

BY WALLACE T. BROOKS

STAFF WRITER

Three men, including Southeastern Pennsylvania Trade Union Council President Michael Flood and his brother, Peter, were found shot to death yesterday in what police sources have described as a "mob hit".

Michael Flood, 32, and Leonard Crawley, 29, of Upper Darby, were discovered in the basement of a South Philadelphia row house belonging to William O'Connor, a retired member of the Roofer's Union. Both men had been shot at close range with a shotgun.

Earlier in the day, Peter Flood, 33, was found 100 miles away, in the back yard of his vacation home in Cape May, N.J. He was listed as an officer of the Trade Union Council.

The killings, according to police sources, signal a new chapter in Philadelphia's crime wars, although the exact nature of the dispute—believed to concern control of lucrative union pension funds—is not clear at this time.

Police have no suspects in the killing.

According to police, O'Connor, 77, suffers from Alzheimer's disease and has no memory of the shootings. He was questioned and released.

"It's probably the reason they didn't [shoot] him too," said the police source.

Michael Flood's father—Phillip—like his son, president of the Trade Union Council, was killed 16 years ago when a bomb rigged to his front door went off as he entered his South Philadelphia home.

No arrests were ever made in the killing.

PART ONE

1961

Peter Flood is eight years old, dressed in tennis shoes and a jacket that is too light against the cold and the wind. He dresses himself now; his mother is always tired.

A thin crust of snow lies across the yard, and his sister's fresh footprints lead from the front steps to the spot where she is standing, studying her mitten. Here and there the grass has broken through, and he notices the patches of damp, bent blades—tired, he thinks, from fighting through to the air. And he understands that, not wanting to be covered.

His sister moves, pulling his attention. She squats on chubby legs, rocking a moment for balance, and then slowly brings the snow to her face, her mouth opening a long time before the mitten arrives.

She pulls her hand away, staring at it. Snow sticks to the mitten and it drools down her chin. She looks up at him, her lips are wet and red, and she smiles. He sees dirt in her tiny front teeth, and in a moment it is on her chin too, and then it drips onto the front of her parka.

"Col," she says.

She watches him until he returns her smile, waits for it like a signal, and then, when he has given that to her, she closes the mitten around a stone and brings that to her mouth too.

There is a park across the street; he is not allowed to go there without his father. He has watched other children playing alone in the park—there are some there now—but he understands, without being told, that his life is not like theirs, that he is someone who has to stay in the yard.

He notices a man now, sitting on his heels, boxing with a boy who can barely walk.

His sister stands up, rocking as she achieves balance, and then takes a few steps away from him, in the direction of the street. She looks over her shoulder, teasing him, knowing he will chase her now and catch her before she is out of the yard, and carry her back to the steps.

Her head turns and she begins to run.

He crosses the yard in a few strides, his tennis shoes breaking holes in the snow. She shrieks as she hears him behind her, and ducks her head into her shoulders, waiting for the feel of his hand on her hood.

And then he touches it, careful not to take any of the hair underneath, and stops her. He puts his arm around her waist and lifts her off the ground, and feels the sudden change in her as he carries her back to the steps.

She screams at him, "No!"

And he feels the heels of her rubber boots kicking against his legs, and understands that in this moment she would kill him if she could.

And then a moment later, back on her feet in the snow, she smiles at him again and tries to say his name.

"Peener."

He sees the dog mess then—that's what his mother calls it, *dog mess,* but he knows the real word—lying in a smoking pile as big as the animal's head on the other side of the driveway. There is no snow on the dog mess, and it glistens in the sun.

Peter feels a familiar tightening in his legs and looks across the street into the park again, listening for the sound of tags on a collar. He is afraid of dogs, especially this dog, but he keeps it hidden. Somehow he is expected not to be afraid of dogs, just as he is expected to stay in the yard.

There is nothing as clear to him as what he is expected to be.

The dog itself is white and has red eyes, crusted black in the corners, and when it looks at Peter, everything inside the animal is in those eyes, all of it held back by a single thread, something he has been taught. And the boy can feel the dog straining against the thread, and knows that nothing the animal has been taught will change what it is.

The man who owns the dog lives in the house next door. The place smells of garlic, even from the sidewalk, and there is always polka music coming from inside. Peter sees the man pounding the animal's chest sometimes, and pulling its ears and throwing balls across the street into the park for it to retrieve. Sometimes he invites Peter to touch the dog himself—"C'mon, Paulie, he don't bite nobody but crooks. He's trained. . . ."

The man calls him Paulie, sometimes Phil. He remembers his father's name, though.

Mr. Flood.

And Peter will walk across the driveway and touch the animal's head, his fingers in the matted coat, while everything inside the dog is in his eyes, held back by the thread, something he learned from this man who cannot remember his name.

"See? He don't bite, he likes you. . . ."

Peter looks up the street now, looks for the man's car. The sound of it will draw the dog from the alleys of the neighborhood, from the hidden places behind the house and the yard where Peter lives. It is a red car with black tires—not whitewalls, he gets his tires from the police garage—and a top that comes down in the summer. An antenna is fastened to the trunk.

He looks for the car, but it isn't there.

His sister falls suddenly, for no reason he can see, and lands on her bottom. There are diapers under her snow pants. She looks at him a moment, waiting to see if she is hurt, and decides she is not.

"Boom," she says.

She stands up, her hands flat against the ground as she straightens her legs. The snow has stuck to her bottom and the spit on her chin has turned the color of mud.

And then he hears the car, distinctly hears it, coming faster than it should and from the wrong direction. As he turns toward the sound, his sister bolts—a hundred disjointed movements collected in a white bundle and headed for the street. He hears her shriek even before he moves to reel her in.

And as he moves, he sees the dog. It has heard the sound of the car too, and comes from behind the man's house, tail and chin in the air, half running. The dog spots Peter and stops, lowering its head until Peter can see the bones of its shoulders.

Peter stops too, unable to move. The animal's lips pull back, almost a smile, and it fixes its eyes on the boy and forgets the car and the man and everything else. It only bites crooks, the man says, but there is a secret between Peter and the dog the man does not know.

He sees his sister now, a movement somewhere beyond the dog, crossing the yard toward the street. She squeals, sensing that she's gotten away. He tries to go after her, but the dog is waiting for him now, waiting for him to move so that it can move too.

He tries, but he cannot make his feet do what they will not do. He hears the car again, closer, moving too fast. It crosses his line of vision still in the street, hits ice and skids into Peter's yard.

His sister has slowed, is turning to see if he is chasing her, to ask why she has won the game. And she is looking back at him, drooling dirt and smiling, when the car picks her up and throws her into the sky.

He watches her ride through the air, rolling once as she comes to him, a splash of red on her white parka now, her feet apart and disconnected like one of her dolls. Her eyes are open, looking someplace he cannot see.

Watch your sister, he thinks.

The car skids across the lawn, the bumper hitting the single, small tree in the front yard, tearing it out of the ground. The dog moves a step closer and waits.

She lands at his feet; her eyes are still open, looking beyond him a thousand miles. One of her arms is folded behind her back, hiding the hand. Her other hand lies palm up, an inch or two off the ground, held there by the padding in her coat. A mitten is in the street.

The boy stands still, understanding that something has happened, not knowing yet what it means, and then the dog is coming across the yard after him, head close to the ground. The boy begins to run, but then stops, before he has even moved, and turns to face the animal, and for a moment everything in the yard is calm and slow. He sees the man's face as he opens the car door, he sees the muscles in the dog's chest, the bits of snow its feet throw up behind as it comes across the yard. He thinks perhaps his sister saw things in this slow, calm way as she sailed to him through the air.

The dog closes and the boy holds the ground over his sister, knowing exactly how the fur and the weight will feel on his face, knowing he cannot leave this spot. He closes his hands into fists and waits.

The car door is open now, the man has one foot outside. His face behind the windshield is terrified, and Peter sees his expression and is terrified too. The man yells something he cannot understand, and a moment later the dog is there, growling from that place inside his chest where nothing the man has said or taught means anything. Where it is only the dog.

He steels himself and closes his eyes.

Nothing.

The growling changes pitch, nothing else.

And then Peter opens his eyes, and his sister is in the animal's mouth. It is holding her at the shoulder and neck, shaking her side to side. It lifts her off the ground and then drops her; it finds a new hold, one of her legs, and lifts her again, shaking her and tearing her snow pants.

He throws himself into the animal the way he throws himself into the waves at Atlantic City. He closes his eyes and dives, reaching for whatever is beyond the fall. He lands on the animal's back and feels the bones under the coat, then slides slowly down to the legs. He presses his cheeks into the legs as they jerk, holding them as if they were his sister herself.

The man is out of the car, running across the snow. Peter sees him or feels him coming—he isn't sure which—putting his hand inside his coat. He slips and falls to one knee, screaming at the dog, and Peter knows that the dog hears him, he feels the animal change.

"Oh, Jesus," the man says, right over him now.

He hears the sound as the man beats the top of the dog's head with the butt of his gun. With the third sound, the dog drops the boy's sister and cries out.

7

"Fucking God," the man says, and drops over the little girl in a posture that seems to resemble the dog's.

Peter sits up and rubs his cheek. He is scratched and bleeding. The man begins to rock now, back and forth over his sister, saying the same thing over and over. "Oh, fucking God. . . ."

The dog walks back into the other yard and lies down, watching the man, its chin flat against the ground between its paws.

The man stands up with Peter's sister in his arms and hurries to the front door, pounding on it with the flat of his hand, looking back over his shoulder at him once as he waits for an answer.

Peter's mother comes to the door holding the top of her robe together with one hand. She sees the man first, then what is in his arms. Slowly, her hand comes off the robe and goes to her mouth. Her robe falls open and Peter sees her breasts.

The man takes Peter's sister inside, leaving the front door open. Peter stands up, his legs shaking, and moves halfway up the steps.

The man puts his sister on the davenport and opens her parka. His mother is crying now, he hears her but can't see her from the steps. The man picks up the telephone on the glass coffee table in front of the davenport and dials a number.

"Tommy," he says, "I need an ambulance right now . . . my place . . . yes, goddamnit, an ambulance, there's a fuckin' kid ain't breathing. . . ."

He hangs up and then, perhaps hearing the words himself, he looks for a long minute out the door, right into Peter's eyes.

The man puts the phone against his ear again and dials another number. His fingers are shaking.

Peter's mother comes back into his line of sight. She stops at the davenport, looking down at the motionless child, and then touches her, straightening one of the legs.

She looks at her own hand and it is bloody.

The man holds his forehead while he waits for someone to answer the phone, trying to hold himself still. He looks again at Peter, then turns away to speak.

"Sally," he says, sounding relieved, "it looks like I got a problem here at Charley Flood's."

Charley Flood is the boy's father, although the boy has never heard this man use his first name before.

"There was an accident in front of his house, his little girl . . . yeah . . . I don't know. The car slid and there she was. . . ."

The boy looks back into the yard where the car is still sitting with its door open.

"No," the man says, "it's worst than that."

There is a long pause while the man listens. "I appreciate that," the man says finally. "If you could come over and wait for him, make sure he don't do nothing premeditated . . ."

The man nods into the telephone. He stops for a moment and looks behind him at the davenport.

"Look," he says, "he ain't going to like this at all."

Peter looks at the davenport too, and thinks of his father, who is unhappy for reasons he glimpses in the silences at the dinner table, when they are all forced to sit together in one place. Before dinner and after, he lives in this house without seeing Peter, or his mother. He only notices the little girl.

Except sometimes in the park. In the park, he is changed, and turns to Peter sometimes, inviting him to share her.

Ain't she something?

And in this way, Peter knows, the little girl is the connection between them.

He wishes suddenly that he were lying there with her, that he had been hit by the car too. He understands that the blood on his cheek is not enough to save him, that he hasn't been hurt badly enough to be forgiven.

The man hangs up the telephone, and then turns back to Peter, walking toward him as if he were angry. He stands still, aware of the trembling in his legs. The man comes through the door and down the steps, hurrying, as if something outside could still be saved. He reaches into his coat as he passes, and then his hand drops behind his back as he walks away, hiding the gun.

The man crosses the yard to the dog. Peter sees the animal's head come up, the tongue falls out of its mouth.

There is only one sound from the dog, so close behind the shot that it's hard to separate one from the other. And then there is another shot, and another, and another.

The man shoots the dog until there are no more bullets in his gun. The air smells of gunpowder, the shots echo back from the houses on the other side of the park.

Between the shots, he hears his mother crying in the house.

He stands on the steps, watching himself from another place, lost in this moment that collects and shapes the small pieces of his life.

Lost in the surprise of who he is.

Late at night, Peter hears his father in the driveway. He knows the sound of the car, the sounds of all the cars that belong on this street.

He is sitting at the top of the stairs, his face pressed into the banister railings. There are other men in the house now, men who work with his father and have been here before. They have been coming and going all day. His uncle is sitting at the dining room table with his mother, his arm all the way around her back, his thin fingers, patched with hair, cup her far shoulder and pull her into him.

Comforting is unnatural to his uncle, but something holds him in this awkward place. He has seen his father held in this same way at funerals; he has seen him disappear into words and manners that were not his.

He thinks of the thread that held the dog next door.

His father opens the door, takes a step into the living room and stops. No one in the room speaks, no one is willing to meet his eyes.

His mother covers her face.

"What is it?" he says.

The room is quiet, and then the one named Sally pushes himself off the davenport and touches his father's arm.

"Come sit down," he says.

His father stays where he is, looking around the room now, as if finding the secret in this place can change it. "Charley," the man says, and tugs at his sleeve, a child's gesture. Peter's father follows him to the dining room table, where they both sit down. The man puts a small glass in front of him and fills it until it spills over the lip.

"Drink this, and then we talk," he says.

His father drinks what is in the glass, taking it all at once, and then returns the glass to the same spot, fitting it into the half circle it left on the table when he picked it up.

His mother is crying into her hands; she cannot lift her eyes to look across the table, and he understands that, understands the weight.

"It's the baby," the man says softly.

From the staircase, he watches his father. Nothing seems to change. He stays exactly where he is, staring across the table. His pulse is in his temple, one of his hands is still wrapped around the small glass.

"She got hit with a car," the man says.

Hearing this, his mother begins crying out loud. His father does not move. "It wasn't nobody's fault," the man says. "The guy hits some ice and he slid . . ."

A tear appears suddenly in the corner of his father's eye and runs the length of his face, dropping straight and fast, like sweat on a glass.

"What guy?" he says.

One of the men in the living room walks to the dining room table and stands quietly beside the one who is talking.

"Victor Kopec," says the one named Sally.

The boy's father moves then, turning slowly to look at the man who has said the name.

The man nods. "He slid into the yard . . ." He rubs the back of his neck, looking for the words to say the rest. "He hit her clean, Charley. She didn't feel a thing. Afterwards, his dog, you know, they get excited, but it didn't make no difference by then. You can ask the doctors. It wasn't the dog, it was the car."

His father stands up and the man steps in front of him and shakes his head no.

"Ask your brother if what I'm saying ain't true."

His father tries to step around the man, but the man moves in front, stopping him. His uncle's arm moves in a slow arc over Peter's mother; he pulls a cigarette from his shirt pocket. His face is pale in the kitchen light, and the pockmarks deepen at the movement, throwing a shadow across his face.

"Charley," he says, "it was his fault, he'd be dead. I've got a kid, I'd done it myself. . . ."

Peter's father doesn't seem to hear him. He puts his hands on the shoulders of the man in front of him, almost gently, and moves him out of the way. The other man—the one who walked in from the living room—grabs him from behind, hugging him around the waist.

The man holds him, then they are all holding him. Peter's uncle has the feet. His father turns left and right, kicking, and his strength moves the huddle of men back and forth across the room.

And all the time, the man named Sally is talking. "You can't kill him, Charley," he says. "Constantine don't want him hurt."

A chair turns over, a lamp falls from a table. The boy hears his father hissing through his teeth as he fights. All the other noises in the room are soft. The boy pictures a neighbor walking past the house on the sidewalk, pausing for a moment to look at the lighted windows, and then walking on.

"Listen to me, Charley," the man says.

His father stops struggling and hangs for a moment in the center of the red-faced men holding him, hangs as if he were in his hammock in the back yard.

"Listen to me," the man says. "Listen to what I'm telling you. She didn't feel a thing."

And in that moment, hanging helpless, his father turns his head, as if to remove himself from the one who is talking, and in doing that his eyes move to the corner of the room, and are somehow drawn to the staircase where Peter is sitting with his face pressed into the banister.

"I want your word," the man says. "I can tell Constantine they ain't nothing to worry about here now."

Behind the men, Peter's mother is crying.

"Later you want to do something, you can talk to Constantine yourself, right?"

His father doesn't answer and his eyes stay fastened to the staircase.

"All right?" the man says. "Lookit, you got things to take care of right here anyway . . . Charley?"

His father rolls his head then, slowly, and looks at the man who is talking, and in a movement so small Peter is not sure he sees it, his father nods. His uncle drops his father's feet and the ones holding his waist and arms set him upright and then step back, wary.

The men flex their arms and necks, some of them out of breath. His father's shirt is ripped along two lines that follow the muscles in his back.

The one named Sally waits a moment and then kisses his father on the cheek and walks out the door. The other men follow him, each of them making some gesture. His uncle is last out of the house.

"I would of killed him myself, Charley," he says.

Peter's father does not answer. He waits until the uncle is gone, then closes the door. He walks up the staircase slowly and pauses for a moment in front of Peter, studying him as if he cannot remember who he is. Then, absently, he reaches out, touches his hair, and walks past him toward the end of the hall.

He stops before he gets to the end, though, and stares into the pale light of her room, as if memorizing what is inside—a place full of stuffed animals—and then he closes the door.

Certain things come to him without his knowing how. He sees the fragile looks between his mother and father, and understands that in those gestures there is a certain panic.

It is as if they were tied head to foot with ropes, unable to move an inch, struggling one moment, giving in the next. And they cannot touch each other at all.

And they cannot touch him.

That is what he wants now, to be touched.

The things he knows settle on him with a certainty that precludes mistakes or misunderstanding; he knows them as well as the room where he sleeps or his own face in the mirror.

He walks into the living room and finds his father sitting in a chair by the window, staring across the front yard, and knows that there is nothing he can say that his father will hear.

His father sees him, then looks back out the window, silent. He was silent before the accident, too, but it was a natural part of the rooms of the house then; now it is unnatural, and the rooms are unnatural too.

His mother comes downstairs only to cook and to eat.

He sits down on the floor next to his father, wanting him to touch his hair again. He thinks of the night the men held him while the one named Sally talked. He wishes he had thrown himself into them, dived on them from the top of the stairs. He judges the distance now, imagining his path through the living room air and the stillness in his chest as he falls, the spot he would land.

He imagines himself broken and still on the floor, and something in that stirs him. He wonders if they would lay him on the davenport too.

He looks quickly at his father's face, then follows his line of sight out into the yard. The tire marks are still in the snow— trampled and dirty and stained with dog urine, but unmistakably there, leading across the sidewalk from the street, up a small rise and stopping at the spot of bare earth where the only tree in the yard was uprooted.

The boy follows the tracks the other way, back out to the street. There is a car there, four doors and green, with a man sitting behind the wheel, eating. A steady white smoke comes from the exhaust pipe. The boy knows this is a policeman too, like the man next door. He is there because the man next door is afraid of his father.

When his father finally goes into the house next door, though, this policeman in the car will not stop him. Peter knows that when his father goes into the house next door, no one will be able to stop him.

He looks at his father again and thinks of the men who held him that night, how he fought all of them back and forth across the room. He thinks of his uncle, struggling with the feet, and the bigger men, stumbling with each turn of his father's body.

He wishes he could have that night again and throw himself into them from the top of the stairs.

In the breaking of his own bones he could mend what had happened.

Peter's uncle comes to the house in the afternoon, smelling of liquor. Uncle Phil. He is smaller than the boy's father, and older, and smiles when there is no reason to smile. His mother is repulsed by his uncle; he has heard her whisper it in the kitchen, "I *skeeves* him, Charley."

She is Italian.

Peter answers the door eating cereal out of a box. His uncle sways in the doorway, looking inside. "Your dad here?" he says.

Peter opens the door wider and steps out of the way. When his uncle is far enough in, he closes the door and walks upstairs, down the long hall to the room where his parents sleep. He knocks quietly at the door, and then hears his father's voice on the other side.

"What?"

His mother spends all day in this room now, with the lights off and the shades drawn. Peter does not want to say the uncle's name out loud and instead opens the door a few inches and puts his head inside.

The room is dark and still. He smells his mother's skin. She is lying in bed with her head against the pillow, her neck bent until her chin almost touches her chest, staring at her hands, or perhaps her feet. Something in front of her. His father is sitting in a straight chair beside the shaded window which overlooks the house of Victor Kopec. He turns from the window, still holding the shade slightly away from the glass, and studies the boy a moment.

He slowly stands up and comes to the door.

His mother doesn't move, her eyes do not follow the motion in the room. His father steps into the hallway and closes the door.

"Uncle Phil's here."

His father nods and starts down the hall. Peter follows him a few steps but then his father stops, turning to look at him again, and shakes his head.

Peter walks into his room and listens to his father on the stairs. His steps are heavier than they were before the accident, and slower. Sometimes he hears them and thinks a stranger has come into the house.

"Charley," his uncle says.

His father says nothing that he can hear.

"I come by to see if there was anything I could do."

"No," his father says, "there ain't nothing you can do."

"You mind if I sit down?" He hears the uncle move across the floor. "You got a beer or something?"

His father walks into the kitchen, slow and heavy. The icebox opens and shuts. "You don't mind my saying so," his uncle says, raising his voice now so that it will carry into the kitchen, "it wouldn't hurt nothing, you had one yourself. It wouldn't hurt you had a beer and put this away."

The uncle says this while his father is still out of the room; Peter doesn't think he would say it if his father were there.

His father comes back and his uncle says, "What? Are you gonna give me a fuckin' beer or hit me over the head?"

His father says a few words; the boy can't make them out.

"That don't do nobody any good," his uncle says.

"You're comin' in here, telling me what I'm gonna do?" his father says. The boy pictures his father now, standing over his uncle, watching him as if the wrong answer to that question could be anywhere in his face.

16

"I'm telling you what you ain't going to do," his uncle says. "Now gimme the fuckin' beer or brain me and put me out of my misery."

It is quiet in the house for a few moments; the boy pictures his uncle drinking the beer. He pictures his mother lying in her bed, her eyes wide open. Nothing moves. It seems to him that she has lived in two places a long time, here in this house and somewhere else, and that since the accident she cannot stand to be here at all. She comes back only to eat.

"I talked to Constantine myself," his uncle says. "He thinks maybe you take little Pete and your wife up into the Poconos a while, stay at his place up there if you want. . . ."

"I ain't going to the Poconos," his father says.

"The shore then," his uncle says. "Constantine don't care where you go, except he don't want you going next door . . ."

The living room is quiet again.

"He's helpin' them on some things, Charley, and Constantine don't want him hurt."

"There's a lot of cops helpin' them on things," his father says. "How come this one's got to move in next door, into a house a cop can't afford, drive up and down the street in his big convertible like some center-city pimp . . ."

"He ain't so bad."

"I'll tell you what he is. He's one of them guys it ain't enough he's got more than he's supposed to, it ain't no good to him unless everybody knows he's got it. And that ain't enough either so he drives into my yard and takes what I got, him and that fuckin' dog, and now he's pissed his pants and cryin' to both sides for help."

"He shot the dog," his uncle says. "He done that out of respect."

"Is that what he said? What are we, fuckin' Italians—'Out of respect'?"

"It was a gesture."

Peter sits down on the floor of his room, his back against the door, and remembers the look in his sister's eyes as she came to him through the air.

"Charley," his uncle says, "the man skid. I got a child too. If it was something else, I'd of taken care of it myself, right there that afternoon. . . ."

His father doesn't answer.

"Charley? You listening to me here?"

He hears the icebox door open and shut, his uncle getting himself another beer.

"I would of got a bat and beat the eyes out of his head," his uncle says, back in the living room. "Family is first with me, and Angela's my niece. She's like my own daughter. . . ."

A moment later, he hears the front door open. "The long and short of it, Charley," his uncle says before he goes outside, "Constantine don't want this guy touched right now. There ain't nothing you can do about what happened, and there ain't nothing you can do about the cop."

"First they're in our business, now they're in my house," his father says, speaking of the Italians. The boy has heard them talk about the Italians before.

The front door closes and a moment later his father is on the staircase. He climbs to the top and then walks to the door outside Peter's room. He stops a moment, his shoes close enough to block out the light, and then walks the rest of the way to the end of the hall without stopping, past the room full of stuffed animals, and into the room beyond that, where the boy's mother lies in the dark.

Where he will pull back the shade and watch the house next door from the window.

Peter Flood returns to his school.

Just as before, he is taken in the morning by his father, and just as before, a man who works for his father is waiting in front of the school at the end of the day to take him home. The man does not speak to him on the ride home and the boy understands he does not like this job.

And each day when he comes home, the rooms of the house are filled with the accident. The place seems even quieter now, coming in from the movement and noise of the school, than it had in the long weeks he spent inside afterwards, overseeing the motionless panic of the only two people he loved.

Visitors come into the house at night. Often it is only his uncle, but sometimes he brings some of the men who held his father that first night, and kept him from going next door.

His father accepts his guests, standing to the side as they come in, not offering them a chair or a beer, simply allowing them to take what they want. The presence of the guests makes no difference to him at all.

Peter sits in his room or at the top of the stairs, listening to the men talk. They complain that the Italians are trying to take more of the money than before.

His father rarely speaks—he no longer cares who gets the union's money—and his mother's room now is as still as his sister's.

His uncle has his opinions about the Italians, though. He says they will get one more cent out of the union than they get now over his dead body.

On a Friday night, Constantine himself comes to visit.

Peter has heard the way the man's name is spoken by his father's visitors, and he is surprised now at his appearance. A gray-haired old man in a black coat and glasses fogged from the cold, he stands in the center of the room, holding his hat, not moving from the spot until he is offered a place to sit.

"Sit down," his father says, and Peter hears something in his voice that is not there for the others.

The old man unbuttons his coat and one of the men who has come here with him lifts it off his shoulders. He takes a wooden chair near the dining room. He crosses his legs carefully and removes his glasses, wiping them clear with his handkerchief.

"How are you doing with your tragedy, Charley?" the old man says.

His father shrugs and looks around the room. The old man fits the glasses back on his nose.

"Who can say?" his father says.

The old man nods, as if that is an answer. He is soft and slow, and the boy cannot imagine that he can tell them all what to do.

"That's what I heard," Constantine says in a sad way, and then he falls silent.

The boy's father stands in front of the old man, wordless.

"What I heard," he says suddenly, "you ain't let it cool down enough yet that you can see it's an accident."

His father shakes his head.

The old man smiles in a kind way. "What, you think he did it on purpose? He drove up in your yard and hit the little girl on purpose? It was an accident. . . ."

"The word don't mean nothing," his father says, and his voice is hard and clear and stronger than the old man's. His voice makes Peter afraid.

The old man holds up his hand. "You know this guy, Charley?"

He shrugs. "I lived next to him two, three years," he says.

The old man closes his eyes. "You and me, we ain't so different from everybody else," he says. "We have accidents too."

His father turns away and stares at the man holding Constantine's coat.

The old man seems to weigh that gesture. "Charley," he says finally, "do me a favor."

His father turns around to face him again, and one of the other men in the room looks quickly at Peter's uncle, and there is something between them, something they both know and his father does not. The old man sits patiently in his chair, looking at this Irish Charley Flood, waiting for an answer.

"Tell me what it is."

Another look passes between his uncle and the man standing nearest his father. Peter understands that his father has said something just now that his uncle, for all his talk about fighting the Italians, would never say.

The old man doesn't seem to notice. "A simple favor," he says, and waits.

His father shrugs. "I'll do what I can."

The old man brings the fingers of his two hands together and lets them touch. "I want to bring this guy over here," he says, looking at the fingers. "Let him tell you he's sorry."

His father begins to shake his head; the old man holds up his hand. "I want you to see this guy, Charley, let him explain what happened."

His father stands completely still.

The old man closes his eyes. "I want to bring him over, you can see him for yourself."

"He don't belong in this house," his father says.

Something in that makes the old man smile. "He's helped us out a few times, Charley," he says.

His father doesn't answer.

"And now he says to me, Constantine, I need a favor too. I got to talk to Charley, set this straight. He says Constantine, I can't live next door to this crazy Irish bastard, he's thinkin' these things about me."

His father looks away from the old man, out the window and then at the men standing in back of him. He looks at Peter's uncle.

"I ain't having him in my house," he says.

The old man studies his fingers and nods, and when he speaks again the kindness has gone out of his tone. "Yeah, you are," he says. "He's gonna come in here, say he's sorry, and that's the end of it."

He looks up at Peter's father, his eyes angry and wet behind the glasses. "You heard what I said? That's the end of it."

His father crosses his arms and stares at the old man.

"It ain't just for him," the old man says. "Something like this, you got to put it away or it affects you." His finger makes a circular motion in the air near his ear. "The first thing you know, you're loco."

His father begins to say something more, but the old man interrupts him. "You been grieving long enough," he says. "It ain't doing nobody any good."

The old man nods at the man who is holding his coat, and that man walks out the front door and is back in half a minute with Victor Kopec.

Victor Kopec is wearing a dark, expensive suit, and he blows on his hands as he walks into the room and rubs them against his face. Peter wonders how long he has been waiting out there, for Constantine to tell his father that he wanted him to come in.

Victor Kopec looks around the room, smiles at the boy sitting at the top of the stairs. "My man," he says.

Peter pushes himself away from the railing, crablike, using the heels of his hands and feet, until he is out of the line of sight. He flattens his cheek against the wall, and listens to himself breathe.

"Mr. Flood," the man says.

There is a long silence, and then the sound of Constantine's voice. "Charley," he says, "it can't hurt nothing to look at the man when he's talking to you."

Peter edges his face around the corner until he can see the living room again. His father is still standing in front of Constantine, and as the boy watches, he turns and puts a murderous, black look on Victor Kopec, daring him to speak.

Victor Kopec is not afraid, though; the old man makes him safe. "Mr. Flood, I want to thank you for allowing me to express my sympathy for what happened," he says.

Peter hears how easily the words come out of Victor Kopec's mouth; he hears the insult.

His father takes a small step closer and Victor Kopec takes a small step back. There are some things that having Constantine in the living room does not change.

"I wanted to tell you what happened was I hit some ice in the street out there, and the car gets sideways where I can't steer it, and the next thing you know I'm in the middle of this. And then the dog, the crazy bastard's got these instincts . . ."

The man's confidence grows as he speaks, as if he cannot see the way Peter's father is looking at him.

"I shot him right there in the driveway," Victor Kopec says. "I had him seven years, since I left K-9. I eat with him, watch television with him, sleep with him. So what I'm saying, I lost something here too. . . ."

His father stares at the cop until he runs out of words, and then, when the room is quiet again, he turns back to Constantine. "Is that it?" he says.

Constantine looks from his father to Victor Kopec, perhaps measuring the distance between them. Victor Kopec shrugs, comfortable, as if the men in the room will be with him forever.

"Is that it?" his father says again.

The old man shakes his head. "That's what I was gonna ask you," he says.

His father turns and considers Victor Kopec. Without another word, he reaches across the space between them and takes the policeman's hand. Victor Kopec is startled at first, and then seems to relax.

"My sincere condolences," he says.

His father shakes the hand and nods.

"Now it's over," the old man says.

His father looks into Victor Kopec's eyes.

"Something happens, you got to either forgive somebody or kill them, it makes you loco the thing ain't settled," the old man says.

The room is quiet again while the words themselves settle.

"Charley?" the old man says.

"Everything's settled," he says, still looking at Victor Kopec.

Constantine takes off his glasses and wipes the corners of his eyes, as if he has been crying. "That's good," he says, the handkerchief still in his eye. "Victor helped us out a lot of times, and this way, we're all friends and he ain't dead, he can help us out some more."

Victor Kopec begins to nod, but in that same moment Peter sees him reconsider, as if he realizes something has changed between himself and the men in this room. That he has been threatened.

Victor Kopec smiles now, no longer sure of himself, no longer so comfortable.

"Constantine," he says, "my sincere appreciation for working this out between us."

The old man stirs in his chair and pushes himself slowly to his feet and smiles. "You're neighbors," he says.

Then one of the men places the coat over his shoulders, centering it carefully, and another opens the door. On the way out, the old man suddenly stops and looks up the staircase, directly into Peter's eyes.

He holds on to the banister, frozen. The old man lifts his hand, his thumb comes up, turning it into a gun, and pretends to fire a shot.

The men leave, the front door shuts, the house is suddenly quiet. Peter's father stands at the door a moment and then walks into the kitchen.

Peter himself sits on the stairs, thinking of the pistol the old man had made of his hand. Of his crooked fingers that could not point up the stairs.

He is thinking of the moment the old man pretended to shoot when a noise comes from the kitchen, almost a shot itself. He waits, and in the quiet that swallows the house afterwards, he suddenly moves, surprised to find himself moving, running down the stairs, crossing the living room, slowing now as he gets closer, and finally walking, a step at a time, into the kitchen.

He sees the blood first, it spots his father's shirt and his pants and falls in heavy drops on the floor around his shoes. His father is leaning into the icebox with both hands, as if he were holding it up, and then Peter sees the spot between his hands where he has smashed it with his head. The smooth line of the door is dented, as if someone had dropped it off the truck.

His father turns to him, his eyes are black and his face is running with blood—the cut is in his hairline—and for one long moment Peter feels himself in the same place with him, feels himself in the center of the place, in the center of his father's thoughts.

And then it passes.

The blood runs out of his father and the look in his eyes turns dull, and he is seeing something else.

"Go to bed," he says.

I n the morning, an ambulance comes for his mother. It is not as surprising to hear the noise in the hallway, or—after he has climbed out of bed—to see the men carrying her down the stairs, as it is simply to confront her appearance. She is a ghost. Her face, framed in a pillow at the top of the stretcher, is as thin as the bones underneath it, and she is the color of bones too.

When did she become a ghost?

He stands in his pajamas and watches the men turn the corner at the landing with his mother between them, stepping carefully, the man in front going backwards, feeling for the step behind him with his feet.

His father is at the bottom of the stairs, waiting. There is dried blood in his hair and in his eyebrows, and his eyes are as dull as they had been in the kitchen.

His father opens the door for the men when they are off the stairs, and then follows them outside to the ambulance.

Peter walks down and stands in the doorway, the cold wind coming up his pajama legs. The men load his mother into the back. He steps into the yard.

The neighbors are at their windows now, one or two are standing on their porches in housecoats. They do not leave their homes, though. A dozen times he has seen these same neighbors gather in each others' yards, sometimes in bathrobes, touching those who are crying on the shoulder, at the same time seeing for themselves if the person on the stretcher is dead. But no one comes to the driveway to touch his father now.

Doors close and the ambulance is sealed. Its lights go on but there is no siren. His father waits on the street until it is out of sight. Then he turns the other direction, staring at the house of Victor Kopec. He stares as if there were something to see, but Peter looks at the house too and there is no light, no sign of movement inside. Shades are drawn in every window.

His father walks back to the house, crossing the car tracks that still divide the yard in half, and stops for a moment when he sees Peter standing in the cold, wet grass in his bare feet and pajamas.

"Get inside," he says quietly.

Peter turns, without a word, and walks into the house. He feels his father close behind him, behind him and above, floating.

"Is she sick?" he says after his father has closed the door. His feet hurt and he is shaking in the sudden warmth of the room.

His father begins one direction, then changes his mind. He sits on the davenport and puts his elbows on his knees and bends forward to run his fingers through his hair. Tiny bits of dried blood sift onto the coffee table in front of him.

"What happened to your mother," he says, "she got scared of things that wasn't there. First she wouldn't go out by herself, then she wouldn't go out with me with her, then she got scared to come downstairs in her own house . . ."

Peter thinks of the night the men came to the house, and of his mother in her room listening.

"Finally . . ." his father says, and then stops. He shrugs and nods in the direction of the front yard, and in that gesture is the whole world on the other side of the door, the one his father knows and the boy has glimpsed just once.

"It scared her so bad she's afraid to even move her little finger," his father says. He looks up then and nods. "She's afraid that she moves her little finger, it wakes up and remembers what happened to your sister. She thinks if she just keeps everything still it don't hurt."

He stands up and walks to another chair, as if he is afraid of the opposite thing.

"Did she go to the hospital?"

"It ain't the kind of hospital you can visit her," he says.

And then he moves again, this time to the window, and stares at the house next door.

He wakes up alone in the house.

He feels the emptiness of the place even before the sound—a soft thumping—moves from his dreams into the room, and he opens his eyes, afraid of anything that is not familiar.

He dresses himself, sneakers and pants and his jacket, and walks into the room where his mother slept. The bed is unmade, part of a sheet lies on the floor, a nightgown is tossed across a chair. The room still smells of her skin.

He picks up the nightgown and takes it to a hook on the open closet door. Then, without knowing why, he goes into the closet. He does not belong in the closet, or even in the room, but he cannot bring himself to leave. He stands in the dark, the soft press of her dresses against his face and hands, and feels her absence.

He holds himself—and her—still, his eyes beginning to pick up shapes of things in the back and on the floor. He imagines his mother, afraid to move even a finger. He slows and then stops his breathing, noticing the stillness is more perfect when he is part of it. Moments pass, every other thing is still.

And then enclosed in stillness, a tiny, passing moment stalls inside him, and then takes a shape of its own, billowing like smoke, filling him almost as soon as he first notices it there, filling him until he is suddenly afraid there is no room left inside himself to breathe.

He backs out of the closet, taking as much air into his chest as it will hold, and the moment recedes to the place it had been before, and passes.

He hears the pounding again, somewhere outside.

He walks out of the room and down the stairs. The noise stops and he stops, suddenly afraid that another moment is caught in his chest. He waits, but it takes no shape. He opens the front door and steps out.

A cold mist has settled in, a kind that will last all day. He zips his jacket to his chin and puts his hands in the pockets and looks out across the street. The place on the curb where his father parks—no one else has parked there for as long as he can remember—is empty. The spot itself is dry, the outline of the car against the wet pavement.

Victor Kopec's front door opens and he emerges carrying an ax. He walks to the middle of the yard, hurrying as if he were afraid of being caught at this. He picks up a sign lying in the grass and begins to tap it into the ground with the flat end of the ax.

Peter can't see what the sign says from the steps, and walks toward the curb in front of his house until he can make out the words:

FOR SALE
BY APPOINTMENT ONLY
CALL CATHY AT DUNNE REALTY

Victor Kopec holds the sign with one hand and taps with the other. He taps a dozen times, and then he steps back and swings the ax with both hands. Not a full swing—he brings his hands to a spot in front of his eyes, and then pulls them straight down, as if he were ringing a bell—and an inch at a time, the stake disappears into the ground.

He stops and steps back, leaning on the ax, and considers what he's done. The sign is off center, pitched forward and to the left. Victor Kopec drops the ax and lifts one of his black police shoes in the air and kicks it. The noise is still in the air when he kicks it again. The sign falls back and then forward, as if it's been shot. The next kick turns it sideways, and then Victor Kopec picks the ax up off the ground and swings it from the side, the way Peter has seen Pancho Heurrera swing at baseballs at Connie Mack Stadium, and hits the sign square in the face.

Out of breath, Victor Kopec turns to see if anyone is watching. An afterthought. And that is when he notices Peter. He considers him a long minute. "How come you ain't in school?" he says finally.

Peter does not answer.

"You better go on inside," Victor Kopec says, "or somebody'll call the truant officer."

He doesn't move. The man is angry and afraid at the same time. The words are not the ones he wants to say.

"You want to make something of yourself, you got to go to school," he says.

Then Victor Kopec turns to his sign, which is bent almost in half, and smashes it again. He walks back into his house and closes the door.

Peter wipes at the mist on his face with the sleeve of his jacket, but the sleeve is wet too, and feels colder than the air. He looks at the sign in the yard, wondering how long Victor Kopec will leave it like that. He thinks of his uncle, who once shot a cat on the steps of his house on Two Street and left it there for a week in a plastic bag, where the old woman next door who owned the animal would see it every time she came out.

He pictures his uncle's face, the pockmarks deep in his cheeks, and thinks of the thing he said to his father in the living room while the men were holding him.

"Charley, it was his fault, he'd be dead. . . . I'd done it myself. . . ."

He knows his uncle would kill Victor Kopec, but not for what happened in the yard. His uncle's reasons are never the ones he gives.

His father gives no reasons at all. His are shaped out of sight by weights the boy only glimpses at work in the momentary changes that cross his face and disappear.

His sister could touch that face, put her fingers in the creases and over the eyes, and understand him in ways Peter never could.

A breeze blows across the park and rattles Victor Kopec's broken sign, and Peter walks back into the house to wait for his father.

He is alone in the house all day. He sits on the floor in front of the television set, turning off the sound, and eats marshmallows. He hears Victor Kopec slam his car door outside, then start his engine. He hears him leave, hears him return. The phone rings, he does not answer it. He is not allowed to pick up the phone when he is alone; he doesn't know the reason. He counts the rings—eight of them—and then the phone is quiet, and in the silence that is left behind, he hears the last ring hanging in the air.

He lies on the floor, his cheek resting against his hand, and watches soundless cartoons.

His uncle's voice wakes him up, talking to his father outside. He opens his eyes, stiff and cold, not sure where he is.

"Lookadit this way," his uncle is saying, "you talked to him once, what does it hurt to talk to him again?"

He sits up. His hand has gone to sleep under the weight of his head and he holds it in his other hand, lifeless and white. He thinks of his sister's hand, the mitten in the street. He hears the key in the door.

Peter pushes himself up off the floor; his dead hand doesn't feel the wood underneath it. His father comes through first, holding a bag of groceries. His uncle is behind him, pressing close as he talks.

"I'm tellin' you, the guy's callin' Constantine eleven times a day, sayin' you're gonna do him. He says he's gonna sell his house and move to Fort Lauderdale. . . ."

His uncle notices him then, standing in the room whose only light is the television set. "Hey, Petey," he says, "how you doin'?"

Peter nods, shaking life back into his hand.

"Just like you," his uncle says to his father, "he don't say nothin' . . . Hey, what's wrong with your hand?"

"Nothing," the boy says.

His father walks past him and puts the groceries on the dining room table.

"How come you're shakin' it, then?" his uncle says.

"Went to sleep," he says. He looks around himself at the darkened room, surprised that the day has passed without him.

His father turns on the lights in the kitchen and dining room, opens the icebox door and comes back with two beers. He gives one to Peter's uncle.

"I'll fix us something to eat later," he says, "but leave me and your uncle talk a minute first."

He nods and goes up the dark staircase to his room.

"You ain't listenin' to me," his uncle says after the boy closes the door. He hears them as clearly as if they had come up the stairs with him.

"I heard you," his father says.

"Then say something back."

It is quiet a long moment, and then his uncle is talking again. "What Constantine said, he don't mind that the guy's frightened. He likes him a little nervous, it makes him easier to work with. But he don't want him nervous enough he moves to Fort Lauderdale."

"He ain't going to Fort Lauderdale," his father says.

"It's what he told Constantine."

It is quiet again, a long time. "Wait a minute," his uncle says. "We been through that, right? You told Constantine you ain't gonna hurt him. . . ."

Again it is quiet.

"You're fuckin' crazy, Charley," his uncle says. "I sincerely mean that."

His father says something back, speaking too quietly for Peter to make out the words.

"Constantine ain't going to put up with it," his uncle says. "He's told the guy it's forgiven."

"It ain't up to him," his father says.

"And who decides that? You?"

Peter hears a different tone in his uncle's voice then, a conciliatory sound, as if he has won the argument and is trying to show his father that he has lost.

"Constantine forgave him," he says.

Not long after that, Peter hears his uncle leaving the house. The front door opens and closes.

Peter finds his father sitting at the kitchen table holding a bottle of Pabst Blue Ribbon beer in his hand, tearing a path through the label with his thumb. He works from the top down, and when his thumb breaks through at the bottom the two sides of the label open like the doors on a barn.

His father rolls the paper under his thumbnail into a ball until it is perfectly round. "Your Uncle Phil," he says, smiling, and shakes his head. He looks at him then, without the smile. "You hear what he said?"

Peter nods.

"Always makin' things big. . . ."

Peter sits down at the table and almost at the same time his father gets up. He goes to the refrigerator and finds a fresh beer and then, before he closes the door, he looks at him and says, "You want a beer?"

Something depends on the answer.

"Yeah," Peter says, "I'll drink a beer with you." The way his father says it.

A smile—the shade of a smile—crosses his father's face, and then is gone. He reaches into the icebox with the hand holding the beer, and when it comes out, it is holding two. He sets them on the table and then hands Peter the bottle opener.

"The first thing about drinking beer," he says, sitting down, "don't ever take the cap off with your teeth."

Peter stares at his father, wondering what is happening. "It don't matter if all your friends use their teeth, in the end they're gonna break one off, wait and see." He looks at him and waits. Peter picks up a bottle and the bottle opener and pries off the top.

"It's the same thing as hittin' walls," his father says. He takes the open beer out of his hand, brings it to his lips and tastes it.

Peter reaches for the second bottle and stands up to get better leverage on the bottle opener.

"There's always going to be some guys hit walls," his father says. "They go to somebody's wedding, drink the wine, say the wrong thing and the first thing you know they're punching holes in the reception hall." He looks at Peter again, the smile pulling at the corner of his mouth. "Your Uncle Phil was a great wall puncher."

Peter nods, picturing it.

"The thing about that," his father says, "besides it's stupid, is that you can't always tell where the studs are, especially you drank enough champagne to want to punch walls in the first place. And it's one thing to put your fist through drywall, it's something else when you hit the studs. . . ."

His father falls silent a moment, and Peter is afraid the moment is over. That his father has said as much as he can.

His father shakes his head. "More people broke their hands at weddings than fights," he says. And then he touches the side of his bottle to Peter's and drinks again.

Peter lifts his own beer off the table and carefully brings the cool, wet circle at the top against his lips. The smell is different this close, and then he lifts the bottle and the beer is bitter and alive in his mouth. His eyes water and he swallows, feeling his father watching.

"There's no excuse, hurting yourself on purpose," his father says. "The Italians know that, the Irish don't. It's why they run things."

And then he seems to go away for a little while, perhaps thinking of Peter's sister.

Peter brings the bottle to his mouth again, taking more of the neck into his mouth than he means to, and then taking more of the beer. He coughs, and his eyes water again.

His father seems lost.

He takes the bottle out of his mouth, and feels beer on his chin. He wipes at it, and coughs again. His father comes back, looking surprised to find him there.

"You like it?" he says.

Peter thinks a moment, not wanting to lose him.

"No," he says.

"Then don't drink it."

On Easter Sunday, the city holds its egg hunt in the park. Two months have passed now since the accident; the only evidence of it left outside the house is a bare spot in the front lawn where Victor Kopec's convertible tore the tree out of the ground and the For Sale sign that sits off center and bent in the yard next door.

Inside, the damage is everywhere.

The days bleed into nights, and into each other, becoming weeks; nothing starts or ends. A coma. In the morning, light comes through the drawn shades and turns the walls a quiet orange, and at night the lighting seems always to come from other rooms. There is a slowness to everything inside the house, a heaviness that Peter notices most when he steps outside, and is no longer heavy and slow himself.

The hunt for Easter eggs begins late in the afternoon, after the Broad Street parade. Peter's father is somewhere with his uncle, doing their work for the unions. His car is gone, but even with the hundreds of people who have brought their children to the park, no one has taken the space where he parks.

He sits on his knees on the davenport, his chin resting on the back cushion. The children are gathered at the far end of the park, standing behind a ribbon that is held on one side by the mayor and on the other by someone in a rabbit suit.

A man Peter has seen on television, on the show *Bandstand*, is next to the rabbit. His name is Larry Tock; Peter says it out loud, listening to the sound. Larry Tock, the king of Rock. He is not a dancer, but the one who introduces the music. For that reason, and perhaps for his clothes, he is the star of *Bandstand*.

Larry Tock picks up a microphone and begins talking to the

crowd. The speakers are mounted on the white Cadillac which brought him into the park. Peter hears the words once as they are spoken, and again as they echo off the houses across the way.

Larry Tock starts to count. "One, two, three . . ."

On "three," the mayor and the rabbit drop the ribbon and a wave of children with Easter baskets breaks over the opening between them, the bigger ones pushing the smaller ones out of the way, pushing two of them down.

As Peter watches, the wave spreads and slows; some of the children trail their older brothers and sisters, some move off in their own directions, searching the grass and shrubs, stopping now and then to pick up one of the eggs. The parents come behind them, taking pictures, and in the background, Peter hears the voice of Larry Tock over the speakers, calling, "Happy Easter."

The children cross the park. A few of them are Peter's size, but mostly they are smaller, three and four years old. A few are as small as his sister.

He picks out one of the smallest and follows her, watches her run in circles in the grass, lost in her own purposes, dropping the eggs out of her basket as she bends to pick others up. The wind blows her hair and the collar of her coat into her face and she stops, tossing pieces of hair and material behind her, as if she were unattached.

She runs a few steps and another egg rolls out of her basket, a silver egg that lies in the grass—she doesn't know that she has lost it—sparkling in the sun. And for a moment he thinks of putting on his jacket and shoes and going into the park too, of picking up the silver egg and putting it back in her basket.

He sees himself doing that, and also sees himself sitting here in the window. One thing as real as the other.

And then he hears the music. Polka music. He walks into the yard and looks at the house next door. Victor Kopec's windows are open, the curtains blowing in, and the music that Peter has not heard since before the accident is loose in the neighborhood; it sounds like drunk men laughing.

He walks back inside thinking of his father, afraid that he will hear the music from Victor Kopec's house too, afraid of what he will do.

He walks into the kitchen and pours himself a glass of milk. Too full, all the way to the brim. He carries it back to the living room, sipping at it as he goes to keep it from spilling, and then, just as he and the milk are settled in their places at the window, his father's long black Lincoln stops in front of the parking place across the street.

His father turns in the front seat and begins to back in. Peter's uncle sits in the front seat with him, talking.

The car moves backward, then forward, then back again. His father straightens the wheels and then climbs out—his uncle is still talking—closes the door without bothering to lock it, and crosses the yard toward the house.

He does not seem to notice the polka music spilling out of Victor Kopec's windows.

Peter's uncle comes out of the car after him, still talking, and follows him.

"You want, me and Theresa could take Petey for you a while . . ."

Hearing those words, Peter understands his mother isn't coming back to the house.

His father opens the door and walks inside, his uncle a step behind. Peter is still facing the window and doesn't look at them as they come in. He stares out at the park, watching the little girl collect Easter eggs, coming back now almost to the silver egg itself, then turning, distracted by her mother and father—she is in a straw hat, he is wearing a suit and tie—who want to take her picture.

"Petey," his uncle says, "how you doin'?"

In the silence that follows, his uncle laughs, and then turns to Peter's father. "He's more like you all the time," he says.

Peter's father sits heavily on the davenport and closes his eyes. Peter watches him a moment, over his shoulder, then turns away from the park and the hunt for Easter eggs and drops down next to him. He feels the heat of his father's body. His uncle stands in the middle of the room, smiling, suddenly out of words.

"I gotta go," he says finally, "let you talk things over with Petey."

His father nods.

His uncle says, "Be nice, Charles. Don't do nothing until you've had a chance to think it over."

His father doesn't answer.

"Promise me," his uncle says.

His father moves his head as if it weighed a hundred pounds and slowly fixes his look on the boy's uncle. "I don't want to go through this promise-me shit right now," he says. "It's the wrong time."

"I got to hear it, I know you."

His father shakes his head.

His uncle begins to say something else, but his father interrupts him. "Nothing's changed," he says. "You want me to promise something, this don't change a thing."

"Maybe," his uncle says, "it was the best thing she left. Think about it that way. . . ."

And Peter's father stands up, takes his uncle to the door and opens it for him.

"I'm just sayin' it might be for the best," his uncle says. "They get like that, they ain't the same afterwards. It's like a scar . . ." He makes a cutting motion across his cheek. "It's there where you see it all the time. . . ."

His uncle stumbles down the steps as if he had been pushed. His father stands in the doorway.

Across the street in the park, Larry Tock takes over the loudspeakers and begins singing. "In your Easter bonnet . . ."

Peter's father closes the door.

His father stands at the door a long time after it's closed, until the Easter song is finished and all the music that's left outside is a polka.

"What would you say," he says finally, "you go stay for a while with your uncle?"

37

Peter doesn't look at his father; he shakes his head no. "Your Aunt Theresa, she thinks you're her kid already." He smiles, making a joke.

Peter looks straight ahead, and watches his uncle walk up the street toward his own car.

His father moves away from the door and sits in a chair, holding his face. He stands up, he sits down, unable to make up his mind.

"Your mother ain't going to be around now," he says finally, and the boy nods; he already knows that. "She decided she don't want to live here anymore."

"Where is she going to live?" he says, feeling himself beginning to cry.

His father looks around the room, and then at the ceiling, and finally back at him.

"It might be better, you was to stay for a while with your Aunt Theresa," he says again. And Peter shakes his head; the tears drop off his cheeks onto the davenport cushion. He feels his father watching and turns his face away.

"I don't know what to tell you," his father says quietly, "things ain't going to be the same." And then he stands up and walks upstairs and down the hallway.

He wipes at his eyes and looks into the park, trying to find the little girl. He stays in that same position for half an hour, listening to the sounds his father is making in the bedroom upstairs. She is gone.

He stays here until the children begin to leave the park, holding on to their baskets and their parents' hands; until the mayor and Larry Tock and the man dressed as a rabbit get into the white Cadillac and drive off to their offices in center city.

Peter envisions these offices, quiet, dark places full of servants and secret drawers. There are reports in the drawers, and one of them is his.

He saw the policeman write down his name after the accident.

When there is nothing left to watch outside, he backs slowly off the davenport, climbs the stairs and walks to the end of the hall. He does not enter the bedroom, but stands just outside. All his mother's dresses from the closet are lying on the bed. He stares at the pile, recognizing the dresses, the sleeves he has touched while her arms were inside them.

He takes a single step, entering the room. All over the floor are drawers that have been pulled from the dresser and emptied into boxes. What is left of the dresser is like a skeleton.

Her shoes are in another box, sitting on a chair near the window, thrown carelessly inside. He thinks of tangled feet. Of accidents.

The bathroom door is open and his father's shadow lies across the bedroom floor. Peter steps farther into the room until he can see his back. He is standing in front of the medicine cabinet, its doors wide open, emptying the things inside into a wastebasket that sits in the sink.

He sees a toothbrush, a pair of tweezers, combs that she used to hold up her hair. A razor for her legs. Perfume, mascara, lipstick. His father picks each thing off its shelf, looks at it, and then drops it into the wastebasket. He is in no hurry, and gradually the sounds that her things make falling into the basket change as they no longer hit the metal bottom, but fall onto each other.

Glass against glass, it is almost music.

He thinks of the music next door. He wonders if his father noticed it, with his uncle following him across the yard, talking.

Yes, he noticed.

There are three shelves inside the medicine cabinet, and when they are emptied his father shuts the door. Peter and his father find each other in the mirror.

He comes out of the bathroom, carrying the basket. "Things ain't the same," he says again, sounding not so unsure of himself now, almost angry.

Peter sits on the bed. The movement in the room has filled it with the smell of his mother. He holds himself still as his father begins carrying the boxes through the open door and down the stairs. He remembers that she had been afraid to leave this room, to move even a finger; he remembers the feeling as he stood in her closet and quieted himself and then stopped breathing.

He remembers these things, trying to glimpse her, but even with her smell in the room and her things on the bed, he can't find her in the way he wants. Not for even a moment.

His father is back on the stairs when Peter notices a small, round compact lying on top of the things in the wastebasket. He stands up and moves to the basket, and puts it in his front pocket.

He feels it there against his leg as his father reaches past him for the dresses on the bed.

He wakes up early in the morning. The sky outside the window is dark, and he cocks his head, following the almost soundless steps of his father as they pass his room and then descend the stairs.

The front door opens and closes, and Peter puts his feet on the cold wood floor and feels for his sneakers.

His jacket and pants are tossed across the foot of the bed and he dresses in the dark, listening to the sounds of his skin passing through his pants legs, of his own breathing. He fits his feet into the cold sneakers without putting on his socks, and ties the laces in double knots. He stands up and walks into the hall, and then goes down the stairs too.

At the door he stops; he has never been outside alone at this time of the morning. He weighs the darkness outside against the darkness in the living room; he touches the place where the door meets the frame and finds his father has not closed it completely, not wanting to make the noise.

Peter opens the door. His father's car is parked across the street; in front of it is the green car with the antenna mounted on the trunk. The windows of the car are fogged; a policeman is inside.

He holds himself still and looks across the yard to Victor Kopec's house. Nothing moves. He takes a few steps and then stops, afraid of making the smallest noise.

He hears a bus somewhere in the distance, and then a dog, farther off still. The sounds relieve him.

He moves again, walking away from the house until his line of sight clears the edge of Victor Kopec's porch and he sees the front door. There is a lamp above it that Victor Kopec keeps on even during the day, and in the orange light he sees that this door is not flush against the frame either.

When he steps again, the surface beneath his tennis shoes changes and he finds himself standing on the bare spot where the convertible uprooted the tree. He moves off the spot—he has avoided it since the accident—and then, faintly, hears a drowning voice inside Victor Kopec's house.

"Fucking God," it says.

A moment later something breaks on the floor, and then the house is quiet. Peter stands a few feet behind the bare spot in the lawn and waits. Time passes, he doesn't move. He stares at the front door and wills his father to come out.

The sky in the east turns pink, a boy comes past on his bicycle, one of his pants legs rolled to his knee to keep it out of the chain, tossing newspapers backhand onto the steps. His bag says Daily News. Something moves inside the police car, moves and settles.

And then the front door to the house opens, and Peter's father comes out, carrying Victor Kopec over his shoulder, wrapped in a sheet.

He walks without hurrying across the street and stops behind the red convertible, the body still draped over his shoulder, going through the keys in his hand to find the one to the trunk. In a moment his knees bend and he lowers himself until he is even with the lid of the trunk. His back is straight and his arm embraces the sheet to steady the load.

The sheet moves and Peter sees Victor Kopec's bare feet.

There is a popping noise and the trunk yawns open. His father bends farther forward and ducks his head, bends until the body drops of its own weight into the trunk of the car. Peter hears a soft thud, almost as if Victor Kopec has sighed; the bumper of the car dips and evens.

His father straightens himself and looks into the trunk, as if he wants to memorize what is inside it, and then he closes the lid carefully and walks back across the street to Victor Kopec's front door. He pulls the door shut and locks it.

Peter sees the blood on his father's sleeves.

His father crosses Victor Kopec's yard and enters his own. Peter hasn't moved. His father nods at him then, as if he in some way expected him to be there. He returns the nod, the movement strange after holding his head still so long, and then follows him into the house.

His father walks into the kitchen and turns on both faucets in the sink. Peter watches the muscles move under his shirt as he washes his hands. He wonders if he will have muscles in his back: if the slow, merciless engine that is hidden inside his father is hidden inside him too.

His father washes his hands twice, the steam coming up over his shoulders, and then carefully cleans out the sink. He shakes his hands and turns to look for a towel. His hands have turned pink in the hot water.

"Things ain't the same, Peter," he says.

His father picks up a dish towel and dries his hands. He watches his father's fingers roll over each other inside the cloth. He waits for him to finish, and then waits for him to begin something else. He has been waiting since the afternoon of the accident.

"The men are going to be mad," Peter says.

His father smiles at him, and Peter sees that he is happy in some way that things are not the same, that something has finally changed.

It occurs to Peter that his father has been waiting too.

"Yeah, they are," he says, the smile gone now.

Peter looks at his hands. "Then what are we going to do?"

"You're gonna be all right," he says quietly.

He looks at his father, waiting for an answer.

"I did what I'm going to do," his father says. "Now we'll see what happens."

Peter thinks of the old Italian Constantine, the way he spoke to his father, his crooked finger pointing up the staircase at him, making a gun. He feels his lip tremble and touches it with the back of his hand, quieting it.

"There's nothing settled until everybody's dead, right?" his father says. "Things can be worked out."

Two hours later—it is eight o'clock in the morning—an unmarked police car rolls slowly up the street on heavy tires, crosses into the oncoming lane and parks close to the green sedan sitting in front of Victor Kopec's house. The policemen in both cars roll down their windows and then lean into them to talk.

The traffic coming up the street moves around them until an Allied van which cannot fit into what is left of the street stops in front of the parked car and waits, blocking traffic, for them to finish.

The policemen don't acknowledge the truck or the cars backed up behind it, honking.

Peter watches them from his bedroom. As they talk, the one who has been there all night comes through the car window, his thick forearms crossed against the door. He laughs at something he says—his own joke. Peter's gaze moves four cars up the street to the spot where Victor Kopec is lying in a sheet in the trunk of his convertible.

He wonders if his father has taken care of both of the policemen, or just the one he can see smiling in the window of his car.

He hears his father in the hallway then, coming to take him to school. He puts his books into a satchel and checks his shirt and tie in the mirror. They walk out of the front door together, in clear view of the police and the convertible, walk across the yard and the street and climb into his father's Lincoln.

The policemen don't seem to notice them, no one seems to notice. The air inside the car is warm and the seat behind Peter's back is cool and soft. His father puts the key in the ignition, stops for a moment, deciding something, and then starts the engine.

He looks once to the side, and the car waiting there next to his backs up, making a small opening, and his father takes it, without looking at the driver, and then points his car into the other lane. He stops once to back up, changing directions, and then drives away.

Peter is almost breathless. Passing right in front of the police, driving away. It makes him think of falling, of the secret stillness of a fall. He turns in his seat to see where they have just been.

"We could get away," he says. It hasn't occurred to him before.

His father nods. "The way you do that," he says, "you stay right where you are."

And Peter and his father stay where they are, and Victor Kopec's convertible stays where it is too, untouched. It is there the next morning, and the morning after that. And each morning Peter and his father walk past it and the policeman sitting in the green sedan, and get into the Lincoln and drive to school.

And each afternoon, the man who brings Peter home drives past it before he stops to let him out.

On the third day the man turns the corner at the park and suddenly speaks.

"Uh-oh."

Just that. Peter is in the back seat and pulls himself up to see. There is a nest of police cars in front of his house. An ambulance is in Victor Kopec's yard. Lights are flashing, doors are open everywhere—the police cars, the ambulance, the front door to Victor Kopec's house.

The man who drives him home from school slows as he comes to the house, trying to see inside. There are men with cameras and flash attachments standing near the door, half a dozen policemen in uniform holding them back.

The car passes Victor Kopec's house and stops. The man who drives it looks back at Peter, not knowing what to do. "You want we should go find your father?" he says.

He thinks for a moment and then opens the door and climbs out.

"You sure you don't wanna . . ."

He closes the door and walks across the yard to his house.

The driver watches him a moment, undecided, and then he leaves.

A colored man in a suit comes out of Victor Kopec's house and speaks to one of the photographers. "They was bleeding in there like a pipe broke," he says.

"Let somebody in," the photographer says, asking a favor.

The man in the suit shrugs, and all the photographers go past him into the house.

Peter fits the key into his front door and walks inside. He goes upstairs and undresses, hanging his school clothes over the back of his chair, and then putting on his sneakers and his jeans and his jacket.

He returns to the front steps and sits down to wait. The police seem to be waiting too. Some of them are sitting on Victor Kopec's front steps, some are in the yard, talking to each other as they hold back the neighbors. A police car appears, coming across the park, lights on, and the policemen who are sitting down stand up, and the ones holding back the crowd suddenly begin to push.

"I want everybody in back of the sidewalk," one of them shouts, and the neighbors give ground, a foot at a time, until they are off Victor Kopec's lawn.

The police car stops across the street. The back door opens and an angry-looking man in a uniform climbs out, slams the door, and walks through the neighbors to the front of the house. They move for him; he is the chief of police. The boy recognizes him from television; he is as famous as the president.

The chief climbs the steps and stops there to speak with a sergeant, looking around as he listens to the sergeant's report, then turns his head and stares directly at the house next door— Peter Flood's house—and then at Peter himself. Peter stares back.

The police chief turns and tells the sergeant something else, pushing his finger into his uniform just below his chin, and then walks into the house. The sergeant and some of the men left outside give each other looks, and then follow him in.

A moment later the photographers exit the house all at once, as if they were blown out; some of them looking back where they have been, some of them holding on to their hats. Peter hears the chief's voice, yelling at the policemen left inside.

"I'll throw you cocksuckers off the roof, you let anybody in here," he says.

Peter looks at the pitched roof and imagines it. Policemen coming through the air. He does not think the police chief would do that, but the policemen outside the house give each other nervous looks now, as if they are not sure.

The chief stays inside a long time—perhaps as long as Peter's father had—and then emerges, quieter now, angry in a different way.

"You find the body, Frank?" one of the photographers says.

The chief turns to the photographer but doesn't answer. Half a dozen flashbulbs go off; he straightens slightly, but offers them no change in expression. In Peter's experience, photographers always want you to smile.

When the bulbs have stopped, the chief turns to the sergeant who has followed him into and out of the place and says something Peter cannot hear.

The police and the photographers turn together and survey the cars parked along both sides of the street. "I think it's the convertible," somebody says, and the crowd in the yard separates as the chief and half a dozen of the policemen come through on the way to the car. The photographers follow the police, and behind them are the neighbors.

Peter feels something like a tuning fork in his balls.

The chief gets to Victor Kopec's car first, dropping his head even with the window to look inside. He checks both seats and then he walks straight to the back end and stands still, looking at the closed trunk. One of the policemen steps in with a crowbar and wedges it under the lid. There is a popping noise, not much different than the noise it had made when the boy's father opened it with the key, and the trunk comes open.

The flashbulbs explode again—more popping—and the photographers crush into each other, fighting to hold their places around the trunk while the policemen push them away and tell

46

them to get back. The chief stands quietly in the middle of the movement and noise, looking inside the trunk.

Then he turns and stares again at Peter, and then he starts across the street.

Peter watches him come. Behind him are the other policemen, and then the photographers. The neighbors stay in the street. He hears the sound of the police chief's polished black shoes on the sidewalk, the creak of the belt that holds his gun, the sound of the change in his pocket.

The police chief squats, sitting on his heels, and looks into his eyes. Peter smells shoe polish.

"Where's your father?" he says.

Peter shakes his head, and the chief looks over him toward the house.

"You know where he's at?"

One of the photographers steps around a policeman and takes a picture. Peter sees colored circles. The chief turns, still on his haunches, and says, "Get them people out of here," and the other policemen push the photographers back.

"You know where he's at?" the chief says again.

Peter shakes his head.

"When he comes home, tell him I want to see him. Tell him I'll be back to see him. . . ."

Peter nods, understanding that he is part of it now. He stares into the chief's eyes.

The chief rises slowly and looks at Victor Kopec's convertible. It seems to Peter that the chief is going to say something more, but he reconsiders it and heads back into the street. The reporters walk backwards, just in front of him, asking their questions.

"Who's that kid, Frank?"

The police chief doesn't answer. "Did the guy have a family? Frank?"

"Where's he assigned to?"

"Frank, did the guy have a family?"

The chief of police walks to his car without answering the questions, then stops a moment before he gets inside.

"Lieutenant Kopec was an excellent police officer," he says. "Any further statements will come as the case develops." And then he turns away from the cameras and drops into the front seat of the police car and points, with one finger, toward the other side of the park.

The reporters shout more questions, but the car rolls out across the grass, leaving tire tracks.

The reporters come back to the convertible, the trunk is still open. A rope barrier has been set up around it, and investigators in white coats are going through what is inside.

The reporters look at each other and shake their heads. "Frank's pissed," one of them says.

They remember Peter then, and come back across the yard, smiling. Peter gets up and goes into his house. In a moment, he hears them knocking on the door. He sits down on the floor and turns on the television set, loud enough so he can't hear the knocking, and waits for them to leave.

Bandstand.

The phone rings sometime after dark.

He picks it up and presses the receiver against his ear, cold and hard, and listens.

"Who's this?" It is his uncle, something in his voice.

"It's Peter," he says.

"Your father there yet?"

Peter looks across the empty room to the front window. There are lights outside, a policeman is still guarding Victor Kopec's convertible. Victor Kopec himself is gone now, he watched them lift him out of the trunk.

"No."

"You tell him as soon as he gets in to call me, all right? . . . You understand me? As soon as he's in the door."

He hangs up the phone. The television set glows in the corner, lighting the room, and the light changes with the scenes; the whole

48

room seems to blink. He thinks of the reporters who would not go away. He thinks of them talking to each other, laughing on the other side of the door.

He goes into the kitchen and makes himself a jelly sandwich. As he eats it, he remembers one of the reporters who stood in the front yard pointing at the house, arguing with the photographers.

"Get a picture, get a fuckin' picture. . . ."

Time passes. Outside a car engine races and stops, not his father's. A door slams. Peter goes to the window and sees his uncle on the sidewalk. The streetlight throws a shadow across half his face and makes the pockmarks deeper in the lighted side. He imagines a pain which could cause such marks.

His uncle knocks as if he were in a hurry to get inside. Peter opens the door and he steps through it without a word. He looks around the room—a familiar gesture, but this time he is not thinking he would like the place for himself.

"He ain't home?"

He shakes his head.

His uncle closes the door as if it were his own house and walks inside. "How come you got it so dark?" he says. He smiles, but something is strained in his voice.

Peter shrugs. "It doesn't matter to me," he says.

His uncle goes to the wall switch and the room is suddenly filled with light.

"I think you spent too much time alone," he says. Peter understands that is a joke, he doesn't know what kind.

He shrugs again and his uncle bends over the television set, and the sound of voices fills the room. Ralph and Norton, planning to get rich. He knows the words by heart.

His uncle sits on the davenport and lights a cigarette. "You got a beer in the icebox?" he says.

Peter nods.

His uncle watches him in a way Peter has seen before—never when his father is there with them, though. "So?" he says, "you gonna get me a beer or what?"

He walks into the dark kitchen and opens the refrigerator door. In the light he sees the jelly knife lying on the counter, the open bag of Wonder bread. The bottles of beer are on the bottom shelf, where the icebox is coldest, and he takes one of them out. He finds the church key in the drawer next to the icebox, holding the door open with his knee for light. He takes the bottle and the church key to his uncle, and then wipes his hand against his shirt.

His uncle lays the cigarette on the end of the coffee table, the ash suspended over the edge, and opens the beer. In the moment just before the glass touches his lips, Peter sees the trembling in his hand.

"You got something to do?" he says after a while.

Peter shakes his head. His uncle picks the cigarette up between his thumb and middle finger, carefully choosing a halfway spot, as if the ends could hurt him.

The boy sees it again, that his fingers are trembling. He draws on the cigarette and holds the smoke inside a long time, and then a trace of it appears under his nose and hangs there for a moment like fog. He puts the cigarette back on the table and stands up, taking the beer, and walks to the window to look at Victor Kopec's car.

"They said the guy's head was cut halfways off," he says. There is a tone of admiration in that, but it passes even before the words are finished.

Peter thinks of the sounds from the house:

"*Fucking God,*" the man says. Something falls and breaks, and then it is quiet. He imagines Victor Kopec's head, cut halfway off.

His uncle turns away from the window and lights another cigarette. "You can't tell your old man nothing, never could," he says.

Peter doesn't answer.

"He'll stand there, just like you, listening to somebody as long as they want to talk, and then go do exactly what he was gonna do anyway. You can't tell him a thing because he thinks he already knows everything you know anyway."

He feels his uncle pulling him into his side of an argument now; he holds himself out. His uncle shakes his head, then looks again out the window.

"You know what it is?" he says. "He's got to be the one that decides. He's always got to be the one decides. . . ."

He pulls at the cigarette and finishes the beer; the smoke simply disappears inside him. He drops the cigarette into the mouth of the bottle; Peter hears it hiss as it hits bottom.

"You got another beer?"

He gets him another beer; his uncle lights another cigarette. Except for the sounds of the television and his uncle inhaling the cigarette, the room is quiet.

"How old are you, anyway?"

"Eight."

"You supposed to be up . . ." He turns his wrist and lifts his hand to check the time. "Nine-thirty," he says. "You supposed to stay up till nine-thirty?"

Peter shrugs; an ash drops off the cigarette onto his uncle's shirt. "You're lucky," he says. "Your Aunt Theresa don't let Michael stay up at all."

Michael is Peter's cousin. He is a year younger than Peter, and he climbs out of the window of his room onto the roof sometimes while the families are visiting and, holding on to the window frame, pisses onto the sidewalk.

Peter has been farther out on the roof of Michael's house; he has walked to the edge and unzipped his pants and then looked back over his shoulder at his cousin's face and seen the excitement inside him.

Michael has tried to get him to jump.

There is a tuning fork going inside his cousin all the time.

"Right after he done his schoolwork, it's up to his room," his uncle says. He looks around the room, reminded of something. "You got homework?"

Peter doesn't answer. He does his work at the school. The nuns go over the same arithmetic every day, the same reading words, and he does the problems they give him to take home while they are teaching; sometimes he even knows what they will give the class to do later. Peter doesn't memorize things; he sees them, the way they are put together. A kind of second sight that is so natural he hardly notices it is there.

No one knows that, it is one of his secrets.

"You got to keep up with your books," his uncle says, repeating something he has heard; talking now only because he is uncomfortable with the silence. He looks at the television set and watches Ed Norton making an onion sandwich. "You don't do your books, you end up like that. . . ."

His uncle finishes the beer and walks upstairs to the bathroom and urinates without closing the door. The sound stops and starts; he pisses a little at a time, like he was emptying his pockets. The toilet flushes and then his uncle is back on the stairs.

"Your father's got a nice house here," he says. He stops on the stairs and looks at the ceiling, shakes his head in an admiring way. "They didn't built the houses on Two Street like this—there ain't no cracks in the walls, right?"

Peter shakes his head.

"Big rooms like this," his uncle says, "a nice park right across the street . . ." He comes the rest of the way down the stairs and then stops again, looking outside.

"Your father must sleep like a baby," he says.

Again he doesn't answer.

"You like your neighbors?" he says. "I bet you got neighbors in this place, you want to borrow a cup of sugar, the lady next door don't say, 'Fuck you,' from behind the door, am I right?" He surveys the room, smiling.

"Dentists live in houses like this. . . ."

Peter stares at him, thinking of Victor Kopec. The same thought seems to occur to his uncle, but in a different way. "I wonder if that house is still for sale, now the guy's dead."

He comes the rest of the way down the stairs and goes into the kitchen for another beer, and Peter hears his father's car in the street.

The car backs into its parking place. The engine stops, the lights go out. Peter starts for the door, but his uncle comes back into the room and stops him.

"Hey, where you goin'?"

"It's him," he says.

"He don't want you runnin' around outside this time of night. He'll be here in a minute."

Peter stands at the door and waits for the sound of his father's shoes on the steps. He wants to tell him something before he gets inside. He doesn't know how to say it but he would step through the door and try—he is not afraid to disobey his uncle—if his uncle were not there at his side. It is about his uncle. He is here to hurt him.

The door opens and his father steps inside, and it is too late.

"Charley," his uncle says, "where you been?"

His father does not answer him. "You get something to eat?" he says to Peter.

He nods.

"Go on upstairs," he says, "lemme talk to your uncle."

He nods again, but he doesn't move. His father waits; Peter waits. He waits for him to understand why he isn't moving.

"You didn't hear me, or what?" his father says.

"He's just like you," his uncle says, "he don't listen."

Peter holds the spot as long as he can and then starts up the staircase. "Go on," his father says. "And I don't want to look up the stairs and see you sittin' at the top."

He goes into his room and closes the door. He stands in the middle of the floor, in the dark, holding himself still and listening. He hears a prayerlike mumbling at first and then, as he accustoms himself to the quiet, he begins to hear the words.

"He ain't that pissed," his uncle says, "but what he wants, he wants you to sit down with some people, explain what this Gypsy motherfucker did. That's all, just explain to these people, cool them down so this don't come back and hurt us. . . ."

It is quiet a moment.

"It don't have to be tonight," his father says.

"There you fuckin' go. It's gotta be tonight because he says it's tonight."

"Constantine don't decide everything."

"He ain't unreasonable about something like this, your family was involved," his uncle says. "He respects you for it; that's what he said, God as my witness, 'I respect what the man done.' But what he wants now, what he's sayin', let's get together with some people tonight, before the police do a number on us all, and explain how it happened."

It is quiet a long time downstairs; Peter hears the television set, Chester whining at Doc.

"It ain't like he's askin' you to apologize," his uncle says, "just explain where everybody understands people ain't started taking people out . . ."

It is quiet again.

"Where is he?" his father says.

"He's waitin' for us right now. We go over somebody's house and sit down and talk. That's all."

"Whose house?"

"A guy's house Constantine knows. What fuckin' difference does it make whose house?"

They are quiet again and then Peter hears his father on the stairs, and then the door opens and his father is there in a wash of light.

"I got to go back out a little while," he says. He leans in the doorway, his feet still in the hall. His face is troubled, as if something in the room were out of place.

Peter feels himself beginning to cry.

"What's wrong with you tonight?" his father says, staying in the doorway.

Peter shakes his head, denying it. "Nothing," he says.

"This takes maybe an hour, I'll pick up a pizza."

He doesn't answer.

"You don't want a pizza?"

"He's funny today," Peter says, looking downstairs. He hears himself say the words.

His father peers at him from the door, framed in light. "Phil's always funny," he says.

Peter shakes his head. "He's . . . fucked up."

The first time he has ever said the word in front of his father. A cloud moves across his father's face and when it is gone he suddenly begins to laugh. He laughs in a way Peter has never heard before; something comes out of him that he didn't know was inside.

"Jesus," he says, "that's too good."

And as Peter looks carefully, he sees his father is not just laughing, he is smiling at him too. Shining.

"I'll get us a pizza," he says, and he closes the door and goes downstairs. Peter stands in the darkness, listening to his father and his uncle leave the house; he goes to the window and opens it, and listens to them climb into his uncle's car.

The engine starts, the lights go on, and they are gone.

He lies on his bed with his hands folded behind his neck, staring at the ceiling and holding on to the sound in the room as his father laughed. Picturing the shine on his face.

He doesn't sleep or move, he simply lies on his bed in the cold room until morning, when his uncle comes back to the house alone, opening the door with a key, and climbs the stairs to his room to tell him something bad has happened to his father.

The boy walks straight to the window and jumps.

PART TWO

1966

Nicholas DiMaggio is sitting by the window in Ed's Diner, making circles on the table with the bottom of his water glass. He is holding half a dozen thoughts at once, moving from one to the next, trying at this moment to imagine how the water gets on the bottom of the glass—not the word *condensation,* he knows the word, but how it works. If it is something you could see with a microscope.

He wishes he had spent more time in school when he was in school.

He thinks of school.

He looks at the circles and then his hands, grease in the lines of the joints. He will scrub that out later, before he goes home. He never goes home to his wife with dirty hands. He thinks of her sitting straight-backed in a slip in front of her mirror, studying her face. He holds her shoulders in his hands; he can feel her pulse.

He closes his hand and opens it, estimating how much he's aged by the pain in his knuckles, comparing it to what he remembers from last winter.

It's always the winter that brings on pain.

He feels the cold pressing on the window, feels its breath through the glass, and looking that way, into the street, he notices it has begun to snow.

He hasn't seen the sun in a week.

Ed moves behind the counter. There is no one else in the place, and he is waiting to close. Three-thirty in the afternoon.

"You want more coffee, Nick?"

"No," he says, "the kid should be done all the work by now."

He pushes himself up out of the booth, watching old Ed smile, feeling the plastic seats stick to his pants, and puts a dollar on the table next to his empty cup. It sits off center in the saucer, a little coffee collected in the low side.

"How's he doin', anyway?"

"Real good," Nick says. "I left him today, he's got a water pump all over the sidewalk, probably won't take me two, three hours to find the pieces, get it back together."

"What is he, twelve?"

Nick stops for a moment to think. "No," he says, "he's only nine. You're making me older than I fucking am."

"Somebody said he was already pretty good."

Not meaning engines now.

Nick shrugs. "He's doing all right," he says. "Come up sometime and see for yourself."

The old man behind the counter looks down the slope of his apron and grabs his crotch. "I would," he says, "but you know Annie. I got to beat her off this thing with a spatula."

Nick opens the door, and feels the wind blowing up from Broad Street. He turns his back into it and zips his windbreaker. Ed's face appears at the window, smiling a few inches away, and then the shade drops.

He sees the white kids first, two blocks away on the other side of McKean Street, coming home from public school. The short one's got a behind like an old lady's—the kind that sticks out so far that walking with it is something you have to think about, like carrying a suitcase—and he's smoking a cigarette.

The short one, he knows, is Phillip Flood's son.

The other one is his nephew. Charley's boy. They all live together in the house across the park from Nick's that once belonged to Charley. How that happened, he doesn't want to know. The little girl got killed, the wife went crazy, Charley disappeared . . .

It seems to Nick that all these things happened a couple of months after they found the cop next door in the trunk of his convertible, but time moves for him in a different way than it used to; the order of things isn't as clear as it was. He isn't sure.

He remembers watching the boys in the park—it seems to him they were both riding one bicycle—and feeling bad for the one that belonged to Charley. He never walked over and talked to him, though, the way he would any other kid. He had a house of his own and a son of his own, and did not want the entanglements.

These guys, you did not want the connection.

Nick drops his chin until it rests on the jacket, protecting his face from the cold—everything but the top of his forehead—and pushes through the wind. How many fighters had broken their hands on Nick DiMaggio's forehead? He goes back, remembering three. He figures that means there were probably a dozen.

It makes him smile, the way his memory blurs. It seems to him that it started about the same time he was beginning to see what things were about. But what he remembers and what he understands are not the same thing, and he knows that, and this part of his life is as good as the part that came before.

The smile is still in his head when he senses the movement from the other side of the street.

Four of them come out of the alley half a block away.

Phillip Flood's son and his nephew are passing the cigarette back and forth, probably discussing how to get into some girl's pants—it terrifies Nick sometimes, thinking he might have had a daughter—and they don't see them until it is too late.

Nick comes to the intersection and looks down the crossing street—Chadwick—to his garage. The door is open, an eight-year-old Cadillac sits underneath it, half in and half out of the shop. Harry is on his tiptoes, bent into the engine.

He wanted to put the water pump in by himself—Nick could see that, so he went to Ed's for coffee. He wonders if the kid has even noticed the way it got cold.

Nick stands for a moment at the corner, absorbed in the ordinary sight of his garage and his son leaning into the open hood of a car, and then, standing still, he is visited by the feeling that he is watching the place from his old age, remembering it. He moves, turning away, frightened, and looks up the street to see what will happen with the boys.

He wipes cold tears from his eyes and finds a place against the wall where the wind isn't as strong.

The short one sees them first. He looks up and seems to stumble; the cigarette falls off his lip and blows up the sidewalk to meet them. He turns his head, looking for someplace to run. A house or a store, a fire station.

The taller one stops too, but he only looks at what is there in front of him.

The colored boys close the distance. Nick sees the short one is pretending to have something in his pocket.

Nick crosses his arms and waits. The colored boys collect in a circle over the white boys; as big as men. They look up and down the street.

One of them notices him then, half a block away. He stares at Nick, deciding something, then slowly smiles, as if there is an understanding between them.

Nick feels himself deciding to walk away. He looks down Chadwick again, at the open door and the sign over it—NICK'S AUTO REPAIRS AND GYMNASIUM—his kid leaning so far into the Cadillac's engine that it looks like he is going to fall in.

He decides to walk away, but he doesn't move. He was born on the second floor of a house a block and a half from his shop and the neighborhood is still his, even if he lives two miles away in a better part of the city. He knows the history of this street and all the streets around it—he is part of the history—and he knows the faces, even if he can't always remember the names.

He remembers the names later, sitting at dinner, or lying in bed. Nothing is lost, only stored farther back. That is what lets him smile.

He pushes himself off the wall and moves toward the boys until he can hear them over the wind.

"Let's see them pockets."

The white boys go into their pockets and come out with a dollar or two in change. The colored boy who noticed Nick before turns and looks at him again, surprised to find him closer.

"You crazy, motherfucker," he says.

Nick doesn't say a word. Phillip Flood's kid notices him then, thinking at first he is help, then deciding he isn't. The other one, Charley's kid, stares at the dark faces in front of him, holding himself straight. He reminds Nick of Charley, the way he holds himself. Charley had worked with his hands before he moved up in the union. He'd spent time on roofs and looked it, nothing like his brother.

Phillip never was part of it until his brother was running Local 7.

One of the colored boys takes the money. He studies it a moment, then says, "Shit," and puts it into his pocket. "Let's see them shoes," he says.

Nick folds his arms again and spreads his feet. The white boys take off their shoes—new, white sneakers—and the colored boys take them too. Nick feels something stir, but he thinks of the Cadillacs that come and go in front of the house across the park, all hours of the night, and stays where he is.

He does not want the connection.

"Let's see them other pockets," the colored boy says, and the white boys look at each other and then pull their coat pockets inside out too. A comb, some matches and cigarettes, something that looks like a lady's compact. Nick squints; and yeah, Charley's kid has got a lady's compact. His hands are pink from the cold, the nails are dirty. The compact is round and almost the color of his skin.

The colored boy reaches for the compact too, but the kid pulls it away. The colored boy smiles.

"Let's see that," he says.

The boy shakes his head no.

"I gone whip your white ass right here," he says. The kid who looks like Charley doesn't say a word. His cold hands roll into fists and he waits.

"You think this old motherfucker gone help you?" the colored boy says, nodding to Nick. "He ain't gone do nothing but get fucked up hisself. He probably like to get his ass beat, make him feel good."

The boy holding the compact is as grim as this street. The other one, his cousin, stares at him, waiting for him to give the colored boys what they want.

And if he does that, Nick will go back to the garage and look at the water pump. That's the contract he makes. If Charley's kid stands up, it's another story. Nick won't leave him in this alone.

The colored kid stares at the boy with the compact, a smile breaks his lips.

Nick waits.

He doesn't want the connection. He doesn't want to be a thought in Phillip Flood's head; it gets turned around.

He sees something change in the white boy's posture; he senses this kid who looks like Charley Flood is going to turn over what is in his hand. Its value has changed.

He is relieved and let down at the same time.

And then, almost in the same moment, the boy surprises him. He takes a step forward, claiming the empty space between himself and the colored boys, and throws a soft-looking fist at one of their heads. He is off balance and scared, his thumb is tucked inside his fingers. He hits the colored boy's mouth as hard as he can; the colored boy barely moves his head.

A gesture, nothing else.

The colored kid runs his finger over his nose and checks it for blood. "Now I gone kick both your asses," he says. "See what you done?"

He smiles again, showing a slice of pink inside his lips, as if he had been opened up. The short white boy ducks his head and bolts. One of them reaches for him, but he is gone. Faster than he looks. He crosses the street and goes into the alley where Nick first saw the other four, and is almost to the next block before he looks back and sees that no one is following. Then he stops, shoeless and red-faced and out of breath, and screams one long, furious word.

"Niggers."

The word dies in the wind.

"Give them their shoes," Nick says.

The colored boy who is holding the shoes turns to look at him, but it is the other one—the one Charley's boy hit—that Nick is talking to. He is the one who will decide.

He smiles again. "Man, you must be comical," he says, and it's done.

Nick tosses a meaningless slap at the boy's ear, bringing up his hands, and then hits him as hard as he can in the ribs, feeling the bones through his jacket. He stands still, watching him fall to his knees and then to the sidewalk; he watches him curl.

Nick stares at the kid holding the shoes. The kid turns and runs, into the wind, the shoes bouncing against his leg.

"Robert ain't but fifteen," one of them says, looking at the boy on the sidewalk.

The boy on the ground fights to breathe. Nick thinks of the feel of his bones underneath the jacket, wonders if he's broken his ribs.

Charley's kid stares at him, as surprised as the boy on the ground. The other one is still in the alley, watching.

"His brother gone find you, man," the colored kid says. "He gone kick your ass for sure."

The kid on the sidewalk gets to his knees, his face still resting on his arm. He holds the other arm motionless and tight to his body.

"What do you think, everybody in the world's going to give up their shoes?" Nick says to the kid on the ground.

His blood quiets, and he is beginning to feel sorry. There was no fight. For a little while it felt like one, but it went away before it started.

He is sorry for what happened and he is sorry for what didn't.

From the alley, Phillip Flood's kid screams again.

"Niggers . . ."

The colored boys look at Nick as if he'd said it too, all except the one on the ground. He is making small, crying noises as the air comes in and out of his chest. His breathing is shallow and quick. A line of spit connects the boy's mouth to the sidewalk. It bends in the wind and breaks.

"You got a father?" Nick says.

Charley's boy looks up quickly, as if Nick might be asking him.

"His father gone whip your ass for sure," one of the colored boys says.

The word comes across the alley again, under the sound of the wind. "Niggers." It is like a howl.

Nick squats next to the kid on the ground and uses the arm he is resting on to get him to his feet.

The boy stands, bent to his right, holding his ribs.

"Somebody be back to see you," one of them says, moving farther away; ready to run.

"This is where I am," Nick says, "right around the corner." He points behind himself to Chadwick Street.

The colored boys walk into the cold wind, the one that Nick hit is bent at the waist and stops now and then to catch his breath. Charley Flood's kid watches them, still holding the compact in his hand.

"You better get home," Nick says.

The kid hears him, but he doesn't move.

"They ain't going to bother you anymore," he says. He looks across the street to the alley. "Tell your cousin to watch where he steps; people throw glass in that alley."

The kid puts the compact into his jacket pocket, then touches it from the outside, through the material, to make sure it is there, and starts across the street in his socks.

Nick watches him go, and thinks of getting in one of the old cars sitting in front of the garage and driving the boys home. That's what he would want someone to do if it were Harry. But then, Harry wouldn't have given up his shoes, not to four of them, not to all of them in the city. Someday that will get him hurt, but when you're hurt that way, it heals. He thinks of Phillip Flood's boy, leaving his cousin and running. How long does it take to get over that?

He walks back to the garage, feeling unsettled. Wondering if he should have taken the boys home. In the end, he doesn't know.

In the end, all he knows is that he doesn't want the connection.

Peter walks home in his socks. His feet ache from the cold and he steps on small stones when he crosses streets.

He walks into the pain, accepting it, and then through it. On the other side, he is an observer, watching himself make his way up the sidewalk, a few yards ahead of his cousin. It is a talent he has developed, this removing himself from the moment.

His cousin had cut himself on glass, and Peter hears him in a distant way—as if he were on the other side of a door—making crying noises.

He stops and turns around. His cousin stops too and looks down at his feet. He says, "Jesus Christ . . ." Whatever else he meant to say is gone. His eyes fill and tears run from the corners down his round, wind-burned cheeks.

"It isn't that far," Peter says.

His cousin sits down on the sidewalk. "I can't walk no more," he says. He picks up his feet and holds them in his hands. "They're froze solid. . . ." He looks up at Peter for help. As if he had shoes to give him.

Peter leaves him and walks in the direction of the house. When he has gone half a block he turns around and sees that his cousin is still sitting on the sidewalk. He goes back.

"C'mon, Michael. It ain't far now."

His cousin gets slowly to his feet and then limps a few steps before he stops again. He looks up the street, then back at Peter. "The old man's going to kill us," he says.

"C'mon," Peter says, and begins walking again, and in a moment he hears his cousin behind him, breathing through his teeth.

"What are we going to tell him?" he says after a while. Peter doesn't answer; he isn't going to tell his uncle anything. "He's going to be pissed," his cousin says.

A cop walks past them, looking quickly at their shoeless feet, then disappears into a bar on the corner. "Peter?"

"He's pissed anyway," Peter says.

It is quiet a few minutes as they turn the corner and head up Twenty-second Street, six blocks from home. "We got to think of a story," his cousin says.

Peter shakes his head. He isn't good at stories, and his uncle thinks everything he hears is bullshit anyways. Peter wonders what kind of stories he makes up himself, to think everyone else's are bullshit.

They walk another block in silence, as his cousin tries out different explanations in his head.

"The niggers got us," he says finally.

"That isn't a story, it's what happened."

"Grown-ups," he says, "and they beat us up."

His uncle talks about the niggers all the time now, how they are trying to get into some of the unions. It isn't the niggers he is mad at, though, it's the Italians, telling him what he's got to do about it. That he's got to make it look like the niggers can work if they want to.

Peter turns and studies his cousin. "He isn't going to believe we got beat up by grown-ups," he says.

They walk farther, his cousin forgetting his feet to think of a story for his father. "He's going to fuckin' go crazy," he says finally.

Peter shrugs.

"He don't touch you," his cousin says, and he is close to tears again. "He never touched you in your life."

True.

He has never come after Peter with a belt. They have lived in the same house without touching each other from the morning he stepped into Peter's bedroom and told him something had happened to his father. His uncle had moved his family in even before Peter was out of the emergency room.

He understands that his uncle has been pulled two directions ever since; wanting to hurt him, wanting to be forgiven. Natural enemies. He takes Peter and Michael twice a year to Connie Mack Stadium to watch the Phillies, Christmas Eve they go to church.

He delivers lectures on girls and cops and school, sending Aunt Theresa into the kitchen for the parts he does not want her to hear. He tells them, again and again, that they are brothers, flesh and blood.

And sometimes when he says that he watches Peter's face to see if he believes that the words change what is there between them, if he believes the words can recast events that have already passed.

It infuriates him that he cannot change what Peter sees.

"You ain't got nothing to worry about," his cousin says. But Peter has seen the way his uncle looks at him—has seen the way he looked at his father—and knows that isn't true.

The black Cadillac passes them a block from the house, tires popping on the street. The side of his uncle's face is in the back window, looking strained. Peter knows that look; it's the Italians.

Phillip Flood is standing in the hallway waiting for them when they come in. Still in his coat. Peter stops cold, caught in his uncle's stare.

He looks at Peter, then at Michael. He looks at their feet.

Michael sits down just inside the door and peels off his socks. He feet are pink and tipped white, and one of them is cut. He holds them in his hands, rocking back and forth on the floor. His father watches him a moment, then turns back to Peter.

"It was the niggers," Michael says. "Big ones."

"What niggers?" he says, still looking at Peter. Peter doesn't answer. He notices his feet are beginning to burn in the warmth of the house. He thinks they have been out in the cold too long to be comfortable now inside.

"The niggers took your shoes?" he says.

"There was six of them," Michael says, and then bends over his feet, as if to cradle them in his arms.

"You ain't hurt," he says to Michael, and then looks again at Peter. "So where were these niggers?" he says.

"McKean Street," Michael says. "They were as big as you . . . bigger."

"Are they still there?" he says.

Michael shakes his head. "A man chased them off."

It is quiet a long moment. Peter hears his aunt moving around upstairs. Probably making the beds.

"They were big," Michael says.

"You didn't fight them for your shoes?"

"The man came along," Michael says. "An old guy."

"So how did they get your fucking shoes?" He whispers that, not wanting Aunt Theresa to hear him use the word in the house.

"After they got them, then he came," Michael says.

Phillip Flood takes one more long look at them and then climbs the stairs. Aunt Theresa passes him on her way down. She looks at his face, then at the boys beneath her on the landing.

"Michael," she says, hurrying now, "what happened to your feet?" She washes down the stairs like a flooded bathroom.

"He ain't hurt," Peter's uncle says behind her.

She pays no attention. She hurries past Peter, smelling of onions and garlic, and kneels in front of her son. "They're frostbit," she says, and looks up the stairs. "We got to get them in warm water."

His uncle stands where he is, looking down. "If me and Charley ever come home without our shoes when we were kids, we'd come home without feet."

The house is suddenly quiet. Phillip Flood doesn't mention his brother's name in this house. A rule that no one realizes is there until it is broken. He is still a moment, hearing what he has just said, and then he turns suddenly away and walks down the hallway into the back.

"You see what you've done?" Aunt Theresa says to Michael. "You've upset your father."

Late in the afternoon Nick is standing in one of the windows overlooking the street, deciding if he wants to box. A nice-looking

Jewish kid from the neighborhood is beneath him on the street, practicing dance steps. He uses the street sign as a partner. The kid calls himself Jimmy Measles, and he is on television all the time, dancing on the show from West Philadelphia. Nick can't remember what they call it.

The kid believes he is a television star, and maybe he is. The neighborhood girls are around him all the time. He sometimes sees the kid patting their fannies.

The gymnasium sits over the garage, connected by a steep, unlighted stairway. Nick hears the door open downstairs and promises himself that he's going to put up handrails before someone falls.

He has been thinking a lot about lawsuits lately, expecting a colored lawyer to walk into the shop any day now and hand him the papers for breaking the boy's ribs on the day Harry took apart the fuel pump.

He checks the cars outside, looking for something that a colored lawyer might drive, but there is nothing out there he doesn't recognize. A dozen cars are parked on the sidewalk, waiting for rings or voltage regulators or hoses. Most of them are old; Chevrolets, Fords, Pontiacs. He won't work on foreign cars; he doesn't even own a set of metric wrenches.

He turns to the stairs, catching the sight of Harry shadowboxing in the ring, all the rules of boxing and science distilled into seventy pounds. Nothing wasted, every moment in balance.

Nick hears steps on the stairs then; slow and heavy, they stop twice on the way up, resting. He watches the top of the staircase, and an old man gradually appears, his hand flat against the wall for balance.

When his head has cleared the landing he stops again—still on the stairs—and looks at the ring in the middle of the floor, and Harry moving around inside it.

The old man doesn't say a word. He climbs the rest of the way up, carrying a paper bag with underwear spilling out of the top, and then carefully sets the bag in a corner and sits on it. The skin over his eyes is baggy and scraped; it looks like a week since he had a bath.

Nick moves off the window and crosses the room. The old man glances at him as he approaches, then focuses his attention back in the ring.

Nick stands over him and waits, not wanting to be disrespectful. The old man could be eighty; he could be sixty. He isn't a fighter; he's taken some beatings, but they aren't old, they aren't inside him.

There is a timer on the wall which goes off twice every four minutes, marking the beginning and end of each round, and the minute's rest in between. It buzzes now and Harry drops his hands and begins walking quickly around the ring, close to the ropes, and there is an economy even to that. Nine years old, he treats training like he was fighting on television next week. Sometimes Nick worries that the kid is too serious.

"How you doin'?" Nick says.

The old man looks up at him but doesn't answer.

"You like the fights?"

The old man makes a noise Nick cannot understand; he spits as he makes it. Nick looks at him, nodding.

"You want to sit here a while and watch, it's all right," he says. The old man doesn't seem to hear. His eyes go back to the ring where Harry is walking in circles, waiting for the timer to go off again.

He is the kind of kid that you don't ever have to tell him something is serious. You have to tell him when it isn't.

"What I mean is," Nick says, "you can stay a *little* while. Until we turn off the lights, right? When I turn off the lights, out you go."

The old man watches Harry shadowbox and jump rope and hit the heavy bags. An hour later a couple of colored fighters from North Philadelphia come in with a trainer and work five rounds without headgear.

The trainer stands in the corner, impassive, blood-red eyes, watching his fighter, whispering to him between rounds. The other fighter he ignores.

The bell rings, starting and stopping the rounds. Heads collide, an eyelid swells shut, blood shines beneath both their noses.

Nick imagines it through the old man's eys. It must look like a war, and in a way it is. But the issue being decided is between the fighter and his trainer; the other fighter hasn't got anything to do with it.

Probably paying him five dollars a round.

Harry watches the fighters too, doing his sit-ups on a board propped against the side of the ring. Nick sees him figuring them out, what will work.

Other kids from the neighborhood wander in. They sense violence, here and on the street; they are drawn to it.

Most of them have boxed a little themselves, were brought in here by their fathers with bruised lips or scraped foreheads after a fight, their hands in their pockets; embarrassed and scared.

And the fathers would take Nick to one side. "Nick, do me a favor. Don't baby him. . . ."

As if that were the reason they couldn't fight, they were babied.

As if the family names had been insulted.

As if the fathers had been fighters themselves.

Nick remembers the fathers, though. He remembers what kind of fighters they had been.

And they would leave their sons, as scared of Nick as anything outside, and Nick would show them, each in his own time, that it wasn't so bad getting hit. That was as much as he could give most of them, without their giving something back.

A month later, they would quit coming by, except to watch. They disappeared into games that were played with balls, games Nick did not play himself.

Or turned into dancers.

Not that he blames them. Fighting isn't for everybody, it isn't supposed to be.

"Who's the old guy?" one of them asks.

Nick shakes his head. "He just walked in."

"What's he doin?"

"He ain't hurting nobody," Nick says. "Maybe he was cold."

The middleweights finish five rounds, the trainer presses a cold silver dollar into his fighter's swollen eyelid.

The fighters dress without showering, and start down the stairs. Nick can't see going out into the weather with a fresh sweat, but he can't think of a good way to tell them it's all right to use the shower. Trainers don't like anybody telling their fighters anything. They tell them not to use the showers, they don't use the showers. Somebody tells them it's all right he might as well of changed the Ten Commandments.

The trainer crosses the room to shake Nick's hand. "Thanks, Nick."

"You getting him ready for something?" Nick says.

"Gettin' him ready for my fucking heart attack, he don't listen to what I tell him."

Nick shrugs. "He don't look too bad."

"The minute he's out of my sight," the trainer says, still holding on to Nick's hand, "he's fuckin' everything he can find a pulse. He got a communicable disease right now; he ain't fought without the clap, one kind or another, in a year. He's got to make up his mind, does he want to fuck or does he want to fight."

Nick shrugs, thinking he is just as glad he didn't say anything about the shower.

"You're thinking rubbers," the trainer says. They always liked to tell you what you were thinking. He shakes his head. "You can't talk to George about no rubbers."

The trainer leaves, the neighborhood kids leave with him. Nick likes kids, the life in them, and when they are gone he feels the change. Something goes out of the place besides the noise.

He realizes he's given up on training today; there isn't anyone around except Harry to box with anyway, and that's not what he wants.

He wants what he almost had earlier—was it last week already?—with the colored kids on the street.

He wants somebody he can hate a little while, but that's harder to find than it used to be. Somehow, he has ended up under-standing too much; and what he can understand, he can forgive.

He unbuttons his shirt and pants and hangs them on some nails pounded into the wall near the shower. He takes off his socks and underwear and hurries into the single-stall shower before he turns on the water.

He doesn't want anybody coming up the stairs and seeing him naked.

When he comes out a few minutes later, dripping water and scalded red, the old man is sweeping the floor. Nick wraps a towel around his waist and hurries across the room to stop him.

"Hey, don't do that," he says. He steps in front of the pile of dust and balled tape riding the old man's broom, holding the towel together. "You don't have to do that."

The old man makes a shooing gesture with his hands and spits out a word Nick cannot understand.

Nick steps out of the way, and the old man pushes the broom through his wet footprints.

He sweeps from the edges of the ring out into the room, fin-ishing in the corners, working around Harry, who is standing on a box underneath the speed bag. He picks up one of the boxing magazines piled beside the toilet and uses it as a dustpan. The old man is thorough and slow, and Nick wonders if he's got a couple of dollars in his pocket to give him, or if he's got to go downstairs into the cash register in the garage.

He wonders how to give the old man the money without having him show up again tomorrow.

The old man wipes up the last of the dirt with a towel caked with dried blood, and then hangs the towel on the middle rope of the ring.

Nick reaches into his pants to see what he's got. "Thanks," he says. "These fuckin' kids, they don't pick up nothing."

The old man doesn't seem to hear him. He puts the broom back in the corner and picks up a pile of hand wraps lying in a corner. One by one, he smooths the hand wraps flat and hangs them over the chinning bar to dry. He has to stand on a chair to reach it.

Harry has finished on the speed bag now and steps into the

shower. The water goes on, steam rises above the glass door. Nick looks out the windows and sees the lamppost swaying in the wind.

When the shower stops, he hears the building creak.

The old man finishes hanging the hand wraps over the chinning bar, replaces the chair, and turns to inspect the room. He checks the floor and the ring and the walls; he doesn't look at Nick.

Nick stands still, watching him. His hand is touching the folding money in his pocket, but it's hard to bring it out. He knows what it's like to be cold and not have a place to go.

He remembers a New York hotel they put him in after a fight; 1951. The place cost fifty cents, and with his hands swollen, he couldn't even turn on the radiator.

He can't remember the fight itself—the fights are all the same now, they have blended somehow into the same fight—but he remembers the hotel room down to the frost on the window and the pattern of the water stains on the ceiling.

The old man is suddenly staring at him, having put off the moment until there is nothing else to do. Nick looks into tired eyes; he looks until he can see himself alone in New York City.

"Just tonight," he says quietly.

The old man blinks, then moves slowly to his bag of clothes. He sits down heavily and drops his head back into the corner of the wall.

"You can unroll one of them mats," Nick says, pointing to his mats, "but it's just tonight. Tomorrow, you got to go back to your own place."

Harry is out of the shower and dressed. Nick takes one of the bills from his pocket and leaves it on the bench, and then starts down the stairs. Harry is behind him, carrying a bag with his schoolbooks. At the bottom they stop, and Nick takes the two-dollar reading glasses out of his pocket and holds them in front of the thermostat, magnifying the numbers until he can read them.

The place costs him a fortune to heat, the winter months it goes a hundred dollars. He feels his son watching him. He shakes his head and puts the glasses back in his shirt pocket.

"Shit, we'll leave it on," he says. "It's only one night."

Nick wakes up in the night, thinking of the hotel room in New York again. Emily is lying on her side, her hand under her cheek, prettier now, he thinks, than she was in those days. Softer. Her face makes him happy.

He remembers the hotel room; he tries to remember the fight. It won't come; just the room and his hands and the sounds in the hallway. He lay on a cot freezing, afraid of the noises outside.

He'd had thirty fights, and still couldn't get used to being away from home. Thirty wins, no losses. But in those days thirty fights wasn't anything. He was still making seven, eight hundred dollars, sometimes he got cheated out of that. Now, a kid gets fifteen wins, they got him fighting for a title.

But not his kid, he thinks.

It isn't something he'll have to tell him, it's something he already understands. Nick has spent enough time in fifty-cent hotel rooms for them both.

He looks at Emily again, and sees his son in her face. Her relatives didn't want her married to somebody who was beat up all the time, so he gave up fighting. They were college people, connected to the city, and after they were engaged, her father got him a job in the police garage. Nick could always fix engines.

He didn't run, he didn't go near the gym. And then one Sunday afternoon at Emily's house, her mother makes a nice chicken, and who walks in the front door but Slappy Grazano.

Nick leans back into his pillow and sees it happen again. He smiles.

Slappy looks at the table and then all the people sitting around it in their church clothes and napkins; this is a man who does not understand the uses of a fork. Not which fork to use, but why use them at all.

"So, Nick," he says, "we got you a fight."

Nick says, "Slappy, I don't want no more fights."

"One more, Nick. Somebody you already beat."

"I can't fight nobody," Nick says, "I'm not in shape."

Slappy says, "For this guy, you don't need to be in shape. Come on, Steve wants to see you."

Nick remembers the table getting so quiet he could hear the icebox running in the kitchen. He doesn't want trouble with Steve Grazano, so he stands up and puts two chicken legs in the pockets of his jacket and goes with him.

He remembers the look on Emily's face.

Yes, she's prettier now.

At Steve's place he says the same thing: "I can't fight nobody, Mr. Grazano, I'm not in shape."

But in the end, he's got to do it anyway, and before he leaves Steve says, "By the way, you got another one of them chicken legs?"

So he gets his dinner too.

The fight itself.

He remembers a heaviness that was never there before settling over him in the fourth round. He can see himself getting tired, beginning to hold on to the kid. Del Conners is refereeing, and he keeps slapping Nick's gloves off when he holds, telling him to fight, taking points. People booing; Nick never got booed in his life.

Finally, in the seventh round, Del pries him off the kid and says, "Nick, you don't stop hugging this nigger, I'll stop the fight. I mean it."

And the kid says, "Nigger?"

And Nick says, "I don't give a shit."

Del says, "I mean it, Nick."

Nick says, "So do I," and Del Conners stops it right there and raises the kid's hand.

"Who you calling nigger?" the kid says, allowing his hand to be raised.

Del hid from him for two years, thinking he was mad.

Nick lies in bed, wondering why it makes him smile now to think of the things that hurt him then.

He thinks it has something to do with the second half of his life—that at the end, the only way dying can make sense is if you feel grateful enough for what came before. He remembers the nuns in the hospital in Atlantic City had a different idea. He was there almost half a year when he was, what, eight years old? Nine? Harry's age. He imagines leaving Harry in a hospital for half a year.

One of the nuns, an old woman with pale lips whose hands shook as she reached for the thermometer, told him one night that when he was sick enough he would long to go back home to God. "It's what sickness is for," she said.

And she was dead before he left the hospital.

He pictures her standing beside his bed, the shadow that moves across the wall as her hand reaches through the pale light for the thermometer. And then suddenly he is remembering the white kids giving up their shoes in the street.

He wonders if they will think of that someday and smile. He doubts that it will ever make Phillip Flood smile. He puts himself in his place, imagining Harry coming home without his shoes.

Half an hour later, knowing he is through sleeping for the night, he gets quietly out of bed and goes downstairs. He makes himself a cup of coffee and waits for the paper.

Two days pass and the old man is still in the gym. He ties the laces in Nick's gloves before he boxes; he holds the heavy bag that Nick hits afterwards.

Nick prefers to let the bag swing, but he allows the old man his small jobs; he doesn't want to be the one to tell him that he's in the way.

He avoids conversations. The old man spits when Nick talks to him, trying to talk back.

Nick has begun to think that the old man knows something about fighting. He's never done it himself—his nose is thin and straight and there's no thickness in his eyebrows, and he is the kind of old man that if he had fought, he would have been hit— but he seems to know what he's watching. There is a certain impatience that crosses his face when a fighter is flat or tired or lazy in the ring. He reminds Nick of a trainer.

When the old man watches, nobody gets the benefit of the doubt.

Afterwards, when he sweeps the floor, he will push the broom into the feet of the boxers as they sit on the bench dressing.

He makes an angry popping noise, and the fighters move their feet.

Ain't there a number you can call," one of them says to Nick, "they come pick somebody like that up?"

Nick is sitting near the window, watching the old man pick up the pages of the *Evening Bulletin* that have drifted across the floor. He shakes his head. "I don't know what you're supposed to do," he says.

"How long you going to let him stay?" the fighter says.

Nick shrugs. "It's pretty cold," he says, "to put somebody out."

The door opens downstairs, and then closes. Nick is expecting a trainer, an old guy named Louis Grizzert who's got a kid he wants him to work with. He stands up, his legs feel tired and fragile from being outside in the cold all day working on engines, and walks to the head of the stairs.

It isn't any Louis Grizzert on the stairs, though.

Nick stands with his hands on the railing, looking down, and out of the dark Phillip Flood rises into his life. Behind him are the boys who lost their shoes to the colored kids. They are carrying gym bags.

Phillip Flood is wearing a tie and a suit and a cashmere coat that drops to his knees. He looks up at Nick and smiles.

"Nick, my man."

"How you doin', Phil?" he says.

He tries to remember the last time he spoke to Phillip Flood; he thinks it might have been the week he moved into Charley's house.

Phillip Flood takes the last eight steps in a sudden burst, and then pulls off one of his gloves and reaches for Nick's hand. Out of breath.

Nick shakes hands, trying not to give Phillip Flood his knuckles to squeeze. People were always squeezing fighters' hands to show they were strong. Nobody considered how sore fighting made them, not to mention working on engines.

Phillip Flood pulls him close, still holding on to his hand, and hugs him. Nick feels the cold from outside and then the shoulder of the coat against his face, and he is surprised at its softness.

He smells cologne.

"Nicky," Phillip Flood says, "I wanted to thank you, what you did for my boys."

Nick pulls himself back and looks at the boys. The taller one —the nephew—is looking around the room like he might be interested. The other one is bored.

Nick shrugs. "We been there ourselves," he says.

Phillip Flood lets go of his hand. "I don't remember nobody takin' my fuckin' shoes. . . ."

He looks at his son then, the son looks back.

"So what I was wondering, Nick, would you have time to work with them a little . . . You know, show them something for next time."

Phillip Flood brings his fists up on either side of his face, imitating a boxer. His front teeth press into his lower lip, turning it white.

Nick looks at the boys again.

"Those were big guys," Nick says. "Sometimes you just give up your shoes."

Phillip Flood laughs and then puts his hand on Nick's back, guiding him toward the far side of the gym.

"Do me a favor here, Nick," he says quietly.

Nick nods, not enjoying the feel of the hand on his back.

"These kids are dead pussies."

"Those were big guys," Nick says again.

"They come home without their shoes," he says, "I want them to come home bloody. I want them to come home with their balls."

Nick doesn't say anything to that.

"They got to learn how to handle themselves for their own good."

Nick shrugs, thinking that is probably true.

Phillip Flood takes his hand again, and puts something in it. Nick looks down and thinks for a moment that it's a ten-dollar bill. There are too many zeros, though.

"You know what I'm saying, here, Nick," he says. "I don't want them so busted up I got trouble with Theresa, but outside of that . . ."

Nick gives him the money back. "It's ten dollars a month if they like it," he says, "just like anybody else."

Nick says that, but there are only half a dozen regulars—most of them cops—who pay. It costs Nick two, three hundred dollars a month to keep the place open.

"Nicky," he says, "I don't want 'em to like it. They got fucking pizza, they got television. They already got enough shit they like."

He puts the bill in Nick's shirt pocket and pats his chest. "They don't have to win no Golden Gloves," he says. "Just teach them some balls."

And then Phillip Flood leaves.

The kids stand dead still in the middle of the room, holding their gym bags, the tall one watching everything at once. The other one, Phillip's kid, looks bored. Or looks like he's trying to look bored.

Nick feels the money in his pocket, feels a hundred dollars changing the gym.

"You want to try this?" he says.

He wraps Charley's kid's hands.

The other one sits down in front of an old television set by the toilet and adjusts the wire hanger Nick uses for an antenna, and watches the dance show from West Philadelphia.

Nick remembers the name now, *Bandstand*.

Charley's kid looks at his hands after Nick wraps them. That first time, it's like letting them hold a gun.

Nick pulls a pair of sixteen-ounce gloves out of the locker and he ties the kid's laces, and then takes another pair out and has the old man tie his. The gloves are faded and worn, and tufts of horsehair stick out of the seams. Nick holds the ropes and the kid climbs in the ring, smiling at the feel of the mat. The other one, Michael, looks up from the television set a moment, his mouth half open, and then he smiles too. A different kind of smile.

"The first thing let's do," Nick says, "punch me right in the face. As hard as you want."

He drops his face even with the kid's and offers him his cheek. The kid looks at him a moment, then at the gloves. Then he moves his hand, almost slow-motion, until it touches Nick on the line of his jaw. Nick smiles at him. Most kids, they'll hit you in the face with a hatchet if you let them.

"You can hit harder than that," Nick says.

The kid nods.

"C'mon, I want you to hit me a good one."

The kid drops his hands.

"It's all right, I'm used to it."

The kid seems to think it over. "That isn't how you do it," he says quietly.

"It's how you learn," Nick says. "You remember that colored kid took your shoes?"

The kid nods.

"Pretend like that was me."

But he sees the kid doesn't want to hit him.

"I'll tell you what," Nick says, "let's just move around here a little bit, and when you see a chance, you waffle me then."

The kid likes that better. He holds up his hands and follows Nick around the ring. Nick taps him on the forehead once in a while, getting him used to the feeling; the kid doesn't seem to mind. Nick hits him a little harder, then offers the side of his face for the kid to hit him back.

He throws a punch—not as awkward as he was outside—and Nick is surprised at its weight.

He ducks underneath the next one and the kid stumbles into him, and there is a noise as his face cracks against Nick's shoulder. Nick steps back and drops of blood are falling off the end of the boy's nose.

Nick waits to see what he will do. If the blood makes him mad or scared. The kid blinks tears and wipes at his nose with his forearm, then puts his hands back up and begins following Nick around the ring again.

Except for the blood running into his lips, there is no difference in him at all.

Nick notices his cousin has forgotten the television now and is watching the ring. He looks interested in the blood.

"That's good," Nick says. "Now you just do that same thing but step toward me. . . ."

The kid does what he is told. He wipes at the blood with the sleeve of his T-shirt and tries to step in behind his punches. He is not a graceful kid, but he is stronger than he looks and he listens, even with a mashed nose, to the things Nick says.

Nick throws punches that stop just as they touch his face, giving him the feeling. He doesn't flinch. Nick watches carefully, and he doesn't flinch. He just moves slowly around the ring, his right foot trailing the left, following Nick wherever he goes.

The bell rings, and Nick drops his hands, nods at the boy, and takes a towel that the old man has hung over the ring ropes and wipes the blood off his nose and mouth.

"How's that feel?" Nick says, looking at his face. The bridge of the boy's nose is swollen and starting to turn blue. Nick remembers the solid feel as he fell into him; the boy's face didn't slide left or right, he took the shoulder square on.

The kid nods.

"Does that mean it hurts?" Nick said.

The kid shakes his head, as if he doesn't know.

"It's all right to say it," Nick says. "If I bumped my nose like that, I'd say it hurts." Nick waits a minute, there is no answer. "Then I'd get even."

He sees the beginning of a smile in the corner of the boy's mouth. It's there, and then it's gone. "Put your head back," he says, "see if we can get it to stop."

The boy does what he is told; a nice kid, Nick thinks. A nice, polite kid. He looks at the other one, sitting in front of the television.

"You want to move around the ring for a round?" Nick says.

The kid looks at his cousin holding the towel against his face, the blood-soaked shirt sticking to his chest. "Are you crazy?" he says.

He looks back at the television. Nick doesn't blame him, it isn't for everybody. He likes that he said it. He climbs out of the ring, and looks at the television set too. He studies the dancers a moment, and sees Jimmy Measles.

"You see that guy right there?" Nick says, pointing with his glove, "he comes around here all the time."

The kid looks more interested. "Jimmy Measles?" he says.

Nick nods. "That ain't his real name, but he lives right around the corner. He's always out here in front of the place, practicing his dances."

The boy nods, but Nick sees he doesn't believe him.

"So," Nick says, "you want to box?"

The boy shakes his head no; his eyes go back to the screen.

"Maybe tomorrow," Nick says, hoping they won't be back tomorrow.

The kid never looks up. "Maybe," he says.

Phillip Flood comes back up the stairs an hour later. The boys are dressed in their street clothes; Peter's nose is stuffed with toilet paper. Michael is watching cartoons—*Bandstand* is over now—and hardly notices when his father walks into the room.

"They do what you told them, Nick?" Phillip Flood says.

Nick sees that he is talking about his son, not his nephew. Nick looks at the kid in front of the television set. "Sure," he says.

Phillip Flood is smaller than Nick, and ten years older. The acne scars turn his face gray under the lights.

"He looks like he's been to a birthday party," Phillip Flood says. Nick looks at him a long minute, thinking of the way he'd put the money in his pocket and patted his chest.

He doesn't trust himself to answer. The gym is his, he built most of it with his own tools. The floor, the staircase, the ring. Everything but the wiring. Some of it was an accident, the way it turned out, but it was his. When it changed it was because he let it.

"He looks like he's been to a fucking party. . . ."

Nick puts on a pair of six-ounce gloves and walks over to the heavy bag. He begins hitting it without waiting for the timer to start the round. His hands feel broken, but he hits the bag, over and over, until the pain spreads and dulls.

Phillip Flood watches him a moment, and then turns back to his son. "Turn off the fuckin' television," he says.

The boy leans forward and turns it off. "You got your mouthpiece?"

The boys follow Phillip Flood out.

Nick never looks up from the bag.

A minute or two later, the old man appears on the stairway holding a sack of groceries. Nick is surprised to see him there; he didn't notice him leave. The old man is like that, though. He comes and he goes, and mostly he stays out of the way. Like an old dog.

He sees Nick at the heavy bag and sets the groceries down on the floor and hurries across the room to hold it.

Nick does not acknowledge the old man, or the sound that ends the round. He hits the bag until the pain in his hands is in his head, a dull ache. He hits the bag until the punches are useless, and then, in the middle of the round, he suddenly walks away from the bag and the old man, and throws the gloves into one of the metal lockers at the other end of the room.

"These fucking guys," he says quietly.

The old man stays where he is, staring at him, hugging the bottom of the bag, wondering if he's still allowed to stay.

Before Nick leaves, the old man tries to give him a dollar bill.

They are back two days later, Phillip Flood leaves them in front of the gym.

Nick hears the deep sound of the heavy doors slamming and knows it's a Continental or a Caddy. He goes to the window to see if it's a colored lawyer, but it's Phillip Flood's boys, crossing the sidewalk beneath him.

Nick turns back into the room and sits on the window ledge, looking at his place. The old man has cleaned again this morning, swept the floors, scrubbed the ring, stacked all the gloves in one locker; the headgears and cups in another. Nick thinks he must get up before dawn.

He is standing on a small ladder against the far wall now, straightening the old fight posters there, most of them held in place for ten or fifteen years with thumbtacks.

Nick watches him work, his fingers touching the faces on the posters, slow and thorough, taking care of them as if he knew who they were.

Nick hears the boys on the stairs.

Charley's boy comes up first; he steps into the room holding a gym bag and then moves to the corner, understanding the place is not his. Both his eyes are discolored. A nice kid, Nick thinks again.

The other one comes in behind him and drops his bag on the floor and moves in front of the television.

Nick feels a draft and walks to the head of the stairs to check the door. The short one has left it open. The heat is costing him a fortune.

"You're Charley's boy, right?" he says to Peter. He decides to go down later and close the door.

The kid nods.

"How's the nose?"

He shrugs.

"The way it got squashed, I didn't think you'd be back for a while." The kid doesn't answer. The old man makes a scrambling noise and climbs down off the ladder, moves it a yard to the right, and then climbs back up. The furnace comes on, shaking the room and filling it with a faint, familiar smell of oil.

Nick is suddenly as uncomfortable as the kid. "So," he says, "you gonna be a fighter?"

The kid looks at him a moment, considering that, and then he shrugs again. "I don't think so," he says. The kid seems to take the question too seriously, as if what he's going to be is already decided.

"You could," Nick says. He points to the posters the old man is straightening. "All those guys up there walked in the gym the first day just like you, and they weren't champions then."

The kid looks at the posters, taking his time. Nick can't tell what he is thinking.

"We could get you a couple of fights first," he says, "before Sonny Liston."

The kid smiles at that, not much of a smile, and Nick sees it turn before it disappears. "So," he says, "you want to move around a little today?"

Behind him, the television has warmed up and sound of the dance show from West Philly gradually fills the room. The old man looks down from the ladder and spits out words that Nick doesn't understand. The music makes him angry.

Peter lies in his room at night, his tongue running over a lump in his bottom lip where he fell into Nick's knee. He thinks of that moment, his own punch pulls him off balance and his feet cross and tangle and he falls through Nick's gloves—Nick has reached out to catch him—and closes his eyes just before he hits the knee.

There is a hard bump, like a car running over a pothole in the street, and then a feeling that spreads from his lip to his chin, and then Nick is helping him up, smiling at him, telling him that biting knees is against the rules.

He lies in his bed and thinks of that, and in the dark he feels himself smile. He goes over it again.

He thinks of Nick cleaning the blood off his chin after the round, asking if he is sure he wants to be a fighter. He allows himself to imagine that now. Nick smiling at him as he cleans his face. He is bleeding in front of a thousand people and Nick is cleaning his face.

He goes to sleep thinking yes, that is what he wants to be.

In the evening, Peter's aunt disappears into the kitchen to wash dishes, leaving him alone with his cousin and his uncle. The aunt is part of an indistinct balance in this house which protects him, and in her absence, he suddenly feels his uncle staring at him from behind.

He turns to meet the stare, and in the moment it takes his uncle to change his expression, to close the thought off his face, Peter has caught him. He doesn't know at what.

It feeds him, to see his uncle afraid.

The moment passes; the taste remains. His uncle opens a drawer looking for a cigar and then pushes open the kitchen door to say he needs a beer. The taste of the moment is still in Peter's mouth later as he lies in bed waiting to sleep.

It tastes like blood.

His cousin sleeps down the hall, in the room that was his sister's. The smell of cigarette smoke comes through the door, which is always closed. Beyond the door, his clothes are thrown across chairs, his posters are hung on the wall. He hides his cigarettes and magazines in places his mother cannot reach—she is too heavy to get on her knees and look under the bed, too heavy to climb on a chair in his closet.

There is nothing of Peter's sister left in the room, but in his sense of the place, the room is still hers.

He lies in the dark, fingering a lump in his eyebrow, remembering another collision—this one with Nick's head—that afternoon in the gym. It was as if a door had slammed shut, and in that instant he could feel the soft sleeves of the dresses hanging in his mother's closet.

He hears his uncle in the hallway, walking quietly toward his door from the top of the stairs. His footsteps stop, and then the door opens. His uncle's face comes into the room, pushed there ahead of his body, as if in a dream. Peter sits up in bed.

"Get dressed."

Peter smells the black, after-dinner cigar, and then, as his uncle comes farther into the room, he smells the beer. His uncle has been drinking alone downstairs, something he does more often now that he is having the trouble with the Italians.

Peter has watched him, sitting with a bottle or a glass in his hand, staring at the front door.

He pulls on his jeans and the socks from the day before and then ties the laces on his tennis shoes. His uncle watches him, swaying slightly, smiling.

"What are we doing?" he says. Thinking it is possible that he is taking him to the same place he took his father.

His uncle holds a finger against his lips and motions for him to follow. They are out the front door before he speaks again.

"You tell your Aunt Theresa," he says, "we're dead."

Peter follows his uncle, liking the sound of that, to the Cadillac parked across the street, and gets in the front seat. His uncle lights a cigar before he starts the engine. The boy looks back at the house, at the dark window that is his room.

They drive east, crossing Broad, and then all the way down to Two Street where they turn left, heading north. His uncle looks at him twice during this trip, the last time as he is stopping the car. They are in the middle of a block; there is noise coming from a bar across the street.

His uncle opens the door and gets out. "Wait here," he says. He looks back into the car a moment, deciding something, and then says, "Get in the back."

Peter gets into the back seat. His uncle closes the door and crosses the street. He stops at a door next to the bar's, and then opens it. He has his own key.

Peter waits, listening to the pitch of the voices inside the bar. A dog walks past, then a drunk. He is unnoticed, sitting in the dark of the back seat.

A light comes on in the apartment over the door, and then the curtains in one of the windows are pulled aside and he sees a woman looking down at the car. She lifts her hand to her mouth and then Peter sees the point of her cigarette glow red. The smoke rises like another curtain.

His uncle appears behind her. The boy sees him in silhouette, almost as a shadow. He sees him touch her.

The woman turns then and disappears into the room. In a moment, two men come out of the bar, arguing, one of them holding a bottle.

"I told you a hundred fucking times," says the one without the bottle. "How many fucking times I got to tell you?"

The other one does not answer. He stands in one place on the sidewalk, claiming it.

"You hear me? I ast you a fucking question, John. I ast you a fucking question, you say the answer, right?"

The man without the bottle moves closer as he says that, his right hand is a fist hidden just behind his leg, as if it were a weapon. The man with the bottle waits; and in the car, Peter waits too.

"I'm givin' you one more chance," says the man without the bottle. As he says that, he takes a step closer, into the place on the sidewalk the other one has claimed. He lifts his hands, as if to sing.

"You're my brother," he says, "so I'm giving you one more chance . . ."

And as he says that, the bottle arcs in the air and comes down across the side of his face. He staggers and turns halfway around, as if to walk away, but then turns back, lowers his head and charges.

When the door leading to the apartment opens, the two men are lying on the sidewalk, locked into each other's headlocks, hitting each other without leverage, biting each other . . .

The woman stops for a moment to watch them. She is wearing a housecoat and hairy slippers, there is a cigarette between her fingers, lipstick marks on the filter. Peter sees every detail. The men yell and roll one way, then another.

"Youse two again," she says, and walks around their bodies and then crosses the street. She opens the back door without looking inside, and he smells her perfume even before she is in the car. She does not look at him until she has closed the door. Black specks of mascara hang in her eyelashes and there is lipstick on her teeth.

"You smoke?" she says.

He shakes his head no.

She puts the cigarette against her lips and as she pulls the smoke out, her face glows. She moves the cigarette away and then, using the same hand, she reaches across Peter's chest and touches the far side of his neck, pulling him. Her fingers are cold and the heat of the cigarette is somewhere under his ear. He allows himself to be pulled.

He smells her perfume, and then her hair spray, and then her lipstick. Her hair is stiff against his face. Her eyes move across his and then he feels her mouth pressing against his, and then feels her tongue in his mouth. Then her tongue is gone, and in the hole that leaves she blows the smoke in her chest into him.

She moves away slowly, straight back, looking into his eyes. She is smiling. "So now you smoke," she says.

She puts a hand on his chest and pushes him back until his head is resting in the corner between the seat and the window. "What else don't you do?"

He shakes his head, not knowing what to answer. On the periphery of his vision, he sees the two men still lying on the sidewalk. They are fighting quietly now, without words. Her housecoat falls open and he sees bruises, and then the tuft of hair between her legs; he notices the color of her fingernails.

Her hand moves up his leg, touching his penis through his pants, then opening his zipper. "Jesus," she says when she has it out, "you're bigger'n your uncle already."

He stares at her hand, the painted fingernails. The feel of her cool hand. A bead of liquid appears at the mouth of his penis, then breaks and slides down the side. She lowers her face into his line of vision.

"Don't tell him I said that, okay?" she says.

He shakes his head no.

"That's the kind of thing might piss him off," she says. She shakes her head. "You never know with Phil. . . ."

She leans back until her hair spreads out across the seat and then, still holding him by the penis, she lifts her legs over his shoulders and pulls him down on top of her.

"Your uncle's scary when he gets mad," she says.

She moves his penis until he feels it touching something wet. "You know what that is?" she says, teasing him now.

He nods his head.

"That's a nice wet pussy," she says. "Your uncle said you didn't know what a pussy was, wanted to start you off with the best there is."

She watches him a moment, waiting. He doesn't know for what. "Push," she says finally.

And he pushes in, and she closes her eyes.

And someplace behind him, he feels his uncle watching.

Peter looks down at himself in the dark, and sees the glistening of moisture on his penis as it moves back and forth into the opening in this woman; he realizes this is the place his uncle puts his penis too.

And he closes his eyes, holding that idea, and the idea of his uncle somewhere behind, watching, and pushes as deep as he can into this hole.

Poisoning him.

That is his thought.

"Jesus," he hears her say, "you're a natural. . . ."

She leaves the car with no more ceremony than she entered it. She closes her housecoat when he has finished, fits her feet into her slippers, and gets out. He watches her cross the street and then, before she reaches the door of her apartment, she kicks at the two men still lying on the sidewalk.

"Would youse two move it somewhere else for once?" she says. And then she steps over them, walks through the unlocked door, and is gone.

Peter steps outside the car, feeling the cool air on his face. The men lie motionless on the sidewalk. He hears music from inside the bar. He is tired and a disappointment settles over him. He wonders if that is really the best pussy there is. He doesn't think so, it struck him as ordinary.

He stumbles onto the idea that all women may think their pussies are the best. How would they know?

It is another half hour before his uncle appears in the doorway. He hikes his pants as he steps onto the sidewalk, and stops halfway across the street to light his cigar. Peter gets back into the car to wait for him.

The smell of her is everywhere. Her perfume, her hair spray, her pussy. It stirs him, he cannot understand why. It seems possible to him now that pussy is better before and after than it is when you've got a penis in it.

He wonders if that is the secret.

His uncle smiles at him a moment—waiting for some sign, as if there is an agreement to seal. He reaches across the seat and rubs the top of Peter's head. Peter feels the weight of his rings. His uncle puts the key in the ignition and starts the engine.

"So," he says, "I suppose now you want to drive my car." Peter doesn't answer. His uncle laughs and pulls into the street.

"My first piece of ass," he says a few minutes later, "I was fourteen years old. How do you like that?"

The boy shakes his head.

"Went to a house up on Diamond Street and caught a dose first time out of the gate." His uncle drives quietly a moment, smiling, remembering it. The streetlights pass over his face and throw shadows across the pockmarks.

"I always said my kids wouldn't have to go to a whorehouse to find out about pussy."

He looks at Peter then in a strange way. "That's what people want for their kids," he says, including Peter, "a better life than they had themselves."

The car is quiet a few blocks.

They miss the light at Broad, and somehow, in the absence of motion, the silence between them is agonizing. Somehow in the absence of motion, there is nothing there in the car but the man and the boy, and the thing the man has done to him.

"You're a quiet kid, you know that?" his uncle says.

Peter can't think of anything to say; he says nothing.

"When I got pussy the first time, I couldn't stop talking about it," he says. He waits for Peter to answer. The light changes, the boy's uncle does not move to cross the intersection. He sits, looking at the boy, waiting for him to say something. Getting mad. The boy searches for words and there aren't any there.

A horn blows behind them, his uncle ignores it. "Sometimes, I think I brought you two up all wrong," he says. "That you don't do nobody no favors making things easy."

The horn blows again, and his uncle slams the car's transmission into park and steps outside, leaving the door open, and stands in the headlights of the car behind them. The horn goes silent, and his uncle gets back inside.

The traffic light turns red, and his uncle drives through the intersection.

"What you like," he says, calmer now, almost back to the house, "is to know where somebody stands."

Peter looks at him and knows what he is asking.

"I mean, I don't care if a guy's quiet or loud, as long as I know whose side he's on." His uncle looks at him again, making it a question.

Peter doesn't answer.

"Things get tense, the guy you got to think about isn't your enemy, it's the guy you don't know if he's your enemy." He looks at Peter. "I'm telling you this for your own good," he says. "That's the guy that gets you, the traitor."

"I'm no traitor," Peter says.

His uncle stops the car in front of the house. His cigar has gone out and he lights it, cupping his hands. The smoke rises to the ceiling, looking for a way out. His uncle smiles.

"I never thought you was," he says.

A month later, late at night, the house begins to fill. There are men from the roofer's union, who work for Peter's uncle, and there are Italians. The young ones who have come to the house before to complain about the old man Constantine.

Who want to take what he has away from him, but don't have the balls to try.

The first tap at the front door wakes Peter up. He lies still, staring at the ceiling, and listens to the voices downstairs.

"It's done," the man says.

"No fuck-ups?" his uncle says.

"No fuck-ups."

In a moment there is another noise at the door, and Peter edges out of bed and walks barefoot over the cool floor to a spot near the top of the stairs to listen. He presses his back into the wall, hearing the breath come in and out of his mouth. "No fuck-ups?" one of the Italians asks.

"No, everything's good," his uncle says.

Another knock at the door.

His cousin comes out into the hallway then, and makes his way down to the place where Peter is standing. He smells of cigarettes and hair oil.

"They was outside the place on Twelfth Street," someone says downstairs. "Never seen a thing."

"What about the others?" his uncle says.

"The others ain't a problem," the Italian says.

"Jesus," Michael whispers. Peter turns to look at him. "They did Constantine."

"Bullshit," Peter says.

He is telling the truth, though. Michael makes up things he would like to be true, but this time Peter sees it's happened.

His cousin smiles at him in the dark. His voice is trembling and happy. "We did Constantine."

Peter hears his uncle's voice again and it is trembling too, but in a different way.

"What do you mean, they ain't a problem," he says.

"They ain't a problem," the Italian says. "They're all old men. Let them move to Arizona and buy green pants for the golf course."

The room downstairs is suddenly quiet. Peter feels his cousin smiling at him in the dark. "What did I tell you?" he whispers.

"The deal's still the same. . . ." his uncle says.

"Nothing's changed."

But something has changed. Peter hears it.

"We run our business, you run yours," his uncle says. "Nobody comes around wanting to be consultants."

It is quiet again.

"As far as we're concerned," the Italian says.

"What about the old guys?" his uncle says. "They're out of it too, right? You'll take care of that."

"Shit, they're a hundred years old."

"What's that mean, they're a hundred years old?"

"It means you did us a favor with Constantine, we leave you alone," the Italian says, getting angry. "It don't mean we hold your fucking hand. You got a problem with the old guys, you take care of it yourself. It's your business."

Peter waits while that settles.

"Look, these guys are tired," the Italian says. "With Constantine gone, all they want now is nobody does them too. Let 'em alone, maybe throw them a bone once in a while, everybody gets along. There ain't no reason to go hurting a bunch of old men. . . ."

"Shit," his cousin breathes, "we got Constantine." Peter puts his hand over his cousin's mouth. He listens to the men downstairs talk, convincing his uncle that the old Italians are harmless now.

"Things are going to be different," his cousin says. Peter looks at him again, and his cousin whispers, "We can do anything we want."

Nick hears of Constantine's death at seven in the morning at Ed's Diner. The place is full of smoke and all the booths are taken. Ed comes out of the kitchen wearing a clean apron and spots him sitting at the far end of the counter.

Nick has wrapped his hands around a hot cup of coffee, trying to get them warm. Ed moves past Phyllis, his morning waitress, who is bent over behind the counter looking for something in her purse. He lifts his stomach with his hands to squeeze past her bottom, and then gives her a pat on the fanny on the way past.

"Ed, I'm warning you," she says. She comes up red-faced, her lips fastened around an unlit cigarette. She leans into one of the gas stoves to light it, then picks up an order of eggs and scrapple, trying to remember whose it is.

"You got scrapple and eggs, Nick?" she says.

"Nick don't eat breakfast," Ed says, "you know that." She sets the food down farther up the counter and Ed stands in front of Nick and wipes his hands on the apron.

"How 'bout Constantine," he says quietly.

Nick looks up. Ed checks both directions, as if he were afraid of being overheard.

"They got him over on Twelfth Street last night, parked right in front of his house."

"Who?" Nick says.

Ed shrugs. "The Young Turks, I guess. The old guys been holding off the young guys a long time now."

Nick doesn't know any of the Young Turks.

Ed says, "One behind the ear and then one in the eye."

"He was alone?"

"The bodyguard's got a concussion on his head, says they must of knocked him out first." He shakes his head and the men are both quiet.

"You wonder where does a guy like that—the bodyguard I mean—where does he think he's going to hide?" Ed says.

Nick takes a drink of his coffee.

"They must of put him in a corner," Ed says, meaning the bodyguard. "Somebody puts you in a corner, you can't tell what you're going to do."

Nick thinks about that, about worrying over what you should have done. Who you should have done. He thinks that people in Constantine's business must worry all the time. "What a way to live," he says.

Ed looks around his diner. "Myself, I'd rather just work for a living, drive home in an Oldsmobile."

Nick nods and sips at his coffee. Phyllis squeezes behind Ed, carrying two plates to the booths. "You don't mind moving your ass, Ed," she says, "there's people come in here to eat." He smiles at Nick and backs into her a little, moving his behind against her stomach.

"Ed, I'm warning you," she says. "I'm going to put these fucking eggs down your pants."

Ed turns to look at the plates, considering it. "What are they," he says, "over easy?"

Nick goes back to the shop, carrying a cup of coffee in a paper bag. An old Ford Fairlane 500 is sitting in the garage, its hood open, the engine cold and black. Nick opens the bag and puts the coffee on the fender and then hangs a light from the hood release and turns it on.

The car is as old as Harry. The engine is caked in grease a quarter-inch thick, stone cold, and he reaches in and chips at the battery cables where they connect to the posts, trying to knock off enough of the yellowed crust of iron oxide so he can fit a wrench there and loosen the cables.

The man who owns this car lives in a row house with his wife and her mother three blocks from the garage, and has never changed the oil. He doesn't believe in changing oil, he believes in adding one quart when the engine gets two quarts low. He says changing the oil is like having relatives move in; he says it upsets his engine.

Nick clears away enough of the iron oxide to get his wrench around the nut and then presses until feels it give. He pulls the wrench toward him until it hits the engine block, then regrips the nut, and pulls it back again. When it is loose enough, he reaches in with his hand and twists the cable off. Then he begins on the other post.

He hears water running upstairs, the old man in the shower. Nick tries to remember how long he has been up there; he thinks it is probably a month.

Nick isn't sure if he wants him to leave or not. He's clean at least. He keeps himself clean. And if he's upstairs, Nick doesn't have to worry about what happened to him after he left.

Sometimes now in the morning he will come down into the shop and sit in a corner and watch Nick work. He'll bring tools when Nick needs them and then put them back; sometimes he sweeps.

Most afternoons now, when the gym begins to fill up, he leaves. He doesn't like kids, or coloreds. The kids tease him, pretending to steal the bag he keeps his things in, saying "Pop-pop-pop" while he moves around the room sweeping.

The old man will push the broom at their feet or make a spitting noise that is not quite "Pop"—a noise that Nick now understands is as close as he can come to "Fuck"—and then, unless Nick makes them leave him alone, the old man's face will turn murderous and dark, and he will pick up his things and disappear. He has his own key now; Nick doesn't know when he comes back.

The kids are always after him. Nick doesn't know how to tell them to leave him alone without hurting his feelings. He knows he wouldn't want to be protected himself.

He twists the other cable off, and then lifts the battery out of the car and sets it on the sidewalk just outside the open door. The owner of the Ford will want to see it. He's known Nick thirty years, but still he'll want proof he isn't trying to rob him.

He stands up slowly and sees the mail lady walking up the sidewalk. He waits for her there, on the sidewalk, noticing the way the strap holding the mailbag presses into her narrow shoulder. She's got bad skin and two kids and her husband's in the Detention Center on a burglary. Nick knows the house where she lives, but he can't remember her name.

"Nicky, how you doin'?" she says. Her face is covered with powder to hide the rough spots, and she's turned her eyelids blue. Her perfume mixes with the smell of gasoline, and she has a ring on every finger of her right hand.

Earrings as long as her ears themselves. Anything to keep you from looking at her complexion.

"You're going to break your shoulders," he says, looking at the bag. It's stuffed and spilling out the top.

"What's breakin' is my balls," she says, and grabs herself there quickly. Her pants are tight across her stomach, and the material bunches together in the place she touched. It seems to him that she gets her good disposition from that place, he couldn't say why. Other women, he knows, don't like her.

He smiles while she looks into her bag, and then she hands him half a pound of mail from people he doesn't know. He goes through it quickly, noticing a letter for the old man.

Nick looks at the small, careful writing on the envelope.

"Urban Matthews."

The old man is the only person named Urban Nick ever heard of. It's his second letter.

He got the first one couple of weeks ago—a check from the government—and now a letter from Des Moines, Iowa. He wonders if they have Catholic schools in Des Moines. It looks like the handwriting of somebody who went to Catholic school.

"That's it," she says, and she reaches out suddenly and squeezes Nick's hand.

He watches her walk up the street—her pants are tight across the back too—and remembers a morning when she stopped something she was saying about her husband's lawyer to lick her thumb and wipe at a grease stain at the corner of his mouth.

He climbs the stairs with the letter and finds the old man sitting naked, except for his socks and shoes, on the edge of a chair near the mats. He is bent at the waist, his fingers pushed all the way to the knuckles into a hole in one of the mats, retrieving something he has hidden.

The old man starts when he sees him, and drops the mat. Nick looks around the room, thinking there is probably money hidden a hundred places up here.

"You got a letter from Iowa," he says.

The old man accepts the letter without moving off the chair. A scar runs the length of his stomach, dividing it. The skin billows up on each side, hiding the scar itself, all of it but the deep red stitch marks at the ends.

The old man bends again and picks up a towel off the floor and his face is florid when he comes back up. He covers his lap with the towel and looks up at Nick, waiting for him to leave.

Nick looks other places in the room, not to intrude. He blows into his hands and nods toward the window. "Cold today," he says.

The old man waits.

Nick heads toward the staircase. As he starts down, the old man is studying the envelope, as if he were trying to decide how to open it. The towel falls off his lap again; he doesn't seem to notice.

Nick returns to the Ford.

He sets the new battery on the tray in the corner of the engine compartment, and then reconnects the cables. Leaving the hood open, he gets into the front seat and turns the key. The engine cranks and then starts; the garage fills with black smoke.

He parks the Ford on the sidewalk and then backs a Plymouth into the spot where the Ford had been and begins a ring job. He works quickly, to keep himself warm. He thinks of pulling the Plymouth all the way into the garage and shutting the door, but the feel of the place changes when it's sealed off; it's like a hotel room.

Still, he'd like to shut the door. He would if Harry were here to keep him company. He thinks about his son as he takes the cylinder head off, exposing the pistons—the earnest expression that comes over his face when he looks into an engine. He remembers the same look on the kid's face when he was sitting in a high chair, figuring out a banana.

He is reminded suddenly of Charley's son, who is always serious, and can't be talked out of it, the way Harry can. A kid who understands too much, who isn't really a kid at all, not a whole one.

He's got a foot in the world.

Nick knows because he was that kind of kid himself.

Sometime before lunch, he realizes that he hasn't heard anything move upstairs. Even when the old man doesn't come down
in the morning, he hears him moving.

He straightens out of the engine and holds still, listening.

Not a sound.

Nick eats soup for lunch. The diner is full now, everyone
talking about Constantine. He listens to two men at the counter.

"It was drugs. Constantine wouldn't let no drugs on the street,
and it was too much money in it. If it wasn't for that, he's still
alive."

"How old was he?" the other one says.

"I don't know, seventy-eight, seventy-nine, but he was all there,
you know? He knew what he was about."

"Anybody seventy-nine years old ain't all there. You get that
old, you start thinking your own dick's funny."

Nick sits with his face a few inches over the soup bowl, not
wanting to be included. He thinks of his own father, who died at
seventy-six.

"Phyllis thinks my dick's funny already," the first man says.

She hears that as she walks past, carrying dirty dishes. "I think
it's a riot," she says and disappears into the kitchen.

"I ain't kidding," the other one says. "My wife's father, he started laughing at his dick. He'd take it out at dinner and laugh."

"For what?"

"I don't know for what. Like it was a big joke."

Nick blows across his spoon and leans into the steam rising off the bowl. The metal burns his lips and his eyes water. The conversation stops and starts.

"Constantine wasn't laughing at his dick. He knew what he was about."

It is quiet a moment, and then Phyllis comes through the swinging doors, carrying hamburgers.

"You don't believe me," the same man says, "you see what happens now. You want to see some crazy shit, you watch what happens now the young guys take over."

Nick stands up and walks to the cash register. Phyllis takes his money, makes the change. "Give me a coffee and one of them donuts," he says.

She puts a jelly donut and the coffee in the same bag and he carries it back to the garage. The Plymouth is sitting where he left it. He looks at the engine, remembering where he was, and then heads upstairs. The old man likes sweets, maybe the donut will cheer him up.

He isn't there.

His bags are pushed into a corner near the mats and covered with a blanket. He has more things now than when he came; Nick isn't sure what kind of things they are. He keeps them covered. Nick looks at the blanket, estimating the number of bags underneath. Four.

He walks to the window near the old man's things and sets the paper bag on the chair where he will see it. The coffee will stay warm an hour and the donut is good for a week. The old man still eats from garbage cans, he doesn't mind stale donuts.

Thinking of that, Nick passes the trash can on the way back to the stairs. He stops and lifts the top and looks inside, wondering what it would be like. Adhesive tape, a Vaseline jar, old newspapers, dust. Before the old man came, the same stuff would have been all over the floor.

He sees the letter right away, torn in half and then in quarters. The envelope is on the other side of the can, intact. It would be an easy thing to put the pieces of the letter together, and Nick stares at them, wondering what sort of life they might say this Urban Matthews had.

What he gave up for paper bags and a borrowed corner of a gym. Who he gave up.

But it's the old man's business.

Nick puts the lid back on the can and walks downstairs to finish the Plymouth.

Nick is sitting in the window late in the afternoon, watching the street for Urban, when the black car stops in front of the gym and begins to unload. First two men in windbreakers who check the street, then Phillip Flood, then the boys.

The men in the windbreakers stay on the street and Phillip Flood and the boys come up.

"Nicky," Phillip says, "I come over to ask you a favor." Nick doesn't answer. Phillip draws him back to the windows, where he can watch the street as they talk.

"I don't know what you heard about me and Constantine," he says, "but the man was like my own family."

Nick looks at him, surprised. The Lincoln is still sitting in the middle of the narrow street, white smoke coming out of the tailpipe almost the way water pours out of a faucet. The men in the windbreakers have gotten back inside.

"We had our disagreements, but I give you my word . . ."

Nick looks at him, thinking, *So this is who got Constantine? A Mick?*

He remembers the way his hand felt patting his pocket after he'd put the hundred-dollar bill there.

"Like my own family," he says, moving to put his face in Nick's line of sight.

Phillip Flood shakes his head. "On account of the way this happened, I think there could be some misunderstandings, you understand what I mean?"

"Misunderstandings," Nick says.

"And I just want to ask you, you know, to let the boys come up here like before. That's all. And I might have somebody to come up here with them, to keep an eye out that none of this shit spills over onto you."

His hand moves to the side of Nick's cheek. He pats him there, and then on the back of the neck.

"I got people tellin' me to hide until everything calms down," he says. He pauses a moment, as if to think it over, then shakes his head. "That just makes it look worst, right?"

Nick doesn't answer. The hand moves off the back of his neck.

"I don't want nobody in here carrying," Nick says, looking at the car outside.

Phillip Flood smiles. "No problem, Nick. They'll stay downstairs, you won't even know they're around."

Nick nods.

"Is that all right, they stay down there on the street?"

He shrugs. "It ain't my street."

Phillip turns back into the room and watches an old-time trainer working a young colored fighter in the ring, moving his padded catching gloves to call for hooks or jabs. The force of the punches throws the trainer's ancient arms backward, and finally knocks the glove off his left hand.

The fighter waits while he bends slowly to retrieve it, and then fits it back over his hand. A respectful kid, Nick thinks, he won't say anything to hurt his feelings. For the same reason, he doesn't take anything off his punches when he starts in again.

"How are they doin', anyway?" Phillip Flood says, meaning the boys. "They learning to fight?"

"They're doing all right," Nick says. He can't remember the last time Phillip's kid even got out of his street clothes.

It is quiet a moment while Phillip watches the trainer and the colored kid in the gym. When he turns back, something has changed.

"Tell me something, Nick," he says. "If they're doing all right, how come Peter comes home busted up all the time and Michael don't ever get a fucking mark on him?"

Nick takes his time answering. "Everybody's got their own speed," he says finally.

Phillip Flood nods. "Maybe I'll come by some time and watch them mix it up."

Nick shrugs.

"You don't mind I come by and watch," he says, watching Nick, as if he's trapped him. The kid in the ring knocks the glove off the old trainer's hand again.

Nick shrugs. "Nobody has to fight up here," he says, "that ain't the idea. If they feel like it, then they can fight. You feel like it, you can watch."

"They feel like it," Phillip Flood says, and then pats him again on the cheek. "Kids are always fightin', right?" He smiles and then starts to leave, the moist feel of his hand is still on Nick's cheek.

Nick stops him, grabbing his elbow. Phillip Flood looks at the hand; everything in the gym seems to stop. Out of the corner of his eye, Nick sees his son, standing in his socks on the scale, his face perfectly still, watching.

"I don't want nobody up here with guns," he says.

Phillip Flood nods. "Yeah, you already said that," he says.

Nick lets go of him and turns back to the window in time to see the old man crossing slowly in front of the black Cadillac, looking inside. He stops for a moment, as if the car has no business there, and then the driver's side door opens and one of the men in the windbreakers steps out, his head tilted at an angle just behind his left shoulder, and watches him until he moves to the other sidewalk.

The man in the windbreaker gets back inside the car; Nick sees him laughing at something the other man says.

The old man and Phillip Flood pass each other on the stairs, and by the time the old man clears the stairwell, the gym is itself again, full of movement and noise. All of it somehow connected, like an engine.

Harry is tying his shoes, the ancient trainer in the ring shuffles to his right, holding the catching gloves for the fighter to hit. A cop does sit-ups on a board propped against the edge of the ring, a huge white kid who has been training here the last week begins hitting one of the heavy bags.

The place has no memory, and that's the way it is supposed to be too.

Over on the bench, Charley's kid—what's his name, Peter?—is taking off his street clothes to work out. He hangs his shirt and pants carefully from the nails overhead, and puts his socks in his shoes and slides them underneath. He bends over to pull on his sweat socks, still as narrow as a bird across the chest, but he is growing into his body. He is going to be strong—Nick already feels it when they're in the ring—but he's got no talent for this, no instincts. Everything he knows, he's learned.

Not that there weren't fighters who went somewhere without talent, but that kind, there wasn't usually much else they could do. And the payments went up all the time. Even after they quit. Something in that thought—the payments—calls up the uneasy feeling Nick gets once in a while watching Harry in the ring, that this could lead someplace it isn't supposed to.

But it's not the same situation. Harry's protected. And he has talent; he has Nick.

But Charley's kid—something occurs to Nick that's been in the back of his mind almost since the first day Phillip Flood brought him up here.

He thinks maybe Charley's kid likes to get hit.

Peter and Michael sit in the back seat of a car. The two men who picked them up at the gym are inside the gas station while the attendant cleans the windows. He takes a long time, making sure the dirt is out of the corners.

"Jimmy Measles told me he'd get us blown," Michael says.

Peter feels a chill run six ways at once through his body. He thinks of the woman who stepped into the back seat of his uncle's car that night; he has thought of her every day and night since it happened. Repeated the words she said to him, remembering the sound.

"Blown?" he says.

Michael shrugs and looks out the window. "Anytime we want. He'll take us to *Bandstand* and get us blown."

"We can't get into *Bandstand*. We can't dance."

"He can get us in. He's on the committee."

"How come he can get blown at *Bandstand*, he's hanging around in front of Nick's all week dancing with a light pole?"

Michael stares at the men inside, smoking cigarettes, and when he answers his breath fogs the window. "He's scared they're going to kick his ass."

"Who?"

"Kids at *Bandstand,* I don't know. They said they were going to kick his ass, so we go along to protect him and he gets us blown."

"We're supposed to protect Jimmy Measles? You seen those guys on television? They're seventeen years old."

Michael looks at his cousin and smiles. "All we got to do is show up with him."

Peter sits quietly in the back seat of the car, waiting for the men who work for his uncle to come out of the filling station, imagining blow jobs from the girls he has seen on television.

"Nobody's going to fuck with us," his cousin says.

The same two men always pick Peter and Michael up at school and take them to the gym. Ever since Constantine was hit. They wait outside and then drive them home. In between, they leave for half an hour and visit the Rosemont Diner on Passyunk for coffee and Danish.

They aren't supposed to leave, but then they aren't supposed to eat in the car either, and they do that all the time. They are big men with thick necks, and Peter doesn't think they are afraid of his uncle, even though they pretend to be.

They leave for the Rosemont at the same time every afternoon. They order the same Danish, sit in the same table by the window, and are back in thirty minutes.

Michael has followed them, and knows these things down to the number of sugars they put in their coffee.

Eight.

On the afternoon Jimmy Measles is going to get them blown, Peter waits by the stairs, his gym bag at his feet, while Michael watches the street from the corner of the window.

"You ain't going to train today?" Nick says.

Peter shakes his head. He says, "We got someplace we got to go."

Nick nods, looking at him, then at his cousin. "You waiting for your uncle?" he says.

Peter looks into his face and says, "No." He doesn't lie to Nick.

"You going to do something stupid?" he says.

Peter thinks it over; he doesn't know. It feels stupid, but it's something you do a lot when you get older. At least he thinks it is. "Naw, we're just going somewhere."

Nick smiles at him as if he knows where they are going, and a moment later Michael leaves the window and hurries toward the stairs.

"Let's go," he says.

Michael notices Nick watching them, and he smiles. "We got to go back to school," he says. Nick nods.

And then Michael is headed down the stairs and Peter is starting down after him. Nick is still at the top, looking at him in a peculiar way.

"It isn't too stupid, Nick," Peter says.

Nick nods. "Something a little stupid, that's good for you once in a while."

Jimmy Measles is waiting on the sidewalk downstairs. He is wearing new pants and a green jacket and he practices dance steps as they walk to Broad Street to catch the C bus. The toe of one of his black loafers touches the cement behind the heel of the other, his elbows come tight against his sides, and then he spins effortlessly, never losing a step, his eyes closing as he goes around.

Everything is easy for Jimmy Measles.

The sidewalk narrows under some scaffolding, and Peter steps behind Jimmy Measles and Michael, and watches them from the back. Michael has combed his hair back over his ears on both sides, the way Jimmy Measles does, the way Fabian does; it meets in the center of the back of his head.

"Now these chicks, man," Jimmy Measles is saying, "let them suck you and then get rid of them. They're a pain in the ass later. Always wanting you to give them something, or saying they want to go with you. Sometimes they say they're going with you even if they aren't."

"Shit, man," Michael says.

Jimmy Measles nods, and looks quickly over his shoulder to include Peter in the conversation. "They feel guilty after they blow somebody, so they try to get you to go with them, it makes them feel better."

He laughs suddenly; he and Michael laugh together.

"Sometimes, you even got to promise to do that before they'll blow you, but it don't count. It's just something they like to hear before they do the deed. . . ."

He turns again to Peter, his smile stretches slowly all the way across his handsome face. It is the kind of smile that makes Peter wish he could smile the same way back.

"Nothing to worry about, my man," Jimmy Measles says.

Michael turns and looks at him too. "He ain't worried," he says.

They cross Broad Street and wait on the other side for the bus. Jimmy Measles looks at one of them, then the other, and then suddenly he laughs. "So youse want to get blown," he says.

The bus stops in front of them, dripping and filthy, the brakes as loud as the engine. The door opens and they climb up the steps and stop while Jimmy Measles pays all the fares, dropping three quarters into the coin box. The bus jerks forward as they are walking to the back and Peter is thrown ahead, as if he were being pushed someplace he does not want to go.

They sit down, Jimmy Measles and Michael on one bench, Peter across from them on another.

Jimmy Measles dances in his seat, his shoulders moving back and forth. He pulls his fingers from imaginary holsters and points them at Peter. "So, my man," he says, "you ready?"

Peter looks up and down the empty bus. "So who are these guys who want to beat you up?" he says.

T hey take the C bus to Market, and the elevated train out to Forty-sixth. Peter can see the line of dancers waiting outside the Arena door before he gets off the train.

Some of the girls he recognizes from television; he knows how they dance. They are wearing coats and jackets over their skirts, it looks like they all have new shoes. They are chewing gum, smoking cigarettes, doing little dance steps there in line.

Some of the girls call to Jimmy Measles while he is still on the stairway leading down from the elevated stop. They leave their places in line when he gets to the sidewalk, half a dozen girls all around him, pressing against him, pressing against Peter to get close to Jimmy Measles.

Michael is caught in it too. Peter sees his hand touch a tall girl's knee and then disappear up underneath her skirt.

"Jimmy, baby," one of them says, "I got something to show

you." He stops walking to look at the girl, and she turns her head and pulls her shoulders back and moves underneath her skirt exactly the way the woman in the back of the car had moved when Peter was inside her.

Jimmy Measles watches, smiling, until she stops. "Maureen, you know you can't do that shit on television," he says.

He walks toward the door, Michael hurrying to stay at his shoulder, as if he is afraid to be left behind with the dancers. Peter looks up and down the line for someone who might beat up Jimmy Measles, but no one seems to mind that he's there, or even that he is going to the front of the line ahead of them.

Peter walks a few steps behind, thinking they ought to get in the line with everyone else.

Jimmy Measles smiles at the guard on the door—a man, not a kid—and pats him on the shoulder. Then he and Michael walk past, into the building, and Peter goes in after them.

They walk beyond the studio entrance into a hallway that says AUTHORIZED PERSONNEL ONLY—NO ADMITTANCE. Peter stops to look at the sign, but Jimmy Measles motions him to follow along, dancing as he points the way.

At the end of the hallway is a door, marked MANAGER. Jimmy Measles knocks twice and then goes in, without waiting for an answer. Peter stops at the entrance and looks inside. A plump, pale-skinned man with curly black hair that has been oiled until it looks wet is sitting behind the desk, a bottle of vodka sitting with him. There is a glass next to the bottle, empty except for the ice. The man's face is red and his lips are wet.

"Jimmy," he says, "how you doing, my man?"

"Alan, my man . . ."

Jimmy Measles steps behind the desk and kisses the man on the cheek. There is something out of place in it, it is somehow too familiar, too easy. Not formal, the way the Italians kiss each other. "So, who's this?" the man says, looking at Michael.

Peter stays where he is in the doorway.

"This is my man Michael and his cousin Peter."

The man looks from one to the other and then at Jimmy. "How old are they?"

"Phillip Flood," Jimmy Measles says. "That's Phil the Roofer's kid, and that's his nephew."

The man gets out of his seat, shorter than he had looked sitting down, swaying slightly, and leans across the desk to shake Michael's hand. Everything is easy with Jimmy Measles.

"So," he says, falling back into his chair, "you guys are dancers, are you?"

Peter looks at his size 9½ U.S. Keds basketball shoes, the laces knotted where they've broken, and tries to imagine them dancing on television.

Michael is nodding his head.

"We were wondering," Jimmy Measles said, "could we use your office a few minutes before the show. A little business . . ."

The man smiles and gets to his feet. "It's yours, my man," he says. He stands up suddenly, and stumbles as he passes through the door, smiling at Peter with unfocused eyes.

Jimmy Measles goes out of the room a moment later, and Michael walks behind the desk and tries out the man's chair. Behind him, on the wall, are pictures of the man with Fabian, Bobby Vinton, Bobby Rydell, Dion, Frankie Avalon. Most of them are autographed the same way. *For my good pal Louie, all the best . . .*

Peter steps into the office and looks around. There are stains on the floor and the sofa, and a sweet, dirty smell that somehow goes with them. No windows to air the place out. Michael opens a drawer of the desk and looks inside, then another drawer.

He is still going through the man's desk when Jimmy Measles comes back through the door towing the girl from outside. Maureen. He closes the door and she sees Peter, and stops dead. They look at each other, and in that moment he is sorry for coming. Sorry for her, sorry for walking to the front of the line, sorry for what he wants.

"What's he doing here?" she says. And then she sees Michael too, and starts for the door. Jimmy Measles holds on to her hand, smiling.

"They're all right," he says, pulling her back.

She looks at them again. "Not him," she says, meaning Peter.

"I'll do you and him . . ." and she nods toward Michael, "but not him." Jimmy Measles looks at Peter and winks.

"He just wants to watch," he says.

She looks at Peter again, deciding. "I ain't doing this," she says, and moves again for the door. Jimmy Measles pulls her back. Either he is stronger than he looks or the girl is not trying very hard to get out of the room.

"I don't like the way he's lookin' at me already," she says. Peter wonders how he and the girl became enemies. He looks another direction, thinking she is about to start yelling. She is on the edge of that, but the room is quiet.

Peter walks back toward the door, intending to leave, but when he gets there Jimmy Measles is running his hand up and down the girl's back and she has closed her eyes, so she can't see him anyway. Jimmy Measles knows how to touch girls, he sees that.

He leans closer to her and puts his face in her hair. He whispers to her and she nods, without opening her eyes, and in that same moment Jimmy Measles looks at Peter through the girl's hair, and smiles.

"But not with him," she says suddenly. "I'll do you and the fat one behind the desk, but not him."

"Let him watch."

"He can watch, but that's all," she says. "I ain't doing three guys."

Jimmy Measles unbuckles his belt and unzips his pants. Peter sees his erect penis at the same time the girl does. She rolls her eyes, as if this were an old problem, and then drops to her knees in front of him.

"Just a minute," he says. "Wait a minute, will you?"

He lifts one foot and then the other, taking off his pants, and then carefully folds them and lays them across the desk. He puts his hands on top of the girl's head then and she picks a piece of lint off his penis and then, as Peter watches, the penis disappears into her mouth. When it is gone, all the way in, Jimmy Measles winks at Michael, who has come up off his chair to watch.

"Take two extra seconds," he says, "and you don't walk around all day in wrinkled pants."

Michael's lips are open and he is breathing through his mouth.

The girl's head moves back and forth under Jimmy Measles's hands, her eyes are closed tight, her own hands clenched in fists at her side. She could be sucking a lemon.

Peter stands still. Her lips roll back into her mouth as she slides into him, until Peter cannot see her lips at all, then bloom as she pulls away. He studies Jimmy Measles's face—it has changed now, lost its wink, and he is fixed on the girl's head as if he were angry.

It comes to him that he doesn't want to push his penis into somebody's mouth because she wants to be a dancer on *Bandstand* anyway. It comes to him that he is sorry for her, and that she sees it. It's the reason she won't blow him.

Jimmy Measles's hands tighten into fists around her hair and he closes his eyes and slams himself against her face. The veins stand out in his neck.

A second later, the girl coughs, begins to choke, and semen appears in the corner of her mouth and then runs down off her chin.

She tries to pull away, making choking noises, but Jimmy Measles holds her by the hair and moves himself in and out of her mouth until he is finished.

Then, gradually, he relaxes his fist and his face and his neck, and the girl drops back away from him, wiping her chin and mouth with the sleeve of her blouse, and sits on her heels.

Jimmy Measles carefully retrieves his pants and puts them on, checking for creases. She looks at Michael. "C'mon if you're comin'," she says. "We're going to miss the whole show."

The words pass across Michael's face. He comes around the desk, unbuttoning his pants as Jimmy Measles had done, taking them off, folding them and laying them across the same chair. Taking a long time to fold his pants.

His penis looks small and scared. She looks at it and then appeals to Jimmy Measles.

"We ain't got time for this," she says.

"Don't pay any attention," he says to Michael, "that's the first dick she ever saw that wasn't hard."

She frowns and then, giving in, she holds Michael's penis between her finger and thumb and guides it to her mouth. He puts his hands on top of her head as Jimmy Measles had done, but she pulls away and slaps at his arm.

"Do you mind?" she says.

He shakes his head no, and she puts it in her mouth again and begins moving in and out, perhaps half an inch each direction. Jimmy Measles takes the seat behind the desk and smiles.

"She isn't bad, is she?" he says.

Michael shrugs.

She works on him for what seems like a long time and then pulls away again.

"C'mon, Jimmy," she says, "he can't even get it up."

Jimmy Measles leans forward across the desk to see if that is true. Her words cross Michael's face again; tiny muscles shake.

"Maybe it's too many people in the room," Jimmy Measles says. "Some guys don't like having nobody watch."

He smiles at Michael, but Michael is looking at the girl kneeling in front of him.

"Shit, they're starting the music," she says.

Peter listens, and hears the faint sound of *Bandstand*.

"They're just warming up," Jimmy Measles says. "There's plenty of time." She takes Michael's penis in her mouth again and her movements now are more determined.

Jimmy Measles stands up and heads for the door. "Me and Peter are just gonna wait outside," he says. Michael watches them leave, looking as if he would like to leave with them.

Jimmy Measles closes the door and then leans against the wall and lights a cigarette. The sound of the music is louder here and Jimmy Measles begins to dance. Just his body, not his feet. It seems to happen by itself.

"You go in after Michael," he says, moving underneath his coat.

Peter looks at him, not understanding.

"She don't care how many guys she blows," he says. The music is louder now, and Peter imagines her on her knees inside the room, holding Michael's wilted penis in her mouth, hearing the music. Hearing her chance to dance on television today passing by.

"She doesn't want to blow anybody else," he says.

Jimmy Measles shrugs. He says, "What's that got to do with it?"

Somewhere there is a cry. Peter isn't sure where it comes from, but it doesn't seem to be part of the noise that is filling the hallway from the studio.

Jimmy Measles is moving his feet now, the cigarette hanging on his lip, doing some dance Peter has seen him practice outside the gym.

"You hear that?" Peter says.

Jimmy Measles stops dancing and looks at the door.

"What?"

Something breaks inside.

Jimmy Measles takes a last pull off his cigarette, spikes it against the wall, and opens the door. He stands still a moment and then walks in.

Peter hears something unnatural in his voice. "Easy, my man," he says, "take it easy . . ."

The girl is lying on her back when Peter steps back into the room, Michael sitting over her, one knee on each side, holding the vodka bottle by its neck, as if he were deciding whether or not to hit her again.

Her forehead is opened up and her hair is wet and dull with blood. The desk is moved off its spot, the imprint of its legs in the carpet. Jimmy Measles steps behind Michael and, keeping his pants clear, lifts him off the girl.

She does not move when Michael is pulled off her, but lies still, staring at the ceiling.

"Easy, man," Jimmy Measles says. "Calm down." But Michael is already calm. He stares at the girl, breathing through his mouth, still holding the bottle in his hand.

"Jesus," Jimmy Measles says, looking at her.

Michael steps over her to collect his pants. He watches her while he dresses; he seems fascinated that she doesn't move. Jimmy Measles bends over her and looks in her eyes.

"Maureen," he says, "you there?"

He slaps her lightly across the cheek, she doesn't seem to notice. He stands up and turns to Peter. "I think she's got a concussion," he says.

119

Michael stands up to button his pants and then puts his feet in his sneakers. He looks at her in a disconnected way, as if she were something to step over on the sidewalk.

The girl moves a little on the floor; her face turns one way and then the other, and then she vomits.

Jimmy Measles says, "Jesus Christ," and she vomits again. The smell fills the room, the smell and the music. One of her feet begins to shake spasmodically and the shoe on it—a loafer that has already slipped off her heel—drops onto the floor.

Michael sets the bottle back on the desk.

"We got to call somebody," Jimmy Measles says. His fingers run through his hair, and Peter sees that they are shaking. It is quiet in the room for a moment, then the girl burps and a thin, bubbly film emerges from a corner of her mouth.

Jimmy Measles looks up at Michael and smiles in a way that looks like maybe he's going to be sick too.

"What do we do with this?" he says.

Michael studies the girl, disconnected. Something to step over on the sidewalk.

"I'll call my old man," he says.

T he two men who drive Michael and Peter are sitting in chairs in the basement of a house in the Northeast. The wire holding them together cuts into their wrists, and their hands beneath the wire have turned blue.

It is eleven o'clock at night; the girl is at the University of Pennsylvania Hospital and Peter's uncle has not spoken a word since they left the house. Not during the long ride over, not when they stopped in front of the brick duplex and got out. Not when they walked down the stairs to the basement.

One of the men sitting in the chairs looks up at Peter's uncle; he does not speak. His eyes come to Peter, and then move on to

Michael. The other one sits with his head down, knowing there is no help.

"Francis, tell me what I told you."

Peter hears the edge in his uncle's voice. The man who knows there is no help lifts his head and then shakes it. "You said to watch them," he says.

His uncle nods.

"And what'd you do?"

"We went for a coffee," he says.

"Is that how you watch somebody, go for a coffee?"

The man doesn't answer.

"Phil . . ." the other one says.

Phillip Flood turns his head slowly.

"We thought they was with Nick, that's all. We went for a coffee."

His uncle seems to think that over. He thinks it over, and then nods his head, and when he speaks again there is something reasonable in his voice.

"Was I talkin' to you?" he says.

The man drops his head without answering. Phillip Flood picks up a piece of pipe two feet long and steps closer to the men. There are other men in the room; they stand in the corners and wait. Peter looks away just before his uncle swings.

The pipe lands three times, soft landings, and the only other sound in the room is his uncle's uneven breathing.

The noises stop and his uncle is staring at him.

"What are you doing?" he says.

"Nothing."

"You think I brought you down here to look at the fucking floor?"

Peter shakes his head. His cousin stares at the men in the chairs, excited.

"I brought youse down here to see something, right? To see what happened 'cause you didn't stay where I told you."

Peter's eyes move from his cousin to his uncle to the men in the chairs. The flesh on each side of the wires is beginning to swell. One of the men moans.

Peter stares at the broken wrists. The man who moaned leans

forward, his face pale and damp, and vomits quietly onto the cement floor.

And seeing that, Peter vomits too.

His uncle watches, and slowly nods his head.

"That's better," he says.

He climbs out of his window that night and sits with his bare feet against the cold side of the house. He studies the yard twenty feet underneath him, the black car parked across the street with the men inside watching.

The door to his room opens suddenly, and the light catches him on the ledge. He turns and sees his uncle walking in, looking at his empty bed, then, feeling the cold, at the window. It seems to startle him, to find Peter sitting in the window.

"The fuck you doin' out there?" he says. "It's freezing."

Peter doesn't answer; he doesn't know.

His uncle sits on the bed, looking nervous. He takes a deep breath.

"You ain't going to Nick's no more," he says.

Peter doesn't answer. He thinks of the fall last time, of pushing himself off this same edge and the moment afterward, in the air.

"You hear what I told you?"

The boy nods, sensing the fear in his uncle. It's an old, familiar fear, but the boy can't delineate the threat. Only that it is connected in some way to his father. Beyond that, he doesn't know what he holds over him, only that without it, he is helpless.

Except he can fall. The moment is always in his hands.

"I'm telling Nick the same thing," his uncle says. "You and Michael show up, he throws you out. When you two get out of school, somebody brings you straight home."

The boy looks back into the room, and his uncle shakes his

head and laughs in an uneasy way, as if he had forgotten that he was angry.

"You like high places," he says.

He nods again.

"Even after you jumped out the window, fucked up your legs like that, you ain't scared. That's good."

He is trying to tell him something now, trying to get to that thing between them that is always there, and is always beyond his reach.

Without moving an inch, the boy pulls away. His uncle's laugh settles and dies, with nothing in the room to sustain it. It is quiet a long time.

"I want you stayin' away from that gym," he says finally.

Peter begins to shake his head.

"You two don't know better than what you did, Nick don't know better than to let you, after I go up there myself and tell him the situation, then everybody stays home and don't get in trouble."

The boy sees the anger rise in his uncle's face again, and thinks of the two men sitting in the chairs, connected at the wrists with wire.

"I'll stay right there at Nick's . . ." he says.

His uncle suddenly looks at him as if he might stand up and push him off the ledge himself. "You didn't hear what I told you?" he says.

He is angry, and then he is afraid. Peter's father is always there between them. His uncle thinks a long time.

"You heard it that I popped Constantine?" he says finally.

The boy nods. His uncle stands up and walks to the door, and stops there to look at the boy again.

"Anything you hear about it," he says, "it's bullshit. The thing I'm telling you is this: That was for your father."

And then he steps into the light of the hallway and closes the door behind him.

Nick turns the corner, carrying a Danish for the old man wrapped in a napkin in his pocket, and sees the black Cadillac parked in the middle of the street. The old man is standing in the door of the garage, holding a broom behind his shoulder, like a baseball bat. His face is red and he is sputtering at the two men in front of him. The men are both wearing casts from their elbows to their fingers. They stand just outside the arc of the old man's broom, looking at each other as if they don't know what to do.

Nick crosses the street and hears one of them talking to the old man. "Listen," he says, "just go in there and tell Nick that Phillip Flood wants to talk to him. That he's waitin' in the car . . ."

The old man listens to that, then steps forward and swings the broom. The swing is slow, the wind taking away what little power he has, and pulls him off balance.

One of them smiles.

The old man stumbles and then regains his footing and cocks the broom behind his shoulder again. Nick passes the car, seeing the shadow of Phillip Flood's head behind the dark glass windows, and then steps onto the sidewalk and pries the broom out of Urban Matthews's hands. He smells the old man's excitement.

"Leave me have it," he says quietly, and the old man lets go and then steps back into the garage and sits on a box of motor oil. Nick holds the broom and looks at the men in casts.

The back door of the Cadillac opens and Phillip Flood climbs out slowly, looking around as if he had never seen this place before. He looks at Nick without smiling and then walks, uninvited, into the garage. The men with the casts turn to watch the street.

Nick walks into the garage behind him, his sight adjusting to the dark. The old man follows them with tired eyes. He hacks deep in his throat and then drops his head to spit between his shoes.

Phillip Flood stops and turns around. Nick puts his hands in his pockets and waits; he feels the old man's Danish. He thinks of the letter from Iowa, the neat, Catholic-school handwriting.

His daughter. He is suddenly sure that the old man has a daughter.

"I ask you a couple of favors, Nick," Phillip Flood says, building to something. "Teach the kids to take care of themself, watch out for them up here until this thing about Constantine cools off . . ."

Nick takes the Danish out of his pocket, careful to hold it with the napkin, and hands it that way to the old man. "Go on upstairs," he says.

The old man looks at him, not moving.

"It's all right," Nick says. "You hear shooting down here, get your broom and come on back down."

He stands up slowly and heads toward the stairs.

"They're doing all right," Nick says to Phillip Flood.

Phillip Flood makes a circle with his fingers and thumb and moves his hand up and down, as if he were whacking himself off. "One of them's coming home every night all bunged up, the other one's never got a scratch."

Nick shrugs. "One of them likes to fight," he says, "the other one don't." He pauses. "You can't change human nature." He is careful not to say whose human nature he is talking about. Phillip Flood puts the boys together when he talks about them, but they are not the same to him.

"I'll tell you about human nature," Phillip Flood says. But he doesn't. He looks at the ceiling. "I asked you to keep an eye on them two, this Constantine shit going on. The next thing I know, they're in some shit in West Philly, smacking around some Jewish girl. My human nature is, I am very disappointed."

Nick stares at him, trying to imagine Peter smacking around a girl. It makes sense to him that the kid is going to have his problems with girls, but not because he smacks them around. Peter is going to be the one doing the ducking; he'll pick somebody hard to live with.

He shakes his head, and seeing that, Phillip Flood begins to nod. They stare at each other, holding an argument without words.

"*Bandstand,*" Phillip Flood says, still nodding, gaining momentum. "That's where they end up when they're supposed to be with you. A fucking television show."

Nick glances at the two men standing in the door. Their casts fill the sleeves of their coats and they watch the street as if violence didn't matter any more to them than the weather.

Nick has the passing thought that once you start scaring people to keep them honest, you've got to do it all the time. You do it once, nothing else works. He has the passing thought that Phillip Flood had better keep these two scared every minute of their lives.

Phillip moves a step then, back into his line of sight. He cuts off the direct light from the garage door, and Nick suddenly senses himself being pushed into the back of his own place.

He doesn't like that, he doesn't like the way the two men are standing in the doorway watching the street.

"What I come over here to tell you," he says, "is I don't want my boys up here no more. This time, it ain't a favor. They show up, you throw them out."

One of the men in the door hears the change in his voice and turns to watch. His jacket is open, and sags to one side with the weight of the gun in the pocket.

Nick stands still, a foot away from Phillip Flood, studying his face. Watching his intentions change. He sees there is nothing for him now but this moment in this place.

That is his advantage over Nick, not the two men in the door.

He pictures Harry coming into the garage after school and finding him on the floor over next to the compressed air tank, and in the same moment he feels the edge of the workbench against his hip. He has backed all the way to the rear of the garage.

The difference is that he has something to lose.

"You hear what I told you?" The voice is almost a whisper.

Nick holds himself still, allows Phillip Flood to inspect him in the dark, allows himself to be insulted.

"I got work to do," he says finally. "The way I run the place, you decide if you want to come in, I decide if you stay."

Then he steps forward, brushing past Phillip Flood, and walks to the open hood of the car sitting half in and half out of the garage.

Phillip Flood doesn't follow him at first. He stands where he is, still facing the back wall. Nick picks up a wrench lying on a cloth on the car's fender. The car is twelve years old, and Nick covers the fender before he puts his tools there, not to scratch it. He leans into the engine as if there were no one behind him, as if there were no men standing in the doorway. As if he had nothing to lose either.

He hears Phillip Flood's feet on the concrete floor, walking past. Nick feels a chill as he passes: the breeze, or perhaps his shadow cutting off the light from the front door.

"You got a nice place, Nick," he says.

The steps move toward the front door, are almost out the door, when the old man appears from the stairwell, holding the broom like an ax, making a noise Nick has never heard before. A terrified noise that seems, when Nick thinks about it later, as if it might have come from the moment in his life when he stopped talking.

Phillip Flood makes a noise too, a short scream. He falls away from the movement and the noise, stumbling over a jack, and lands on the floor. The old man brings the broom down over his head and hits him in the legs, and then, as fast as he appeared, he is gone, back up the stairs.

The men help Phillip Flood to his feet. There are grease stains on his coat, and his face is dark. Nick watches him a moment longer, then puts his head back into the engine. Phillip Flood doesn't say a word. Nick hears a car door open and close, and then two more doors, and then the Cadillac drives up Chadwick Street and disappears.

A few minutes later, he looks up from the engine and sees the old man standing at the foot of the stairs, still holding the broom.

"Maybe you ought to go stay somewhere else a few days," he says.

The old man stares at him, his mouth beginning to move. Nick shakes his head and drops back under the hood.

"Don't get excited," he says. "I just mean there could be a problem until they cool off."

He says this more for himself than the old man. He knows the old man isn't going anywhere else. He doesn't have anywhere else, that's what going after them with the broom was about.

The first people on Chadwick Street in the morning are the old women. They come out of their doors at daybreak, dressed in their robes and slippers, and sweep their sidewalks and steps.

A long time ago, they swept for their husbands, as their husbands' mothers had done for their men too. They were out there every morning, before the men went to work, showing their husbands—and each other—that they were good wives. They were out there even on the mornings when their husbands were drinking and hadn't come home.

Their husbands are gone now, but the old women are still there, before the paperboy, scolding the sidewalk and the bums who use it, generating movement and heat to hold off the feeling of waking up alone in a cold, empty house.

There are four of them left on this block of Chadwick Street. Two of them are sisters, and this morning the older one steps out of her door and looks at the cold half-dark sky over the roofline of the buildings across the street, and then at her own breath, coming through the scarf she has wrapped around her mouth to keep from catching cold, and then, as she glances up the street in the direction of her sister's house, she senses something is out of place.

She can't say what at first; the street is quiet and covered with frost. She moves her eyes back to the roofline across the street, and then brings them down to her sister's house again, and now she sees something moving.

She crosses the street, being careful to pick her feet straight up and down so as not to slip, and walks to a spot a few feet away from the door that leads to Nick DiMaggio's gymnasium. The door has been splintered and hangs half off its hinges, the top half moving in the breeze coming from the south. Knifelike pieces of it lie inside on the steps, some of them covered by the body of the old man she has seen coming in and out of the place for months.

She stands still and stares at him, feeling her breath against the scarf. He is not a bad-looking man, although he needs a haircut. She thinks he must have fallen down the stairs.

She crosses the street again and knocks on her sister's door, wishing that she'd invited the old man in for coffee, that she'd known who he was.

She hears the locks opening on the other side—three of them—and the door opens.

"Something's happened," she says. "We better call Nicky."

Nick is standing just outside the door when the police come. The old woman who called him is holding one of his arms.

"He must have fallen," she says.

The police get out of their car and stop even with Nick. Urban Matthews is lying with his head in the stairwell, a furious look on his face. One of his eyes is open, the other is missing from the socket. An arm lies across his body, broken in two directions under the shirt.

One of the cops is named Fowler, and he and Nick have known each other a long time. He looks at Nick and waits. "So?"

Nick shakes his head. "Just somebody that needed a place to stay for a while," he says.

The cop smiles. "Another fighter," he says.

Nick shakes his head. "No," he says, "he wasn't no fighter."

It is quiet a moment while they stare at the man at the bottom of the stairs, the strange, uncomfortable angles his body had taken and held. Nick would like to fix his head for him, to straighten it with his neck.

Another police car arrives, and two men in uniforms get out and begin roping off the front of the garage.

"He was quite a smart-looking man, wasn't he?" the old woman says. Nick feels the weight of her hand on his arm. He tries gently to pull himself away—instinctively, he wants his hands free—but she holds on, his jacket bunching under her fingers.

"He seemed to keep himself clean," she says. "He could use a haircut once in a while, but he always seemed very clean."

Nick gets himself loose and goes upstairs with the cop named Fowler. The old man's mat is laid out flat on the floor, the shirt that he stuffed with dirty clothes and used as a pillow still holds the impression of his head.

The first drops of blood are at the top of the stairs, next to his broom.

He got up to meet them.

"So what do you think?" the cop says. "Kids?"

"He kept his stuff hidden up here," Nick says. "I don't know."

He steps over the blood and goes farther into the room. Nothing is out of place. Nick squats at the mat on the floor and puts his fingers into a tear in the material along the side, looking for the things he hid. The smell of the old man is in his bed and in the blanket bunched at the foot. Not a bad smell—the old man kept himself clean—just familiar.

Nick pulls his fingers out of the mat and there is a hundred-dollar bill pinched between them. It is folded neatly in quarters and pressed as if by an iron. He hands it to the cop.

"Jesus knows what he's got up here," he says.

The cop looks around the room. "How long's he been staying with you?" he says.

"I don't know, a few months."

The cop nods, looking at the mat now where the old man slept. He has known Nick a long time. "You leave the heat on for him?" he says.

"It's cold," Nick says. "What the fuck am I going to do?"

He goes back down the stairs, passing the crime scene investigators on the way up. He stops at the bottom, looking out at the neighbors who have accumulated outside the police ropes. He hears the cop named Fowler upstairs.

"Don't tear nothing up," he says. "I want it just like it was when you leave."

Nick walks up to the diner, not wanting to hear them turning the place inside out. It doesn't matter how they leave it.

An old man walks in out of the cold, peeved, you can't understand a word he says, and somehow you agree to that. And then one day you find him in a pile of unhuman angles at the bottom of the stairs, and you've got to agree to that too.

Without wanting to, he thinks for a moment of the letter from Iowa, and then, without wanting to, of Phillip Flood.

He pushes both those things out of his head, afraid where they will lead.

He makes up his mind not to think of them again.

In the afternoon, he meets Harry across the street from the school. He looks small next to some of the other boys, as if the books he's carrying in a strap over his shoulder are as heavy as he is.

Harry sees him right away—he seems to sense him there—and they walk home. The boy understands something has happened, he waits for his father to tell him what. He would protect him if he could.

They walk without speaking half a block and then, still in sight of the children emptying out of school, Nick puts his arm around his son's head and pulls him into his side. Holding him, holding on to him.

And his son allows himself to be held, in front of his school friends, knowing his father wouldn't do this to him without a good reason.

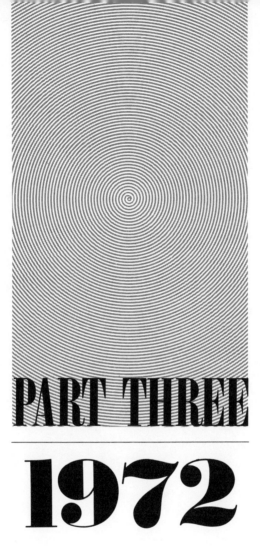

PART THREE
1972

Peter Flood walks in the door of the house where he has lived all his life, but is now, after nineteen years, somehow an uneasy guest.

The laces on his hard-toed work boots are loose and slap lightly against the floor. He stops and takes them off, using the inside edge of the opposite boot to pry one loose, and then the bared sock to get the other. His legs are weak from negotiating a roof all day, and he feels them shake as he pulls out his feet.

There is a letter for him on the table next to the stairwell. He stares at it a moment, and then he looks in the direction of the kitchen, knowing his aunt has opened the envelope and resealed it, wondering if she has heard him come in.

He is late every night now; it is dusk before he quits work. She waits in the kitchen for him and complains about his cold, ruined dinner as if she had to eat it herself.

He thinks sometimes of taking an apartment in another part of the city—the job pays full union scale, he could afford it—but he is tied to the house and the small yard, to the park across the street, to the room where he has waited—it seems like all his life—and received the news of events that have marked his life; the references for everything else.

He is protected here by what has gone before, by an intimacy with the rooms. In that intimacy, there are moments when the people he has loved are close by.

He knows he cannot stay here much longer—the house is more his uncle's and even his cousin's now than his—but he also knows this is the only place such an intimacy can exist.

The things that have occurred here have bled into him and cannot be separated out for someone else to see.

Still, there is less intimacy all the time. Michael intrudes into it; he is in every corner. He has begun to think of himself now in a different way. He has come to believe that whatever is not claimed is his.

The house, Peter himself.

It is part of what he is learning from his father.

The smell of scorched sugar hangs in the air—a half-eaten angel food cake sits on the table, next to a single clean plate. His uncle is out on business, Michael is probably with him. He goes with him everywhere now. Aunt Theresa is in the kitchen watching television.

The letter is from a lawyer.

He climbs the staircase quietly, opening the envelope. The sounds from the television fill the house. His fingers are dirty and he smudges the lawyer's address in the corner.

Cape May, New Jersey.

He walks into his room, shuts the door, and sits heavily on the bed. He pulls the letter out carefully, noticing the weight of the paper.

Dear Mr. Flood:
Kindly contact this office at your earliest convenience in regards to probate of the estate of your mother, Catherine Estelle Flood. Yours Sincerely,
Everett Jordan, Esq.

He thinks of her then, lying in bed in her room. He remembers the feel of the clothes in her closet.

He checks the postmark again. Cape May, New Jersey. All this time only a hundred miles away; it makes him smile. He has imagined her living in California.

He refolds the letter and slides it back in the envelope, and then puts the envelope in his shirt pocket. He puts his feet into his tennis shoes and goes back down the stairs and out the door quietly, not wanting to fight the battle of ruined dinners now.

He closes the door and wanders into the park across the street.

A tire hangs from a rope in the dark—a homemade swing—and beyond it, in the light from a streetlamp, a small black dog worries his way along the curb, his nose to the cement, as if there were not time enough to smell it all.

Peter fits his hips into the tire and feels the branch holding it bend under his weight. He looks up into the tree, remembering small things about his mother, coming finally to the afternoon she stood in the door and saw the bundle in Victor Kopec's arms.

And the moment she understood what it was. Nothing after that counted.

And with that taste in his mouth, he looks across the park and sees a light in Nick DiMaggio's living room window.

He wonders if Nick would remember him after so much time. It is only a thought, but a moment later he pulls himself through the tire and starts out across the park.

And then he is standing outside Nick's house. No idea what he intends to do, he is just there.

He does not touch the door knock—he has not thought of touching it—but in a moment the porch light comes on, and then the door opens and Nick steps out, wearing his reading glasses and a T-shirt. He takes the glasses off, studying him. He begins to smile.

"Peter?" he says. "How you doin'?"

The first time Nick has ever remembered his name.

He closes the few feet to the door, not feeling his legs. "Come on in," Nick says. "You eat yet?"

Peter walks in the house with Nick's hand on his shoulder. The place is warm and smells good. Nick goes to the bottom of the stairs and calls up. "Harry," he says, "come down and see who's here."

Nick's wife sticks her head around the corner from the kitchen. She smiles at Peter without knowing who he is—disappointed, he thinks—then disappears.

Nick is looking at Peter, up and down, happy to see him. "You got big," he says.

Old weights shift, and Peter Flood walks farther into the room, needing to move, suddenly afraid he is going to bawl.

Harry comes down the stairs then, and he has gotten big too.

He stops at the bottom, looking at Peter as if he doesn't know who he is.

"It's Peter Flood," Nick says. "You remember, he used to come up to the gym."

Harry nods, the elements of a smile on his face, but there is no smile there. "How you doin'?" he says. He looks quickly at his father.

"So you been lifting weights or what?" Nick says, touching his arm.

Peter shakes his head. "I got a job," he says.

Which is true, but not completely true. His uncle got him the job—got them both jobs. He thinks of the foreman of the crew nodding as the supervisor told him he had to use them, looking at the ground. He wouldn't look at either one of them.

"What are we supposed to do?" Michael said when the supervisor was gone.

The foreman looked back toward the job, as if they weren't there. "It don't matter to me, as long as you stay out of the way," he said.

Michael found some shade and sat down, and Peter followed the foreman around the construction site all morning until he finally gave him something to carry.

He hauled shingles and nails up the ladders at first, then learned the job itself, squatting all afternoon on roofs thirty and forty feet in the air, the glare of the sun all around him. Surrounded by the noise and movement of the city, but isolated from it too.

He liked it on the roofs, and pushed himself toward exhaustion, and the relief that came on the other side.

Michael quit the job after the first summer and went into the business end of the business. His father was president of the Trade Union Council then; the other unions had seen that he'd cut the guys who ran things in the city—the young Italians who took over after Constantine—out of the roofers' business, and wanted them out of their business, too.

"Lookit this arm," Nick says to Harry. Harry looks at Peter's arm, going along with his father.

Nick sits down on the couch and offers Peter the seat next to him. Harry is still standing at the bottom of the stairs.

"So, what you been doing?" Nick says.

Peter tries to think. "Just working," he says.

"You ain't in school . . ."

He shakes his head. Not for a long time now.

"You ought to come by the gym sometime," Nick says.

Harry looks at his father again, half a second; he bites his lip. Nick's wife puts her head around the corner one more time to see if Peter is still there. Her table is set, and Peter knows from the sounds coming out of the kitchen that she's ready to serve dinner.

"He going to stay, Nick?" she says.

Peter shakes his head no and begins to get up. Realizing that he is still in the shirt and pants and socks he wore to work.

"Stick around," Nick says. "She can cook a little."

"I got stuff to do," he says, back on his feet now, wondering what he will say if Nick asks him what stuff that is.

But Nick lets him go. "You ought to come by the gym, move around a little," he says again, walking him to the door.

Harry stares at him as he goes past on the way out, and then nods, barely. Nick shakes his hand.

The door closes and Peter walks into the park. He feels the letter, stiff against his shirt. He takes it out and reads it again in the light from the streetlamp, and then folds it into thirds and puts it carefully into his wallet.

He carries the letter with him the rest of the week, it and the visit to Nick DiMaggio's living room.

He remembers the words Nick said exactly, the dents in the bridge of his nose from his glasses, the slippers half under the couch, the expression on his wife's face. He thinks of these things in an order that is not quite as he saw them, and settles finally on Harry, standing at the foot of the stairs, dreading to have him there.

He understands that look without knowing the reason for it, and he will not go back to the house.

He thinks of the gym though, all that week as he works his way across the steeply pitched roofs of a development of low-income town houses going up just off Shunk Street deep in South Philadelphia.

A whole block of crumbling row houses was bought and demolished to make room for the development, and for weeks, the neighbors laid themselves in front of the bulldozers to keep them away. But in the end, the federal government waited the neighbors out, and built its town houses for the blacks.

Once in a while, he glimpses an old woman or an old man behind the barriers that the police have erected, staring at him as he climbs up or down—some of them come in the morning with folding chairs to watch the despised buildings going up— and they dread to have him there too.

But he cannot spend his life on roofs.

He cannot stay where he is comfortable forever.

Peter walks into the gym on a Saturday afternoon. Harry is there alone, shirtless, doing sit-ups on an elevated board in the corner.

He looks around the place—it is messier now than he remembers it, but then the old man who liked to clean is gone—thinking of his uncle's admonition never to come here again. His uncle doesn't know where he goes anymore, though, and doesn't ask. He watches Michael himself now.

"How you doing?" he says to Harry.

The kid nods, his fingers laced behind his neck, touching each knee with the opposite elbow and then dropping halfway to the floor and bringing himself up again. The muscles in his stomach appear and disappear under the skin.

Peter studies the walls, the yellowed pictures of old fighters undisturbed since the last time he was here. He remembers that last time, leaving Nick at the top of the stairs and following Michael down, headed for a blow job at *Bandstand*.

The show is still on the air, but it's called *American Bandstand* now, and Larry Tock is long gone. Dead somewhere in Texas.

Harry does a final sit-up and stops, sitting uphill, looking at Peter.

"Your dad around?" Peter says.

Harry stands up, almost as tall as Peter but thinner. "He's supposed to be back already," he says. He checks the clock. "I could give you a few rounds, if you want."

The kid breaks his nose five seconds after they touch gloves.

The bell rings, they come together in the middle of the ring, and he breaks his nose with an uppercut.

Peter hears the sound distinctly, the break and then a ringing, and then he hears his breath leaving his chest as Harry hits him just below his rib cage on the right side.

He covers himself up, stumbling backward into a corner, feeling Nick's kid coming after him more than seeing him. He takes a hook to the head, and then a right hand hits him in the shoulder and knocks him off balance, and then he is hit again below the ribs.

He grabs Harry in the corner, holding on until he can breathe again. Harry jerks back, trying to get loose, twice as strong as he looks, but Peter holds him until the stab of pain in his chest— the thing that took his breath—narrows and shortens, and then he pushes him away, back into the middle of the ring.

Harry is on top of him again before he can leave the corner.

He pounds his shoulders and arms as Peter covers up, hits him twenty times before Peter catches one of his gloves and pulls him in and holds him again. He hears his own breathing against Harry's shoulder, and then the shoulder moves, bouncing into his face, and the kid's hands are loose and Peter is trying to protect himself from punches he cannot see or predict.

He is strangely fascinated by the punches, their speed and ferocity. Even as the numbness settles into his shoulders and arms, the kid's intention settles too. He is trying to hurt him.

He catches one of the gloves again and pulls Harry close, and at the same time the buzzer goes off. Peter feels him relax.

Harry turns away and begins walking in quick circles around the ring, his sweat and Peter's blood smeared across the muscles in his stomach. Peter stands where he is, taking as much air as he can into his chest, wiping at his nose with the sleeve of his shirt.

He has not caught his breath when the buzzer goes off again. Harry turns back to him, looking at him for the first time since the end of the round, and offers one of his gloves for Peter to touch.

A moment later, he hits him again in the nose. Peter is aware of the pain now; it has a rhythm that is almost unconnected to the punches themselves, a hum someplace behind the violence.

A weight tugs him, one way and then another, and Peter fights for balance, using the ropes behind him and then Harry himself when he can catch an arm or his head. He does that, collects himself, and then pushes him away.

The kid relaxes when he is caught and is pushed away, and it is like lifting dead weight, over and over.

Somewhere in the second round, Peter feels fatigue in his arms; he feels the limits of his strength.

He still pushes Harry away—but not as far away now—and he is back a second later, right in front of him, bobbing like a fishing cork, impossible to hit or stop. The punches land once and then seem to echo back a moment later, even as other punches are coming in other places.

The buzzer goes off and Harry stares at Peter a long moment, as if he does not want to stop.

Peter wipes at the blood from his nose and waits for the next round.

A minute into that round, Peter has trapped Harry's arm just behind the elbow and is holding on—all pretense of boxing gone, he only wants to last the round—and as he looks past Harry's shoulder he sees Nick standing in the corner, his arms draped across the ropes.

Nick is smiling, but he isn't happy. He sees what is happening in the ring.

Peter straightens himself up, not wanting to look so sloppy in front of Nick, and throws a surprise right hand that bounces off the top of Harry's head. In return, Harry hits him with half a dozen shots before he can grab his arms again, and stall for a little more time.

The clock always keeps moving.

And then the buzzer goes off again, and Peter climbs between the second and third ropes, spits his mouthpiece into his glove, and sits down on the bench. He drops his head beneath his shoulders, too tired to hold it up.

Nick brings him a towel and holds it against his face.

"What are you guys, opening a blood bank?" he says.

Peter cannot talk yet; he has used himself up getting through the three rounds. Harry is on the other side of the ring, and when the buzzer goes off again he begins pounding the heavy bag.

Peter watches him a long minute, the towel covering all of his face beneath his eyes. He feels himself getting sick, but sits still, fighting it. He pulls his face away from the towel, wanting fresh air. Nick studies him from the side.

Peter goes back to the towel and blows his nose gently into it—not hard enough to make the tissue under his eyes swell. When he moves away again, the blood is running fresh over his lips. Drops of it splatter on the floor between his feet in an uneven line.

Nick crouches in front of him and begins to unlace his gloves. When he has pulled them off, it is easier to breathe, as if the wet gloves had been covering his face. His hands are lighter now, and he moves them with less effort.

He pulls his shirt over his head, and then falls back against the wall.

Nick tosses the gloves into one of the lockers, and Peter stands up and pushes the cup off his hips, and then, nauseated again, he leaves it around his feet to sit back down.

On the other side of the gym, Harry steals a look at him as he hits the bag. Nick picks up the cup and tosses it into a locker too and then nods in the direction of his son.

"He beats the hell out of me too," he says. "I start boxing, but I can't get mad at him, you know? It's probably the same thing with you."

He moves closer and studies Peter's nose. From the front and then from the side.

He smiles, but he isn't happy.

Peter is back the next day.

Harry stays off his face, but leaves red blotches over his chest and sides with body blows. Half a dozen times, he doubles Peter over with these shots, takes the breath out of his body and paralyzes the mechanism that breathes.

There is no blood today, but he is hurt at least as badly.

Nick watches three rounds from the ropes again, pouring water over Peter's head between rounds to cool him off, smiling and worried.

It is like that the second day, and the third and the fourth.

On the fifth day, Harry rebreaks his nose.

Nick drives home in a six-year-old Pontiac that needs a brake job. He looks across the front seat at Harry. The kid has been strangely quiet the last week, even when they are alone. He has been strange in the gym too.

It's not like him to punish anybody the way he is punishing Charley Flood's kid, not even the professionals who come up once in a while and try to rough him up. After he hurts them, his punches always change—an almost indiscernible thing from outside the ring, they come with the same speed, with the same leverage, but at the very end he takes the weight off them, and they are harmless.

If there is a fault his son has in a boxing ring, it is his reluctance to hurt anybody.

"You busted him up pretty bad today," Nick says.

Harry nods, looking out the window. He doesn't answer.

"He ain't good enough, you should be hurting him like that," Nick says.

The car is quiet.

"He do something to you?" Nick says.

Harry shakes his head no.

"So that means you don't want him around the gym?"

Nick takes a cigarette out of his shirt pocket and punches the cigarette lighter into the dashboard. A moment later it pops out, and he steadies it in front of the cigarette as he drives, the orange glow reflecting in his glasses.

"I don't like those people," Harry says quietly. "They ruin the gym. . . ."

"He can't help who his uncle is." Nick lights the cigarette and then looks again at Harry. "Peter ain't like them anyway," he says.

"So what does he want with us?" Harry says a little later.

"Something," Nick says, "or he wouldn't be coming back every day so you could beat him up."

Harry looks straight ahead.

"Peter ain't his uncle," Nick says again.

"It's all the same family."

Nick nods at that. "Maybe he don't want to be in that family," he says.

The car goes quiet, and then Nick glances at his son again. "Trust me," he says. "You give somebody the benefit of the doubt, someday somebody gives it to you."

He sees Harry understands that.

"Besides," he says, "I ain't old enough for you to be protecting me yet."

PART FOUR

1974

Peter at twenty-one:

He is naked in bed, unable to sleep, bothered by the nearness of the girl lying next to him, her arm across his chest, as if he belonged to her.

He does not know this woman well, only that she smokes and talks about clothes, even as he undressed her. He is not used to having someone in his bed overnight.

The phone rings. He turns his head to look at it, listening to the trucks outside, lining up to unload on the docks. The trucks and the wind. He picks up the alarm clock on the floor and studies the position of the hands. Four o'clock. The phone rings again and he picks it up.

"Peter?" It's Michael.

"Yeah."

"Something's happened." He is scared, Peter hears that. The woman on the bed turns in her sleep, pulling the blanket over her narrow shoulders.

Peter waits, the receiver pressed against his ear, the alarm clock rolls underneath him on the bed.

"They got Phil."

That is what Michael calls his father now, Phil.

"Who got him?"

It is quiet a moment. "Constantine's people," Michael says finally. "It must of been the old guys who was still loyal. The other bunch, they loved him. He did them a favor with the old man, it's live and let live ever since."

Peter sits up and puts his feet on the cold floor. His apartment is on the third floor of a building 150 years old, and on winter nights he can sometimes feel the wind through the walls. He feels it now.

"Peter?"

"Yeah, I'm here. . . ." He stands up, holding the receiver against his ear, and goes to the radiator to turn up the heat.

"It was a bomb," Michael says.

"Where?"

"The door. It took out most of the porch, part of the front wall."

He reaches for the radiator and the phone falls off the table next to the bed.

It is quiet on the other end for a moment, and then he hears a noise, it could almost be a laugh. "There ain't nothing left weighs two ounces," Michael says. The connection is quiet again.

"It had to be Constantine's people," Michael says. "Phil had things worked out with the guys that took over."

Peter is quiet, not knowing anything about the guys who took over. Only that since his uncle had killed Constantine for them, they had left the unions alone.

"I'm gonna need your help," Michael says.

"For what?"

"If I'm going to hold on to this, I got to have somebody I can trust," Michael says.

"I don't know anything about the business," he says.

"I got to have somebody I can trust," Michael says, "or I'm as dead as Phil."

The girl in the bed sits up, her mouth and eyes are puffy with sleep. The blanket drops into her lap. He sees the outline of small, round breasts, and between them a gold cross that hangs from a chain picks up light from the street and winks at him.

"Peter?"

"I'm thinking," he says.

The girl begins looking for her clothes. He sees that she is angry.

"Good," Michael says. "That's what you always been good at, figuring things out."

She puts on her shirt and pants, and, as Peter watches, she

suddenly picks her panties up off the floor and pulls them down over his face and ears.

"Peter?"

He looks up at the girl through one of the holes for her legs. She puts on her shoes and coat, and points to the telephone. "Tell her to come on over," she says, "I'm done." She slams the door as she leaves.

"Who's that?" Michael says. "You got somebody there?"

"No," Peter says, "not now."

"So what do I do?"

Peter thinks a moment, asking himself the same question. Flesh and blood. "I'll come over in the morning," he says.

PART FIVE

1986

A warehouse in the south end of the city.

It is February.

Five men climb the fire escape to the roof, the streetlight on the corner turning the wall behind them green; Peter Flood goes up first, then his cousin Michael Flood, then two men who work for Michael—they call themselves Bobby the Jap and Monk— and then Jimmy Measles.

The steps move under the men as they climb, and Michael Flood shakes the hand railing and grabs at his cousin's feet above him on the stairs. The men who work for Michael Flood shake the railings too and pretend to fall.

Beneath them, Jimmy Measles holds on with both hands. This is the first time he has been to the warehouse, and he is afraid of the height.

Peter Flood hears him somewhere below, his noises distinct from the others. There is something wrong with his breathing, and the bottles in his overcoat pocket make the same flat note over and over as they collide. Hundred-dollar champagne, at least that is what he'd said.

Eight feet from the top, the fire escape becomes a ladder, three single bars welded into the wall, two feet apart, another bar fastened to the roof itself. One by one the men climb this ladder, leaning forward at the top, their hands touching the roof to take the long last step.

Jimmy Measles stops on the fire escape beneath it and looks back at the ground. He takes off the new camel hair double-breasted overcoat his wife bought on Chestnut Street for his birthday, rolls it carefully around the bottles and tosses it up to Peter, who is leaning over the side.

Jimmy Measles puts his hands on the bar just over his head and steps up with one foot.

He puts his foot back on the fire escape. "This shit's covered with ice," he says.

To Peter Flood, it sounds as if Jimmy Measles cannot draw a full breath.

Peter sits on the edge of the roof, holding the coat, watching. He doesn't say a word, he only waits. Jimmy Measles does not belong here.

Jimmy takes an atomizer from his pants pocket, pumps it into his mouth twice, and climbs the ladder. At the top he stalls, half on the roof, half off, his feet kicking in the air. Peter puts his fingers through his belt and lifts him the rest of the way.

It seems to Peter that he is almost weightless; that he could be hollow.

Jimmy Measles straightens himself and drapes the coat over his shoulders and walks to the middle of the roof where the others are settling in. He runs the fingers of his gloves through his long black hair, pushing it back over his ears. It falls in place naturally, and holds. Perfect hair.

Using a glove, he dusts a spot near Michael, and then slaps the glove against his trouser leg before he puts it back on, cleaning it too. He sits down carefully, careful not to wrinkle his pants, and begins to open one of the bottles.

Peter notices the shaking in his cheeks and his chin before the cork pops. He sees it again: Jimmy Measles does not belong here, he is too weak.

Jimmy hands the bottle to Michael Flood, who tastes it and hands it back.

Jimmy begins a story.

"I got this stuff from a guy owns a mom-and-pop on South Street," he says.

The men sit quietly on the roof, waiting. This is what Jimmy Measles is for, to tell stories.

"This guy's got a break-in once a month," he says. "The way girls get their period, this guy's got break-ins. He even gets depressed, that time of the month, knowing they're coming. So at night he empties the cash register. He empties the cigarette machine, takes all the cigarettes home. He takes the meat out of his refrigerator. . . ."

It is quiet a moment while Jimmy Measles drinks from the bottle.

"So what do they do?" he says. "They take the fuckin' meat slicer."

Jimmy Measles looks at Michael, who seems to be waiting for him to finish. It comes to him that Michael doesn't appreciate how much a meat slicer weighs.

"Those things must go a couple hundred pounds," he says. "It's like stealing the water heater."

"He ought to get himself a dog," the man called Monk says.

Jimmy shakes his head. "He had a dog; they stole it."

He checks Michael again, to see if he's smiling.

There is no wind on the roof.

Michael Flood carefully pulls a thin knife from a plastic bag in his lap; a drift of white powder lies across the blade. He leans forward, closing one of his nostrils with his thumb, and sniffs with the other. His eyes water and he smiles at Jimmy Measles.

"Tell us that story the lion pissed down your leg," he says. He takes the champagne from Jimmy Measles and has a long drink.

Jimmy Measles shakes his head. "That isn't about a lion," he says, "it's about my pants. Five-hundred-dollar Brooks Brothers suit, one pair of pants, the second time I wore them. Me and Larry Tock were doing a charity appearance for the circus—people called us for that shit every week back then—and so we're standing around the lion's cage waiting for the guy that's supposed to pay us, and this lion, I swear to God, it pisses on me through the cage, and the piss eats a hole in my pants."

Michael Flood smiles as the story comes out; the two men who work for him look at each other. Peter Flood is thinking of other things.

In the dark, Jimmy Measles watches Michael to see how he's doing. "A five-hundred-dollar suit," he says.

"I heard of elephant manure catching fire," says the man called Bobby the Jap. He is the only high school graduate on the roof. "Spontaneous combustion . . ."

The other man—Monk—doesn't understand. He pulls back two inches, as if to get Bobby the Jap in focus.

"Manure," Bobby says. He smiles, showing gapped, uneven teeth. "It means shit."

Monk reaches for the open bottle of champagne, tastes it, makes a face, and then opens his own bottle. Boone's Farm Apple Wine.

The men sit in the cold for more than an hour, drinking Jimmy Measles's hundred-dollar champagne and Monk's two-dollar wine, urinating over the side of the roof, listening to Jimmy Measles talk.

Michael Flood offers the bag of white powder to Peter, who shakes his head no, and then to Jimmy Measles. Jimmy Measles leans forward until his nose almost touches the blade of Michael's knife, and then presses one of his nostrils shut and sniffs.

His speech becomes faster and he laughs at his own stories.

Most of them are about the television program *Bandstand,* the times he got beat up after the show, the times he brought girls into the stage manager's office.

He thinks of another story but doesn't tell it. When he left Michael alone in the stage manager's office with the Jewish girl. He remembers the way she could dance. Maureen.

But that isn't a story to tell, just one to remember.

He talks about the dances he invented, he and his partner Suze. Half the teenagers in Philadelphia were copying the steps they made up before the show.

"You should of seen the letters I got, asking was I porking her," he says.

A moment later Jimmy Measles's lungs seize in the cold air.

He reaches into his pants pocket for his atomizer again and puts it into his mouth, taking deep breaths as he pumps the trigger.

Taking this for an intermission, the man called Monk gets up and walks heavily to the edge of the roof. He stands still, his breath fogging the air in front of his mouth, and then the arch of his piss cuts a line through the light from the streetlamp, and a moment later the other men hear the sound as it hits the sidewalk.

They drink until there are four empty bottles, wine and champagne, in a pile on the roof. Michael Flood sniffs again from the blade of his knife, then holds it for Jimmy Measles.

He doesn't even offer it to his cousin Peter this time; Peter's mind is somewhere else.

"You heard Larry Tock ended up in Texas, right?" Jimmy Measles says; the drug rolls through him so he thinks that he does not mind so much being on the roof after all.

Michael and Bobby the Jap look up, waiting, but as Jimmy starts to lay out the last chapter of Larry Tock's life, he senses that they are waiting for something else.

Jimmy Measles stops his story; no one asks him what happened in Texas. He wishes Michael would offer him something more off the blade of his knife.

Peter stands up then—the first time—and walks to the side of the roof which is protected from the street. Jimmy Measles thinks he has gone there to piss over the side, as the others have. He catches a glint in Michael's eye.

Back at the edge, Peter Flood looks down, pauses a moment, as if he were having trouble opening his zipper, and then, without saying a word, he jumps off.

Michael Flood walks to the edge of the roof, smiling, and looks into the canyon beyond his feet. It is too dark to see bottom.

He knows there is a pile of sand down there as tall as a car, but it doesn't seem to him that it is much of a cushion in cold weather—now that he considers it, about like hitting a car.

He has never jumped himself, although in the beginning it was his idea.

The others stand up slowly, brushing dirt and grit off their pants.

In the beginning, the cousins came here alone. Peter was fifteen, Michael was a year younger. They quit school together, and Michael's father, the president by then of the Council of Trade Unions, had gotten them jobs on the docks.

He could get anyone a job; that was the source of the power. The politicians came to him, and the Italians—the ones who owned the streets—left him alone. What they had given away they could not take back.

With their first paychecks, Peter and Michael Flood got drunk and came to this roof, and Peter had jumped and busted his tailbone.

And Michael thought he understood it then, how his cousin would rather pick up a check for a bad coccyx than unload pistachio nuts with a line of Arabs watching him from the deck of the ship.

But Peter Flood never missed a day's work.

It seems to Michael Flood now, staring into the darkness, that Peter might have kept jumping for the same reason another man who is given, say, the family trucking company for his twenty-fifth birthday might keep a Teamsters card in his wallet the rest of his life.

To prove he is entitled.

Michael Flood turns away and walks back to the fire escape. The others follow him; Jimmy Measles whispering "Jesus Christ" as they go.

Peter Flood is already on the sidewalk below the men, waiting. The stairs shake beneath the men's feet, but there is no play in it now. They descend in the same order they climbed—Michael Flood, Bobby the Jap, Monk and Jimmy Measles.

Michael studies his cousin's posture, weighing the unnatural, stiff way he is standing—a little goofy, is his exact thought. Meaning that he has hurt himself badly. A small, sweet moment passes through Michael Flood as he recognizes pain. It isn't that he dislikes his cousin, only that Peter's pain makes him happy.

But that is as much sign as Peter Flood will give, the way he stands. Michael drops to the sidewalk and shakes his head.

"How the fuck you're still walking, I don't know," he says.

Peter Flood gazes at his cousin without seeming to hear what he's said. Thinking of other things.

Michael Flood believes that there is something in the falling that hypnotizes him. That, or the landing makes him hear music.

He imagines music in his cousin's ears.

He has never seen Peter land. It is always dark on that side of the warehouse and the pile of sand is invisible from the roof, so he disappears before he hits. The sound his body makes as it hits the sand is heavy and solid, it reminds Michael of the trunk of his limousine being shut.

Michael would like to see his cousin hit the sand, the look on his face at the moment it happens. "We got to do this sometime during the day," he says now.

But he has suggested that before, without results. It has something to do with the light, he thinks. Peter never feels crazy during the day, he is strictly a nighttime jumper.

Jimmy Measles is almost at the bottom of the fire escape now, checking each step for ice, wheezing, his calfskin gloves sliding down the handrails. Afraid to let go for even a second.

Peter looks past his cousin and notices the way Jimmy Measles is coming down the steps, thinking anything higher off the street than a curb he loses his personality. As soon as he is off the fire escape he relaxes.

"I shit my pants you went off that roof," Jimmy says to him.

Peter doesn't answer. He holds himself still, trying to recover the other stillness, the thing that was in his chest as he fell.

But it's gone.

He hears words being spoken and feels the tightening in his spine, like ice freezing around tree branches in the winter. He sees Jimmy Measles's smiling, worried face in front of him.

Jimmy Measles moves one of his shoes behind the other and dances—one step and a turn—and stops in front of Michael.

"So, my man," he says, "you want to habituate Catherine Street or what?"

That is where Jimmy's club is, at Ninth and Catherine.

They load into the limo, Michael and Peter and Jimmy Measles all in back, and head for Ninth and Catherine.

Jimmy Measles opens another bottle of champagne, Michael sticks his knife into the white powder.

Peter sits straight up, his hands underneath him on the seat to take the weight off his lower back. The feeling of the fall is too distant now to remember, and each time the car hits a pothole, it seems to crack the ice encasing his spine.

He pictures himself in the gym tomorrow, all the broken ice.

The car stops in front of the club—double-parked—and Michael gets out without waiting for Monk to open the door. Jimmy Measles slides across the seat after him, and then looks back in to see what's keeping Peter.

"In a minute," he says. "I'll be there in a minute."

Michael and the two men who work for him are already headed inside, knowing that Peter likes a little time alone after he jumps.

Peter goes with Michael to Jimmy Measles's club four or five times a week. He and Michael, and usually Bobby the Jap and Monk to watch the door.

Jimmy Measles buys everything; he will not accept Michael's money. Jimmy likes the customers to see him sitting at a table with Michael, making him laugh.

Peter is there with them, of course, but he doesn't laugh; he doesn't see the point.

And he has noticed that Jimmy Measles's wife doesn't see the point either.

She sits apart from Jimmy and his friends, under the stained-glass window which divides the bar from the restaurant, drinking margaritas. The diamond on her finger catches the light from across the room. Her name is Grace.

Grace does not come to the bar to please her husband, but, as these things go, it pleases him that she is here. It makes him happy that Michael notices her and then looks at him, admiring what he has.

Peter watches Jimmy showing off his wife and his friends. Showing off his wife to his friends.

He aches sometimes, at the size of Jimmy Measles's misunderstanding.

The place itself is newly remodeled. New furniture, new floors, new lights. A pink neon sculpture in the window that bears a resemblance to Jimmy Measles's face.

He keeps a fresh carnation floating in a bowl of water on every table in the restaurant. He has hired a $1,200-a-week European chef named Otto and now has a menu no one in South Philly can read.

The European chef has cut the food end of the business in half, and where the restaurant once broke even, serving eggs and hamburgers and chicken, it is now losing twenty-five hundred a month, and the missing customers account for perhaps another two thousand a month of the bar end of the business too.

And while that has been going on, the bartenders have discovered what Jimmy is paying Otto, and are stealing more than they are entitled to stealing like they worked for the city.

Jimmy Measles does not understand it at all. He watches his business stall in the water and begin to sink, but he holds on to his chef. Slow nights, he brings him out of the kitchen into the bar and introduces him around to prove he can't speak English.

And Grace sits in her seat under the stained window, sipping her margaritas, leaving lip prints on the glasses.

She knows he is in trouble, but it seems to her that he has always been in trouble, one kind or another. In some ways she is attracted to that, or perhaps it is the way he accepts it.

Jimmy never worries out loud. He isn't a complainer—not a word, even about his asthma.

But the problems have a circular feel now, as if she and Jimmy have been through them all before.

It has been too long since he surprised her.

Jimmy Measles's wife studies the men sitting with her husband at the table, and finds herself drawn to Michael. He is not the best-looking—but Jimmy has enough good looks to last her forever—and it is not because he is the boss. She doesn't care about that, either.

He has no conscience. She sees that and wants it.

She gets up and approaches the table, carrying her drink. Jimmy reaches for her without stopping his story, his hand sliding around her waist and then resting on the rise of her bottom.

Peter stands up, offering her his chair. An act of will—straightening his back.

He walks carefully to the bar, protecting his back, wondering if he could take her away from Jimmy. He is not happy to be thinking that, but it comes up when he is around her. It is something she puts in the air.

He understands that Jimmy Measles has a way with women, that he is handsome and knows how to touch them.

He understands certain women naturally love bartenders—before Jimmy hired Otto and remodeled, he worked his own bar six, sometimes seven nights a week, and made a living—and that certain women naturally love men who remind them of their fathers, or love men who are funny, or who buy them stuffed animals.

He knows the reasons don't make any sense.

But this time some law of natural selection has been broken and she doesn't try to hide it.

She sits in the chair she took when Peter stood up, laughing at one of Jimmy's stories from the *Bandstand* days, but she isn't paying attention to the story.

Her fingers touch Jimmy's knuckles, and then she glances across the table at Michael, and something touches there too. She smiles at her husband's story, but she isn't anybody to care about other peoples' stories, or stories about other people.

And she isn't anybody to love bartenders.

Peter and Michael are sitting in the car while Bobby the Jap, gun in hand, checks the doors to the house. It is early in the morning, coming in from a night at Jimmy's.

Peter has boxed that afternoon and is sore and tired, and after Michael is inside, he will go back to his apartment and lie in the tub.

Michael closes his eyes and drops his head into the seat cushion behind him. "Somethin' like that," he says, "she falls off the toilet into her own vomit, she's still too good for Jimmy Measles. Am I right or not?"

His eyes open and his head turns in such a way that the streetlight catches his forehead and throws a shadow across half his face, and in that moment Peter can see that he has decided to fuck her.

Peter doesn't answer. He thinks of the way she lifts a margarita to her mouth using both hands, as if it were something she wanted to smell.

"You think it's possible?" Michael says.

Peter shrugs.

It is quiet a moment, then Bobby pushes through some shrubs at the edge of the driveway, coming around from the back.

"What I think," Michael says, "you get with somethin' like that once in a while, you wouldn't have to jump off no roof to fuck up your back."

He leans closer to his cousin, nodding the way he has always nodded when he asks Peter for something he does not want to give up. Intruding into every corner.

"What do you think?" he says "It ain't like Jimmy's somebody we know. . . ."

In the end, without saying a word, Peter agrees to Michael's fucking Jimmy Measles's wife. More precisely, he begins to take Jimmy with him to the fights every Wednesday night at the Blue Horizon while Michael stays at the club with Grace.

Which is the same thing. Peter does not lie to himself about that.

Jimmy is always anxious to go—too anxious to go—but the Blue Horizon is hot and close, and full of black people and smoke, and in that combination Jimmy Measles sweats and worries, and cannot seem to catch his breath.

Week after week, Peter finds himself preoccupied with Jimmy's breathing, and distracted from the fights.

Why do I care if he can breathe? he thinks.

But he knows. Jimmy Measles has attached himself to Peter— when they are drinking he sometimes shows him pictures of his dogs—and in that attachment is a contract, and obligations that Peter is just beginning to glimpse.

Sometimes, he thinks, it's like having a dog of his own.

Reluctantly, Peter quits the Blue Horizon and takes Jimmy Measles to the fights in Atlantic City instead. It ruins the atmosphere for Peter, but improves Jimmy's breathing.

And feeling more comfortable, Jimmy settles into a ringside table and begins, with his first drink, to negotiate a blow job. Some nights, he asks half a dozen times before he finds a prostitute who will go upstairs with him and take his money.

To Jimmy, everybody in Atlantic City looks like a hooker.

Jimmy's interest in the fights themselves never grows beyond the violence of the knockdowns, but he likes being with Peter and he likes Atlantic City, and if the idea ever tugs at him, what his wife and Michael are doing back in town, it never shows.

It tugs at Peter Flood, though.

In its way, what Michael said is true: Jimmy Measles isn't anybody they know. But Michael meant only that Jimmy was a Jew.

Peter takes him out of town and gets him drunk, spends so much time with him now it's like a bad job, and all through the night, everything Jimmy does or says is to cover up something else.

And Peter allows that and encourages it.

It's what makes it possible to take him out of town while Michael is with his wife.

He doesn't know Jimmy Measles, and he holds the door against the day that is no longer true.

Two months pass and Michael and Jimmy's wife become habitual, more than once a week now.

Peter leaves his cousin at the club with her, Monk and Bobby sitting in the bar, and takes Jimmy Measles to Atlantic City every time one of the casinos offers a card. He believes he has seen every four-round fighter on the East Coast.

And she takes Michael across the street.

Monk and Bobby move their drinks to a table near the window to watch the house. At closing time, they get a sandwich and wait in the limo.

In the morning, Peter comes out of his apartment, showered and clean, climbs into the waiting limo and smells Jimmy's wife all over Michael, and cheese steaks and onions all over the car. And suddenly confronted with what he has done, Peter sometimes tries to talk Michael into quitting Jimmy's wife, saying that keeping regular hours with her is a careless way to do business.

And even if careless business isn't his concern—what he is thinking about is the way it feels when Jimmy Measles gets drunk and shows him the pictures of his dogs or calls him his pal—the warning is real.

The Italians remain split into factions, the old and the new. The old men are faithful to the old rules; they worked for Constantine and, twenty years after his death, still powerless, they claim the unions as their own, the way they were before Constantine was killed.

They want nothing to do with drugs or Atlantic City or any of the businesses held by the men who took their place.

The men who took their place, who own the streets, smile at the old Italians now, and overlook it when one of them drinks too much and shoots a roofer or an electrician.

They are sympathetic in a wary way, knowing the old men are not harmless.

The men who own the streets do not smile at the Irish, though. The bargain that was struck with Phillip Flood has lasted so long that all the men who made it are dead, and the jobs are the real source of power in the city—the men who own the streets see that now—and eventually they will try to take them back.

And Peter reminds Michael, this morning in the limo, that it is careless to take the Italians for granted.

Michael leans across the seat, smiling at him, and pats him on the knee. He says, "They're dyin' of old age, Pally."

Peter looks out the window. To his knowledge, Jimmy Measles's wife is the only woman his cousin ever liked better the second time. She is the only one he doesn't talk about, sitting in a booth afterwards at the Melrose Diner, discussing if she liked to swallow it or not.

She is different, but Michael never says anything about what she does, or has him doing.

The closest he ever comes is once at the racetrack, holding eight hundred dollars' worth of winning tickets in his hand while the tote board flashes the word *inquiry* in front of his horse's number, he turns to Peter and says, "You ever wondered while you was fucking somebody if there was hidden cameras in the room?"

A week later—also at the track—Michael asks Peter if he thinks he could keep Jimmy Measles in Atlantic City all night.

Peter covers his eyes.

"You got a headache, Pally?"

"Yeah I got a headache and it's got a name."

"He ain't so bad," Michael says.

"After he gets his blow job," Peter says, "there ain't anything left he likes but to drink champagne. He doesn't play craps, he doesn't want to go to the shows; he wants champagne.

"And with Jimmy and champagne, there's always a point waiting for you where he's gonna do something—paint a happy face on his dick and show it to the keno girl or throw glasses into the fireplace, even if there isn't a fireplace. The only thing distracts him is if somebody remembers him from *Bandstand*."

Michael says, "He ain't so bad."

Peter cannot think of an argument for that and takes Jimmy to Atlantic City for the night. And then another night, and another.

They go to the fights, they buy champagne. Then Jimmy gets blown, and then Peter spends the last four hours before daylight trying to keep him happy, and at the same time trying to keep the moment when he brings out his penis and his felt-tip a little ways in the future.

Ａnd that is where Peter is on the morning the old men in the raincoats catch Michael crossing the street in front of Jimmy Measles's house, heading toward the limo. Peter is in Atlantic City, Monk and Bobby the Jap are asleep in the front seat, Grace is still in the door, watching Michael leave.

The men in the raincoats have shotguns and go for his legs first, intending to finish him after he is on the ground. Michael sees them too late, one on the sidewalk, one in the street. He takes the pistol out of his coat pocket, beginning to run, and shoots four times, blowing out the front window of a poultry store kitty-corner in the Italian Market.

He is hit himself as he hears the pieces of glass drop onto the sidewalk.

A moment later Bobby the Jap comes out of the limo

screaming—a shoeless Kamikaze—and the old men in the rain-coats are so unnerved at the sight of this foreigner that even though Michael is on the ground, crawling toward the car, dragging one of his legs, they don't stay to finish it.

And three hours later when Peter turns his Buick onto Catherine Street, he sees the television cameras and knows what has happened.

Michael is out of surgery at Thomas Jefferson Hospital by the time Peter arrives, and by then the only interest he has left in Jimmy Measles's wife is avoiding her.

Peter never sees him again with any woman he doesn't pay.

When things go wrong, Michael always goes back to what worked for him before.

The man on the television set keeps saying Michael has "reputed ties to organized crime."

He takes off his glasses and looks directly into the camera and reports that the shooting resulted from a power struggle between Michael and reputed mob boss Salvadore Bono for control of the union pension funds. He puts his glasses back on and begins a recitation of the long history of labor and organized crime in the city while the camera plays over Ninth Street and the broken window, settling finally on a few drops of blood beneath the window.

Chicken blood.

"Police were unable to question the president of the Council of Trade Unions," the man on television says, "who is now in guarded condition following surgery on his hip. No suspects have been arrested."

The television sits on top of Jimmy Measles's cooler. Jimmy sits beneath it at the bar on a stool next to Peter's, looking sore-eyed and grim, drinking champagne through clenched teeth. He hardly looks at the customers as they come and go, he kisses nobody's cheeks, pats no fannies. He leans close to Peter to speak, his lips pulled back from his even, white teeth, which are still locked.

"I take this personally," he says, "people shooting my friends outside my club."

Peter doesn't say a word. There is no one in the bar except Jimmy Measles himself who does not know what Michael was doing in front of the place at six in the morning.

"Flood's father, Phillip," the man on television says, "was assassinated in 1974 as he stood on the porch of his home in South Philadelphia. . . ."

Peter waits, but the usual details of his uncle's death—which always seem to follow the mention of his name on television or in the papers—are missing tonight. He feels Jimmy Measles looking at him, and turns in that direction, thinking he has finally begun to wonder what Michael was doing in front of his place.

But there is nothing like that in Jimmy's expression. "His hip, that's it?" he says.

Peter shakes his head. "What the doctor said, a piece of buckshot stayed, more or less—I can't remember the word—it homogenized the head of his dick."

Jimmy Measles takes this news as if the wound were his own.

When Peter arrives at the hospital the next morning, Michael is connected to half a dozen tubes. A machine is squeezing his legs every ten seconds to prevent blood clots, and even with a fresh shot of morphine rolling through him, he is talking between breaths and sweating.

"If I could, Pally," he says, "I'd just shoot the fuckin' thing off. This minute."

He isn't sure if his cousin is saying that because his penis hurts or because it gets him in trouble, but he doesn't ask which way he intends it to be taken. Lying on your back in the hospital, you don't want somebody asking you to explain what you mean, especially about wanting to shoot part of yourself off.

Peter pats his cousin's shoulder and thinks of the effort it takes to be clear. He studies the length of Michael's legs under the sheet.

"So what did the doctors say this morning?" he says.

Michael shakes his head. "You won't fucking believe it," he says.

The buckshot has torn away most of the hip socket and taken the head of the femur with it.

Two doctors come in the door while Peter is still in the room. They report that they are in agreement that Michael needs a new hip. Michael listens to them and then turns his head. He does not care for the idea of manufactured parts, even though the doctors have brought the artificial joint along to show him how it works.

The thing comes in two pieces. There is a plastic socket that screws into the joint and a piece of chrome a foot long that fits into the bone.

Michael studies the two parts and then hands them back to the surgeon. He closes his eyes and drops his head onto the pillow. "It was up to me," he says again, "I'd just shoot the fuckin' thing off."

The doctor holding the parts smiles in a comfortable way, feeling good about being a surgeon and about not being Michael Flood. He says, "You already tried that, Mr. Flood."

Michael opens his eyes and stares at the doctor. It seems to Peter that for half a minute there is no sound anywhere in the hospital, that even paralyzed people are afraid to move.

And then Jimmy Measles comes through the door, carrying pasta from his restaurant that is some shade of green that shows even through the Styrofoam container, and the moment passes.

Everyone in the room is relieved to see Jimmy Measles.

Ten days later, they give Michael the new hip. The operation takes all day—the doctor with the sense of humor explains to Peter afterward that it is easier when the surgeon removes the femur and socket himself than when the patient does it for him.

They keep Michael in the hospital five weeks, and for five weeks Jimmy Measles sends over lunch and dinner every day, and visits in the afternoon, which is when Peter visits too.

Just once he brings Grace.

The moment Michael sees her he begins checking his sheets, making sure he is covered. She walks past Peter to the window; her eyes never glance at the bed.

Jimmy doesn't notice. He checks Michael's toes, has him move his feet, and when he is satisfied he doesn't have a blood clot, he begins a story about his second wife, Rhonda, the one from Vermillion, South Dakota, who tried to have him committed.

Grace is in a chair near the window, all to herself.

"So I been married to Rhonda two weeks," Jimmy says, "and I stay out a few nights to celebrate, end up early one morning in the lobby of the bank at Chestnut and Broad, waving their fire hose around, you know, like it's my dick, and when I wake up again I'm in a hospital for observation, the doctor's outside talking to my wife and she's sayin' she wants me committed. Married two weeks, and she wants me locked up, and I hadn't even been home yet. I guess that's the way they treat people in South Dakota. . . ."

Michael isn't listening. He is preoccupied; he looks everywhere in the room but at Grace.

Jimmy gives up the story and checks the bottles overhead that feed the tubes, making sure the doses haven't changed. It seems to Peter that he knows as much about the operation now as the doctors, nearly as much as the nurses.

"They said your white count's all right?" he says.

Michael doesn't seem to hear him.

"Leg cramps? You got a good pulse in your feet?"

Michael shakes his head and looks at Peter. "It was up to me . . ." he says, and those are the last words out of him until Jimmy Measles takes his wife and leaves.

When she is gone Michael sits up, trailing tubes, and eases his leg off the side of the bed. He reaches for his walker.

"Where you going?" Peter says.

"This place is gettin' on my nerves," he says, but something catches him then and freezes him to that spot, and that moment, until Peter can get him back onto the bed.

The next day they take the drainage tubes out of Michael's leg. Peter watches that, and does not return to the hospital afterwards.

He has Bobby the Jap and Monk take turns at the door and calls once a day, usually in the afternoon from the gym, to see if there is anything Michael wants him to do.

A week after the doctors pull the drainage tubes out of Michael's leg, two detectives walk into the gym to talk to Peter.

They do not introduce themselves, they just begin to talk. "We been thinking," one of them says, "how funny it is that you was in Atlantic City the night Michael gets shot."

Nick hears that and turns his back on the cops and moves to the other side of the room.

The detectives smile at each other, young cops in plain clothes. Peter is half undressed, standing in his underwear. He looks at them a moment, then pulls his pants back on and walks down the stairway without a word. The two cops look at each other, confused, and then follow him down.

The first one outside is grabbed by the shirt and thrown into the garage door. The door shakes at the impact. Nick sticks his head out of the window, then goes back inside.

Peter turns to the other cop, furious, putting his finger in the middle of his chest. "I don't have any trouble, you want to ask me the question," he says, sounding calmer than he is, "but not here. This isn't my place."

The detectives look at each other, not knowing what to do. "Hey, Peter," one of them says, "lookit, we're just doing our job. . . ."

"This isn't the place," he says. "You don't come here anymore. This place's got no connection to Michael."

T here is a call one night from the Italians, the ones who own the streets.

The man says, "I understand you've got medical problems in the family, you might be thinking of takin' over the business."

He doesn't answer.

"You need some business advice," the man says, "you know where we are. Maybe something can be worked out."

The man hangs up.

Peter goes to the gym, he reads the papers, once in a while he drives to the little house his mother left him in Cape May and gets a night's sleep.

It is the only place he can sleep through till morning.

Other nights, he stops at Jimmy Measles's club. Grace is still at her table, as if nothing has changed. He wonders how the shooting looked to her, the shotguns and the glass and Michael lying in the street.

He saw that she didn't like Michael much, even when she was running him across the street two, sometimes three nights a week.

She'd used him up early.

Being shot changes Michael. He hardens and narrows; he gains weight, he stays out of Jimmy Measles's club. He has no patience for business.

He sees the change himself and knows that something has been taken away from him, and sometimes, he finds himself staring at his cousin, wanting to take something away from him too.

They are sitting in the living room together early in the afternoon, Michael's leg elevated by a footstool, his crutches lying across the floor.

Peter is looking out the window to the park, thinking, for no particular reason, of the children who found little pieces of his uncle in the trees over there, and sold them, encased in plastic bubbles they stole from the ring machines at the grocery store, for ten dollars each during the Mummers' Parade.

"You know, everywhere I go," Michael says quietly, "people tell me how funny it is that you was in Atlantic City when this happened."

Peter turns to look at him.

Michael smiles and holds up his hand. "I ain't blaming you," he says. "I know what you was doing there, I don't mean that. But still . . . it is funny, ain't it?"

Peter doesn't answer. He feels Michael studying him.

"Jimmy tells me Nick's kid is something," Michael says a few minutes later.

Peter turns and looks at him again. "Jimmy doesn't know anything about it," he says.

He had taken Jimmy with him to the gym one afternoon and he sat in the corner in his yellow bikini underpants and new tennis shoes, telling stories and smoking cigarettes. Nick thought he was funny, so Peter brought him back a few times.

"So is the kid good or not?"

"He's good enough," Peter says.

"Why don't you talk to him, maybe we get him out of his old man's garage."

"There's nothing wrong with the garage."

"Not for the old man, what else's he got to do?"

Peter stares at the backs of his hands. Michael watches him.

"He's got a nice life," Peter says.

"He does the same fuckin' thing every day."

Peter feels himself rising to that, but in the same moment a spasm grabs Michael's leg and he squeezes his face almost shut, trying to squeeze off the pain, and hisses through his teeth. Peter waits. Michael's thick hands encircle half his thigh—as much of it as he can get his hands around—and then the spasm passes, and the mood between the cousins has changed.

"It ain't nothin' personal about Nick," Michael says. "But what is he, fifty-four, fifty-five?"

"He doesn't sit out on his steps yet nursing his grudges," Peter says.

That is what the retirement years in the neighborhoods are about. The loneliest people are the ones whose enemies have died. They sit in front of their houses in folding chairs, spring to fall, reframing old arguments, saying it the right way this time, saying all the things they should have said, with nobody there to hear them.

Peter knows that Nick is sometimes lonely for enemies, but it's only that he misses having someone to fight. Sparring with Harry or Peter isn't the same thing. He misses hating someone for a little while, not knowing how it will come out.

But hate moves further away from Nick DiMaggio all the time; he understands too much. And what he understands, he forgives.

"He's a nice-looking white boy," Michael says.

Peter nods. Harry could fight main events right now in Las Vegas or Atlantic City, but it doesn't matter. He has no use for those places, or the people in them.

The old man fought up and down the East Coast back in the fifties and knows where it leads, and his son seems to know it too.

They are the same person, thirty years apart.

Michael says, "He could make some money now that ain't going to be there forever. That's all I'm sayin'. Maybe you talk to him, let him know we help him if he wants it."

"They don't need us to make money," Peter says.

He is angry now, and his cousin sees that and smiles.

Sometimes Jimmy Measles wonders out loud why Michael has quit coming to the club. He looks his place over—the bar, the empty restaurant, Otto, his wife—and it isn't enough. "It must be bothering Michael," he says, "getting used to his leg."

Peter tells him the truth. "It ain't too bad, Jimmy."

"Is he pissed at something?"

Peter shakes his head, also the truth. Michael likes having Jimmy Measles around, but there is something left between himself and Jimmy's wife that makes him scared to come in.

Most of the time, Jimmy Measles sits at the bar with a shot glass and one of the bottles off the top shelf, and looks out the window onto Catherine Street. Still regretting what happened there.

Some nights Grace takes a few hundred dollars out of the cash register, and then is gone for the evening. She likes the bars on South Street; Jimmy doesn't seem to care. She kisses him on the cheek and smiles at Peter on the way out, and the sight of her from behind, going out the door, stays with him all night.

On one hand he wants to take her away from Jimmy Measles, on the other hand he doesn't.

It seems to him that Jimmy Measles causes it.

One night while Jimmy is missing Michael out loud, Peter turns in his seat, suddenly furious at him for being helpless.

He says, "What are you, a fan club? You want a fucking autograph or what?"

Then he sees he's hurt his feelings and wants to smack him for that too.

He says, "Jimmy, what I'm saying, you got enough right here to make anybody happy."

But he is talking about Grace now, and when he thinks of the conversation later, lying in bed at the house in Cape May, he sees that he doesn't know anything about what Jimmy Measles has at all.

A car rolls quietly to the south curb of Passyunk Avenue, in front of the Rosemont Diner. A man of Chinese extraction named Robert O'Meara—the police report will say a.k.a. Bobby the Jap—has just stepped out of the place and is walking west toward Broad Street, working a toothpick in the gaps separating his front teeth.

The car moves in front of the man and stops. The back door opens and the man stoops to see the faces inside. The toothpick rolls as he smiles. There is a moment then, which no one on the street can see, when something small changes in his face. A look of recognition.

The toothpick drops from his lips and Robert O'Meara gets in.

An hour later the car stops again, on an access road near the airport. The same door opens and a full garbage bag is wedged out, catching in the opening like something being born, and then, free of the car, slides into a shallow gulley. Inside the bag, Robert O'Meara is tied at the wrists and ankles with wire, and shot behind the ear.

The body is left there, where someone will find it, as a courtesy.

The door closes and the car leaves.

An airplane passes a hundred feet overhead, shaking the sky, and the package lies motionless beneath it in the road.

The news of Robert O'Meara reaches Michael and Peter in the private office of City Councilman Benjamin Taylor.

Recent newspaper stories have revealed that nineteen of the councilman's relatives—including his ninety-two-year-old mother—are now on the city payroll, and the councilman, sensing trouble, has called Michael to see if he can arrange jobs for some of them with the trade unions instead.

Peter and Michael sit quietly, listening while Benjamin Taylor lays out the problem. "It would be extremely helpful," he says, "if these people were viewed as immediately employable in other avenues of life."

There is new carpet in the office, snow-white and three inches deep, which comes up around the visitors' shoes like something that lives on the floor of the ocean. The city councilman finishes speaking without mentioning what he might offer in return, and Michael takes his feet out of his loafers and runs them over the floor.

"You fuck on carpet like this," he says, "you don't walk on it."

The man behind the desk smiles.

There is a wet bar in the corner, mahogany, and a long table by the window that appears to have been made from the same tree; leather chairs a foot or two apart all the way around.

The councilman lives with the fear that someday a constituent will leave this office with the impression he is not stealing as much as the mayor.

Michael looks up from the carpet and says, "Please tell me you ain't asking me to make your mother a roofer. . . ."

The call comes in then, over the private line. The councilman picks it up, flashing cuff links, and says, "Councilman Taylor speaking. . . ."

He listens a moment, and then hands the phone to Michael, who cleans the receiver before he puts it against his ear. He does business with colored people—more and more, they are part of the flow of power—but he doesn't want their germs.

"Yeah," he says.

He listens, not saying a word, and then he hangs up. He looks at Peter. "Bobby the Jap," he says. "How do you like that?"

Benjamin Taylor smiles and rests his chin on his fingers. "Bad news, gentlemen?"

Michael stares at him, perched on his white-tipped fingers, looking for some sign the spook is playing with him.

Benjamin Taylor lets the smile on his face change, a natural-looking change, until there is nothing there but sympathy.

Michael stands up, pushing himself away from the desk, and walks out without another word. Peter stays in the office a moment longer, getting used to the news, a stillness not unlike falling suddenly in his chest.

And then he gets up too.

The councilman watches him from behind the desk, looking uncomfortable. "Tell your brother I am sorry for his loss," he says.

"Cousin," Peter says. "He's my cousin."

Peter walks down four flights of stairs and finds Michael standing outside the north entrance. The limo is cutting across the three lanes of stalled traffic that encircle City Hall, day and night, sparkling in the sunlight. Horns honk, lights change, nothing moves.

"They picked him up on the street, he gets right in the car with them," Michael says. "He don't try to run or anything."

He shakes his head while Peter pictures Bobby getting in the car. It seems to Peter that he had been resigned to something since he started to work for Michael.

"Them people," Michael says, "sometimes you think they want to die."

The limo pulls in front of a city bus and then climbs the curb to the sidewalk. It stops with its back end still blocking a lane of traffic and Monk gets out to open the door.

Michael ducks in and slides across the seat. Peter crawls in behind him. The door shuts, and Michael's voice comes to Peter out of the dark.

"They took him out by the airport and popped him," he says, "but that's it. They didn't do nothing to him."

Monk gets in behind the wheel. "We going to Maryland?" he says. There is a Thoroughbred racehorse in Maryland that Michael is supposed to look at that afternoon. He has been talking about buying a racehorse all spring.

Peter begins to shake his head no.

"Yeah," Michael says, "Maryland."

Peter looks across the seat at his cousin, his eyes adjusting to the dark. Michael shrugs. "I still want my horse," he says.

Monk steers the car back into traffic and heads down Broad Street toward I-95, and then south on I-95 toward the airport. Peter stares out the window at the high weeds between the refineries and the runways. Somewhere in the weeds is a dirt road where Bobby was left in his plastic sack.

"Bobby had kids, right?" Michael says.

Peter nods. "Three of them."

The children lived with his ex-wife in a place called Davie, Florida. Sometimes Bobby would disappear for two, three weeks at a time to see them. He never said where he was going or when he was coming back. Once, when Peter told him he ought to let Michael know where he was so he wouldn't get the wrong idea —Michael had begun to worry that anybody who wasn't around had gone to work for the Italians—Bobby said, "Just tell him I'm on a load, Pally. He ain't going to understand this anyway, the kid's are all girls."

That's where Peter had been thinking Bobby was the last few days, with his girls in Davie, Florida.

"His wife, she divorce him or what?" Michael says.

"Yeah, she left."

"We ought to take care of the kids for him," he says after a while. "But nothin' for her, Pally. Not a fuckin' cent."

They cross into Delaware and pass through Wilmington. Peter notices Michael staring at a stand of trees off the next exit.

"What I think," Michael says quietly, "we got to respond to this a way it ain't going to happen again."

Michael stands in front of the horse for three seconds, his feet spread, his arms folded in front of his chest. The horse is lying on her back, chewing straw. "Fuck this horse," he says.

He turns and walks out of the barn back toward the car.

The man who is showing him the horse hurries to catch up. "Mr. Flood?" he says. "You want to look at her run or something?"

Monk sees Michael coming and opens the back door.

"Tell your boss, don't waste my time," Michael says.

"That there's a excellent horse," the man says, "ain't nothing wrong with her."

Michael gets into the car; Monk shuts the door and then steps in front of the man who is showing the horse.

Peter is still in the barn, wanting to watch the horse a little longer, to see how she gets up. Wanting some time to think about Bobby. He calls the animal, making a kissing noise. She blows back, and dust rises from the straw in front of her teeth.

The man showing the horse meets Peter on his way to the car. "That's a excellent horse," he says. "She's sound. You can't tell nothing just standing in front of her stall."

"She looks like an excellent horse," Peter says, and he steps around the man and gets into the car too. Michael is staring through the dark-tinted rear window at a white, two-story house with columns across the front that sits perhaps a quarter mile away, separated from the barn by a pasture and three rail fences.

"Can you believe this motherfucker tries to sell me a horse like that?" he says.

Peter doesn't answer.

Michael stares at the mansion. "I told them I want a big horse," he says. "That horse look big to you?"

Peter says, "How can you tell, she's lying down?"

"You can tell," he says.

They are crossing the bridge over Chesapeake City before Michael speaks again.

"Jimmy Measles tells me there was a colored guy up to the gym this week," he says.

Peter takes a slow, even breath, centering himself. After Michael lets you see him angry, he believes you owe him something until he sees you angry too.

"A trainer brought a guy over," Peter says.

It is quiet in the car again, Michael watching him. "Jimmy says this guy kicked Harry's ass."

Peter looks out the window at the canal that runs through the middle of the town. Two tugs are taking a tanker west, toward the Chesapeake Bay.

"So?" Michael says, "did he or not?"

"The colored kid was the kind of kid comes in to learn something," he says. "He isn't showing off, and Harry carries him a couple of rounds, lets him hit him a few punches."

"So he didn't kick his ass?" Michael says. Peter sees him begin to smile. "Pally?"

Peter says, "Michael, what do you care about the fuckin' gym?"

Michael stares at him as if he has been slapped, something furious bouncing around inside his head, into the walls, looking for a place to land.

Then finally it settles. Michael smiles.

And seeing that smile, Peter thinks of a Saturday morning his uncle made them wrestle. He was twice as strong as Michael, and held his wrists against the floor until his uncle got bored. An hour later Michael conked him with the hammer, forty stitches. Peter was asleep on the couch, the sports section open across his chest; Michael might have been twelve years old.

He remembers the ride to the hospital, holding a towel against the top of his head. On the way home, his uncle suddenly stopped the car and bought them both bicycles, and Michael smiled the way he is smiling now.

"Youse are brothers," his uncle said.

And one way or another, Peter has been afraid to go to sleep around his cousin ever since.

"Hey, Pally, I was thinking," Michael says later. "If Bobby the Jap's half Irish, how come he looks all Japanese?"

Peter shakes his head. He doesn't want to talk to Michael about Bobby.

Jimmy Measles's wife is alone.

Jimmy has gone to meet Michael at a club on Two Street, and Peter comes here, where he knows Michael will not be, and finds her sitting alone, under the stained glass.

After an argument, he and Michael go different places. An unspoken rule.

He sits down with her.

As arguments go, it wasn't much—only those few words in the back seat of the car—but words between Michael and Peter do not disappear. They settle and last.

Jimmy Measles's wife watches him stab at a wedge of lime floating in his glass.

He looks at her, thinking of Jimmy telling Michael that some colored kid had kicked Harry's ass, always looking for something that Michael will pat him on the head for . . . always putting himself places he doesn't belong.

There is noise in the corner, a couple of Pine Street antiques dealers arm wrestling and arguing over the rules. Peter looks in that direction; they must be seventy years old.

"You're looking for Jimmy, he's gone somewhere with Michael," she says.

He looks at her. "Jimmy and his pals," he says.

"You're his pal." She is playing with him now.

He shakes his head. "I'm his baby-sitter," he says.

"What for?"

"For Michael could visit you across the street."

She motions the bartender, showing him her empty glass. Someone puts money into the jukebox, and when she speaks again she has to raise her voice over the song "Louie, Louie." The kids from the art college will play "Louie, Louie" a hundred times in a row if you let them.

"Jimmy says they shot him in the penis," she says.

Peter sips his drink.

She says, "Was it painful?"

"Yeah, I think that's safe to say that."

They sit in the noise a minute, not trying to talk. She takes a drink, he traps the piece of lime against the side of the glass and spears it. A smile touches the corners of her lips. "Can he still function?" she says.

The bartender rejects "Louie, Louie," and there are boos from the corner.

Peter shrugs. "He isn't hooked up to a bag, if that's what you mean." In the absence of music, his voice carries the whole room.

"That's not what I mean," she says.

A little later she says, "You're cousins," teasing in some way he can't quite find.

He nods. "Michael's father and my father were brothers."

"You don't remind me of each other."

"Cousins aren't supposed to be like each other, that's brothers."

She seems to know where to touch him; he wonders what Michael told her.

"Sometimes they are," she says.

He takes her across the street; she doesn't say yes, she doesn't say no, she just comes along. She unlocks the door, and that is as much help as she offers.

There is a black leather couch against the far wall of the living room; he goes that direction and she follows. All the furniture is black leather, the walls are white. He sits down under a portrait of Jimmy that gives him snow-white teeth and big shoulders, and she stands in front of him, waiting.

He reaches behind her and touches the back of her knee. She doesn't move. He follows the line of her leg up under her skirt. She stands in front of him, watching. The back of her thigh curves under his hand, a defined, muscled curve, and her skirt rides up her legs in front and collects in back across his arm—a soft weight, it could be her hair. He wonders how he looks to her after her husband and Michael, if she is comparing them.

And it is that thought—the way Jimmy Measles looks to her as he sits in this chair—that stops him: a slipper dangling off a skinny, hairless white leg; his legs crossed under a monogramed robe. Thinking of his dancing days.

Peter's hand is on her behind, just above the place her legs come together. She is wearing nothing under the skirt.

He takes his hand off her, the hem of her skirt drops back to her knees. She stands still a moment longer, and if it makes any difference to her if his hand is under her skirt or not, it doesn't show.

He still feels the solid weight of her cheeks in his hand.

She walks out of the room and a moment later he hears her open the back door, and then there are scrambling noises across a tile floor. Two Boston terriers come through the open door, yappy, wet-nosed little dogs that shake, faces that look as if they're pressed into a window. He recognizes them from the pictures Jimmy keeps in his wallet.

He wonders how this happened—that the famous Jimmy Measles put himself in Peter's life, and put Peter in his.

The dogs are smelling his shoes when Jimmy's wife comes back into the room. "Pancho and Boner," he says, pointing in a hesitant way to one and then the other.

She shrugs, as if she cannot tell them apart.

She sits down in a chair opposite the couch and crosses her legs. They watch the dogs smell his shoes. One of the animals jumps onto the couch next to him, pushing its nose under his hand, wanting to be touched. The other one is gray-faced and old, and can't make it up. He sits on the floor and whines.

Peter picks him up and puts them together.

"He doesn't smell good," she says, meaning the one he helped up. "They get old like that, they get gamey."

There is a small pinch of skin at the back of the old dog's neck, the rest of him is as tight as a wiener. Peter rubs the skin and the dog's back leg begins to kick, a scratching motion. Peter stops, it stops. He rubs the spot again, the leg begins as soon as he moves his fingers. It's like an engine.

"Jimmy can't smell it," she says. "He lets them lick his face, crawl all over his clothes."

The other dog has rolled in against Peter's leg and is lying on its back, its tongue spilled out of its mouth and resting on the couch. "They're a little ripe," he admits.

"They get all over him, Jimmy doesn't smell it at all," she says. "All over his clothes too, and you know how he is about them . . ." She shakes her head. "He's got a fetish about his clothes."

It's quiet another minute, and then she stares at him and says, "That's one of them."

His eyes move to the grandfather clock near the door.

She sees him do that, she sees everything. "Don't get nervous," she says, "everybody wants something different."

Peter suddenly finds himself wondering what she's done in this house with Michael, what kept him coming back. He isn't as interested in what she does with Jimmy—there isn't much that Jimmy could want that would surprise him.

The dog pushes his nose against Peter's leg, reminding him he's there. Peter rubs the animal's neck and his leg begins to kick.

"Like what?" he says.

She looks at him then as if she were guessing his coat size. "Diapers," she says finally.

Michael in diapers.

"Naw . . ." he says. He shakes his head.

"Some people like it," she says.

He blinks. *Michael in diapers.*

"They lie on the bed and have a diaper put on them," she says, "and then we go across the street and drink until they have to go so bad they can't hold it anymore, and after that happens we come back here and change."

He finds himself thinking of Michael's mother, his Aunt Theresa, red-faced and out of breath from picking up their dirty underwear off the floor so they would have to wear what was in the drawer. "You get hit by the bus in dirty shorts," she would say, "the nurses at the emergency room gonna think we're trash."

He thinks of Michael in an emergency room in diapers; he thinks of the things that can hit you in the street.

"I never heard of that before," he says. "Diapers."

She shrugs. "Some people like it," she says. And then she puts the dogs outside, and they go back across the street.

T hey sit in the same place under the stained glass and drink, and Peter feels blessed.

It is like the state of grace when he has touched a woman and fucked her and then watched her get back into her clothes for the first time—when that issue is off the table, and before there are new issues on the table that he never imagined were issues —when everything is calm.

And in the calm he sees that he likes the idea of her coming in here with someone in diapers. He likes the idea of the secret. The wet pants, that's still a little hard to see.

"What you were talking about before," he says, "did you mean Jimmy, or was it Michael?"

She looks at him a long minute, until he is sorry he asked the question. Until it feels as if he's done something worse to Jimmy Measles than put a hand up his wife's skirt.

"I wouldn't tell if it was you," she says.

It is storming the afternoon they come to the gym. Peter is sitting in the corner, dabbing at his lip with a stiff, yellowed towel that has been lying on the same spot on the bench for eight years he can remember, getting stiffer and yellower, and has begun lately to taste like fish.

Nick is in another corner of the room, soaked in his own sweat, hitting the soft bag with punches he seems to throw without trying. That is where he always finishes after they box, on the heavy bags. Old habits. There is no one else in the room.

The door opens downstairs, and Peter smells the rain.

They come up slowly, Monk first, his eyes squinting as he clears the darkness of the staircase, then Michael, dripping rain, walking on a cane, then a weight lifter named Leonard Crawley, who has Bobby the Jap's place, then Jimmy Measles.

They stand in a spot near the ring; puddles collect on the floor. Nick hits the bag.

Peter has never spoken to Leonard Crawley, but he has heard him talking to Monk in the front seat of the limo. He wonders out loud sometimes, in a wistful sort of way, what sound a human back makes as it breaks.

The timer goes off and Nick comes around the platform which holds the ring, nodding at Monk and Jimmy Measles, taking off his bag gloves to shake hands. "Hey, Michael," he says.

"Nick, how you been?"

"I been pretty good."

Michael sees Peter on the bench then. "What'd you do, poison my cousin?" he says. "He looks like he ate a fuckin' dog."

"He killed me today," Nick says, a small courtesy. He always says he got killed.

Leonard Crawley looks at Peter, showing his teeth in a way

that could be a smile. Peter has the sudden thought that if you take enough steroids, first you grow muscles in your arms and legs, then you grow muscles in your face.

"What I was wonderin'," Michael says to Nick, "if the kid was around, could he give Lenny here a couple of rounds."

Nick looks at Leonard Crawley for the first time. "He's run to Jersey for some parts," he says.

"He comin' back or what?" Leonard says. His voice seems higher pitched than it ought to be, and out of place in the gym.

Nick crosses his arms and considers him. Leonard shows him his neck, veins as thick as a finger.

Michael says, "Hey, he don't mean nothin', Nick, he just wanted to move a few rounds with the kid. Two, three rounds is all, takin' it easy."

"He isn't here," Nick says. "I told you he's in Jersey."

Michael moves a step closer to Nick, dripping rain, nodding the way he does when he wants something. "You think he might be back, could work a little with Lenny?"

Leonard waits, enjoying the moment, as if Michael has just asked someone what it was going to be, his right arm or his left.

Nick says, "He could be a while, in this weather . . ."

"You mind if we wait?" Michael asks. "Let Lenny hit one of them bags or something."

Leonard Crawley undresses against the bench, hanging his clothes on a nail, taking off his rings and his bracelet and his necklace and handing them and his money clip to Michael.

Nick walks to the other side of the room; he doesn't say another word.

Jimmy Measles follows him over, trying to tell him a story about his dogs. Nick has a dog of his own, but he isn't listening.

Leonard takes a long time undressing, enjoying it. Without his clothes, he resembles a root system. There are stretch marks on his shoulders, and his arms are black with tattoos.

Peter stands up and talks quietly in Michael's ear.

"The fuck are you gonna do?" he says.

Michael watches Leonard wrap his hands.

Peter says, "There's no reason to do something like this."

"I want to see the kid work," Michael says, still watching Leonard wrap. "That's a reason."

Peter says, "How come you can't just come over sometime and watch him, like anybody else? How come you got to bring a fucking monster? It's insulting."

"So somebody's insulted," Michael says. "So what?"

Peter walks away and finds a seat in the window. There are cars parked on both sides of the street, halfway up the block, waiting for Nick to fix them. Old, beat-up cars; Cadillacs, Fords, Chevys. He still won't work on anything foreign. He knows who has money and who doesn't, and he can fix cars a little or all the way, depending on what someone has to pay. He does that without explaining it; he never embarrasses anybody he doesn't have to.

Leonard Crawley climbs into the ring and begins to throw punches, watching himself in the mirrors, checking the muscles in his arms and back and legs from different angles. Nick sits with his own arms crossed, bone dry in a wet shirt, the afternoon ruined.

Jimmy Measles sees something is going on and leaves him alone about the dogs.

For half an hour, no one speaks. Michael waits in an old stuffed chair and Leonard stands in the corner of the ring, his arms resting across the ropes, the muscles underneath sagging from their own weight.

Peter sees Harry turn the corner. He pulls the van up onto the sidewalk, opens the back door and unloads half a dozen mufflers and tailpipes in the rain.

Then he shuts the door and, leaving the truck on the sidewalk, he climbs the stairs three at a time.

He pauses at the top, one long second, seeing it all at once— Michael and Peter and Jimmy Measles and his father all sitting down, Monk looking at the posters on the wall, the guy with the muscles standing in the ring; the whole place dead quiet.

Michael stands up and holds out his hand. "Harry," he says, "how you been?"

Nick's kid puts his hand halfway into Michael's to shake, protecting it. Like his father, he lives his life with sore hands.

"I was wondering could you give my man Lenny here a couple of rounds."

Peter sits in the window, Nick doesn't move off his chair. The kid takes his hand away from Michael and looks at Leonard Crawley.

"Three rounds?" he says.

Leonard moves off the ropes and stretches. He says, "Three, four, five, whatever you want."

Nick gets up off his chair and stands in front of his son while he dresses, as if he doesn't want him looking at Leonard Crawley until they fight.

Michael checks the clock on the wall. Twenty minutes have passed.

Leonard has been standing in the ring so long Peter has gotten used to the way he looks. Harry is in the ring with him now, loosening up.

Leonard follows the kid's movements, looking bored. "Yo, Michael," he says, "we gonna do this or what?"

Harry stops and looks at him, and then nods. He climbs through the ropes and pulls the plug on the timer, and then takes a cup and the gloves out of his locker. Nick helps him pull the cup on and then laces him up.

He climbs back in, looking pale and thin in the same ring with the weight lifter, and then leans over the ropes toward his father to receive his mouthpiece.

"You ready?" Michael says.

Nick nods without looking at him, and Michael plugs the timer back into the wall. It goes off once, a minute passes and it goes off again.

Nick looks over his son's shoulder at Lenny Crawley. "Anybody looks like that could fight, we'd know about them," he says.

Michael stands in the corner, smiling, having a good time now.

A peculiar sour smell fills the air, something Leonard Crawley secretes when he gets excited. He walks across the ring, hands at his chest, and then his right hand makes a long, slow arc through the air.

Harry steps back and watches as Leonard follows the force of the punch, stumbling.

He steps inside the next time Leonard tries to hit him—another sweeping right hand—and then puts the top of his head under the weight lifter's chin and allows him to throw all the right hands he wants, fifty or more, some of them at his kidneys, some of them at the back of his head, furious punches without leverage or meaning.

They walk around the ring in this way, Leonard jerking at him, pushing and pulling; Harry watching it, allowing it, relaxed. He lets it go on as long as Leonard wants, and then, when he quits to catch his wind and drops his head onto Harry's shoulder to rest, the shoulder suddenly moves, and Leonard's forehead bounces off.

Harry takes half a step back and waits until Leonard's head drops toward him, and then hits him in the face with an uppercut. Harry doesn't ordinarily throw uppercuts in the gym, the punch can ruin a nose.

The glove travels just twelve inches, but he turns into it.

Leonard stops, balancing on some shrinking spot on the floor, and before he can right himself Harry steps to the side and digs a hook high into his ribs, popping the cork, and Leonard Crawley begins to pour out all over the ring. He grabs Harry around the waist, holding himself up. Half a minute later, he lifts him off the floor and carries him back into the ropes, making a screaming noise as they move.

Leaving two perfect footprints in the center of the ring, his own blood.

Harry allows himself to be taken to the ropes, patient, waiting to see what the weight lifter will do when he quits yelling.

The timer goes off but Leonard doesn't stop. He reaches around Harry and grabs the ropes on either side of his body. He begins to slam himself into him, over and over. Harry watches a few seconds, covering himself with his arms, timing him, and then, as Leonard Crawley comes again, he lowers his shoulders even with the weight lifter's and brings up an elbow, and the yelling stops.

That is the first thing Peter notices, the quiet.

Leonard lies on the ring floor without moving, and then his knee raises and rolls, and he seems to follow it, over onto his side. The lower half of his face is hidden under his gloves.

The timer goes off again and a new sound comes out of Leonard

Crawley, a long, hollow note which doesn't seem to have a beginning or an end or a purpose, just something that fades in and then fades out.

Nick is leaning over the ropes, unlacing his son's gloves. Michael hasn't moved. Jimmy Measles gets up and walks into the bathroom to urinate.

"He changed his mind, right?" Nick says to Michael. "Four, five rounds, he don't want them today?"

Michael comes over on his cane and puts his hand on Nick's shoulder. "Hey, goomba, no harm, am I right? My cousin tells me your kid's ready to make some money, I just want to see for myself."

Nick looks at Peter half a second; he doesn't say a word. Leonard sits up holding his face, blood dripping off the end of his nose, his jaw hanging wrong, like a door off one hinge.

The timer goes off again with Leonard still on the floor. Monk climbs through the ropes, carrying a clean towel. He cuts the laces off Leonard's gloves and gets him on his feet. On the way out he warns him not to bleed in the car.

Jimmy Measles emerges from the bathroom, and the four men leave more quietly than they arrived.

Nick watches them from the window. "These fuckin' guys," he says, looking back at the blood on the floor of the ring. "Everywhere they go, it's like they broke in."

Peter doesn't know if he is included in that or not.

The timer sounds again and Harry begins hitting the hard bag. The chains bang together as the bag jumps. The only other sounds are the punches and Harry's breathing.

Peter finds a bucket and fills it with hot water and washes the blood off the floor, and when he has finished, has washed as much of his cousin and his cousin's business from the gym as he can, he showers and leaves.

A week to the day after Bobby is left in a garbage bag on the service road at the airport, Michael climbs through the kitchen window of a small brick row house on Snyder Avenue—Leonard Crawley boosting him up, Monk already waiting inside—and takes the old Italian who lives there out of his bed, a confused old man who cannot see them without his glasses, and tapes him to the water heater in the basement.

His wife finds him there, his socks sticking halfway out of his mouth, when she comes back from Levittown. She has been there visiting her grandchildren. The bats they used, stained with the old man's blood, are still lying on the basement floor.

Peter reads the details of the old man's death in the *Daily News*. It says he was naked.

Peter closes the paper, closes his eyes. He listens to the ocean through the open bedroom window; it sounds close enough to be washing over his feet.

He has not seen Michael since the afternoon at the gym. He came to Cape May that night, to his mother's house to sleep, and hasn't been back.

Downstairs in the kitchen the telephone begins to ring. He stays where he is, listening to it, lying in his shoes on a bed that is too soft and creaks when he moves.

All the furniture in the house was his mother's. The desk is still filled with carefully stacked piles of scrawled notes and receipts and newspaper clippings; the medicine cabinet is lined with her bottles of pills. There isn't a picture in the place.

He hasn't thrown any of it out. He can feel the old woman his mother became in the things she left behind, a compulsive order that imposes itself in every room of the house, as if by imposing order in these few small rooms, she could quiet the disorder that had driven her here.

And it is this sense of order, as much that as the ocean, that allows him to sleep.

The telephone is still ringing. He opens his eyes and looks at the light on the ceiling, a milk-colored antique glass full of dead moths and dust.

No one has the number.

It is five blocks from this house to the store. He walks there in the morning for breakfast and the papers. He sees the same people every day, and speaks to them without knowing their names.

The town itself is an hour from Atlantic City, at the southern tip of the Jersey shore. The place is settled, though, unlike the beach towns that lie in between. No one comes through on the way somewhere else, throwing beer cans from cars. Everyone is here on purpose.

The phone goes quiet, and Peter sits up. The bedsprings stretch under his weight, and he looks again at the old man's picture in the paper. The city seems a hundred years away, and he can almost imagine himself sitting on the benches behind the bulkhead with the old ladies of Cape May, shaking his head at the front page of the newspaper, asking what kind of people would do something like that to a retired gentleman in his own basement.

He walks into the bathroom and fills the tub; there is no shower.

He settles into the bath and pictures her in this same place, looking at the ceiling, thinking of him. She thought of him, he knows. She left him the house.

He stays in the tub until the water loses its heat, until in the coolness he separates himself from her and stands up and reaches for a towel. He leaves the bathroom without draining the tub, dresses quickly, and walks out of the house with his shirt still sticking to the moisture on his back.

He locks the front door and heads toward his car in the driveway.

Once before he gets there, he stops and looks back at the house where his mother resumed her life.

A man Peter has never seen before is sitting in the sun on the steps in front of Michael's place. He is shirtless, squinting at every car that passes. He stands up when Peter parks, and then moves to the sidewalk to meet him as he crosses the street. He puts one of his hands into the pocket of his pants and cocks his head.

"Michael around?" Peter says.

"Not to you," the man says. He takes his sunglasses off and holds them at his side.

Peter considers him a moment, the hand in his pocket, the flat look in his eyes. He is younger without the glasses, almost a kid. But the kind of kid who would break your legs for a dollar.

A kid who, anyplace but this street, would never meet your eyes at all.

"Before we do something here," Peter says, "why don't you go inside, ask whoever the fuck you work for is it all right to do it?"

"You got business with Michael," he says, "tell me, and I tell him. That's the way it works, pal."

The front door opens, offering the sight of Leonard Crawley. His nose is taped and his jaw is wired. He is wearing sunglasses, and beneath them Peter can see the discoloration. The effect, in this light, is horrifying. It looks as if someone has burned Leonard's eyes out of their sockets.

"Leave him come in," he says.

There are perhaps twenty men in the living room, sitting with beers and cigarettes, most of them kids like the one outside. A television set is on in the corner, *The Jetsons*.

Leonard and three men Peter does not recognize are standing around a small table near the window, watching the street. They

201

pass a rolled bill, taking turns bending to the table where half a dozen lines of cocaine are laid out on a mirror.

At the edge of the table is a wet towel, and Peter watches Leonard press it into his face after he has taken his turn. He breathes deeply, and when he pulls it away, the towel is spotted with blood.

Peter walks into the kitchen. Michael is in there with Jimmy Measles and Monk and half a dozen people who have worked for him a long time.

"Where you been?" Michael says.

Peter looks over the people in the room; all of them are roofers, none of them have been on a roof in five years. It comes to him that quitting hard work once you are used to it ruins you. That it turns you mean and soft at the same time.

"Pally, you hear what I asked you?" his cousin says. "We made a move night before last, and I asked you where you fuckin' been."

"The shore," he says.

"I been callin' you six times a day, and you're to the fuckin' shore."

"What the papers said, you didn't need me." His cousin knows he wouldn't have gone into the basement to tie an old man to a water heater.

He sits on the counter.

Michael says, "You should of been there, it would have been good for you."

He liked it, Peter sees that he liked it.

"What I wonder sometimes," Michael says, talking more for the others than to Peter, "what the fuck I need you for in the first place. I get shot, you're at the shore. We got somethin' to do, you're at the shore. I come up to Nick's, you act like you're ashamed we're cousins."

He turns to Jimmy Measles and says, "Get me a fuckin' beer."

It is quiet in the kitchen then, all the noise is on the other side of the door. Jimmy Measles gets off his stool and opens the refrigerator.

Michael Flood stares at his cousin.

"So I'm back from the shore," Peter says. "You took an old

guy into his basement and beat him to death, and now you got the posse sitting in your living room. You askin' me what to do next, get them out of here before they burn holes in the carpet."

Michael shakes his head.

"They did Bobby, we did one of them. Now we're going to end this fuckin' thing, is what's next."

"The Italians been around a hundred years," Peter says.

Michael stares at him, wondering briefly if he has been with the Italians and not at the shore. Trying to see what he's thinking. "Everything in this fuckin' city's been around a hundred years," he says finally.

There is a noise in the other room, something falling. "So what are you doing?" Peter says.

Michael smiles and nods toward the living room. "I'm turning them loose," he says.

Peter looks in that direction. "The only way you turn people like that loose," he says, "you tell them exactly what to do and promise to cut off their hands they do one thing different than what you say, and that way they only jam you up maybe half the time."

"We ain't jammed up," Michael says.

Jimmy Measles puts the beer in front of him and settles back into his stool.

"You put them on the street looking for old guys," Peter says, "I'm going to Hawaii."

Michael is quiet a minute, thinking. Then he gives in.

"You go somewhere, Pally," he says finally, "you let me know before you leave, all right?"

It comes to Peter later that Jimmy Measles is borrowing Michael's money. He sees him running errands for him, picking up his cigarettes or pizza or laundry, opening doors.

Michael doesn't thank him.

"You know," he says one night at the club, "there's nothing written down that you got to ride Otto the chef right to the last spin down the toilet."

Jimmy Measles just smiles. He puts himself into Peter's life and draws him into his, but he isn't asking him to carry his problems.

He doesn't complain about his business, he doesn't complain about his disease. He puts the atomizer on the table next to his cigarette, and takes one and then the other, barely able to breathe, and never says a word about it.

And Peter likes him for that, no matter what kind of mess he is making, putting himself in places he doesn't belong. Peter sits at the table now and watches one of the bartenders take four twenties out of the cash register, and then disappear into the bathroom with one of the kids from the art college.

"You turning this place into a commune or what?" he says.

Jimmy Measles takes a drink and lights a cigarette. His wife is sitting by herself under the stained glass, looking bored.

Peter is suddenly furious, he doesn't know why. Jimmy does that to him. "Let me ask you something," he says. "How deep you into Michael?"

Jimmy Measles looks around his place, all the stained glass and fresh paint and new furniture. Two waiters are sitting in the new stuffed leather chairs in his restaurant, half asleep, no one to wait on. The bar is slow too. "You know where I was this afternoon?" he says.

Peter waits.

"The proctologist. My doctor sent me to have a proctologist examination. They got an inverted chair that tilts up, gives them a better look at your ass. And while I'm sitting there looking at this thing, a nurse comes in, all sweet and pressed, and starts laying out all these shiny instruments on the table, two at a time. It takes her six, seven trips. She's checking them too, kind of holds it up to the light the way you pick out a pool cue . . ."

"Jimmy, I'm trying to get to something here."

Jimmy holds up his hand, as if he is coming back to that. "And then she takes a tube of lubricant out of her uniform pocket," he says, "like she carries *lubricant* around with her, squeezes it on her finger to make sure it's coming out, and then she lays that on the table next to the instruments, and then she hands me a gown. She says, 'If you would just slip out of your trousers and underwear, sir, the doctor will be with you in a moment.' "

Peter stares at him, wondering where this is going. Jimmy Measles takes a drink and uses the atomizer.

"I came," he says.

"You whacked off in a doctor's office?" Which is the thing about Jimmy's stories; at some point they bring you in. Which, he realizes, is also the thing about Jimmy. "What if that girl forgets to lay out one of the instruments and walks back in?"

Jimmy shrugs. "It wouldn't be the first time."

Peter squints through the smoke and considers him. "You did that before?"

He gives Peter a smile, an awful smile, and Peter imagines for a moment that he is his brother, sitting in this chair trying to break him of his habit of whacking off at the doctor's. He shakes his head, trying to get rid of the thought.

"If I remember," he says, "all this started, I asked how deep you were into Michael."

Jimmy calls the bartender and points to their glasses. All of Jimmy's bartenders wear white shirts and black bow ties—real ties, no clip-ons. The bartender's tie is perfect, and there is a little white streak in the crease at the side of his nostril. He pours the drinks, waits a respectful time to see if there is anything else he can do, and then returns to his station. He puts the bottle back on the shelf and walks to the other end of the bar.

"I got to hire another bartender like him," Jimmy Measles says. "Only a girl. Real young-looking, named Sam or something, some boy's name. Nothing looks as good as a bow tie on a girl."

"You get another one like him, they'll be robbing the bricks out the walls."

Jimmy shakes his head, looking into Peter's eyes. He says, "I always know when a bartender's stealing."

He glances at his wife, who crosses her legs. Her heel slides out of her shoe, and she reaches under the table to fix it, touching things she cannot see. Jimmy Measles smiles again at Peter, that same awful way.

"That girl at the doctor's office," he said. "I could bring her in here, maybe put her in pigtails, you know?"

Peter puts his hand on Jimmy Measles's arm, just above the elbow. His arm is soft and thinner than it looks. Peter can feel the bone. "You borrowed money from Michael," he says. "Don't sit around here thinking it takes care of itself. It isn't a friendly thing."

Jimmy Measles begins to say something, make one of his jokes, Peter squeezes the arm, cutting him off. "You eat together, make him laugh at your stories, everybody acting friendly, that doesn't make you friends," he says.

"Let me tell you what happened. He tells you, 'Jimmy, you ever got a problem, you let me know,' right? And then one day you're suddenly having a hard time keeping your wife clear with Nan Duskin, plus the car, plus the business expenses—one of which, by the way, is Otto the chef that couldn't open dog food—and you borrow a few thousand from Michael. He hands it right over, doesn't even seem to know how much he gave you, right?"

Peter leans closer; Jimmy tries to pull his arm away.

Peter holds on. "Well, he knows," he says. "He knows what he gave you, he knows what you owe—and you understand those are two different things, right?—and suddenly he doesn't treat you so well. Suddenly you're somebody runs errands, somebody he tells you where to be.

"And you do that shit, after all the guy lent you money, but all the errands in the world don't take cent one off what you owe him. Running you around's what he does, remind you that the debt's still there."

He lets go of Jimmy Measles, sorry for squeezing his arm. "Michael doesn't like anybody that owes him anything," he says. "He's been like that since he was in diapers."

The word *diapers* comes out accidentally, and hangs in the air a moment, growing like some balloon stuck on a helium nozzle. Jimmy Measles doesn't seem to notice.

The smile again.

"All I'm saying, don't get into him too deep, Jimmy. You get in, be able to get out."

Peter walks out of the club an hour later, thinking of diapers and his cousin. He does not see the two old Italians sitting in a cloud of cigarette smoke in their Ford until he is close enough, if it were not for the closed window, to touch them.

The one in the passenger seat watches him as he walks past.

Peter passes the car, looking up the street; he feels a cushion under his shoes, as if he were walking on a mattress. He knows if he hears the car door open, he is ruined here on the sidewalk, but there is no sound.

He puts himself in the old Italian's place.

He is thinking nothing good comes this easy.

In the morning, Peter finds Jimmy Measles alone in the far corner of the club next to a mound of wet, black carpet. The ceiling and roof are gone in this part of the building, there is nothing overhead but clouds.

Jimmy has found a chair that has inexplicably survived the fire untouched—the rest are in black piles all over the club, indistinguishable now from tables and pieces of the walls and ceiling and floor.

Peter smells the gasoline and imagines the path of the fire. It seems to have begun in the basement, gone up the staircase to the kitchen, then into the dining room and bar, looking for a way out, and then finally followed the kitchen flue to the roof.

Jimmy Measles is sitting in his slippers and robe, wheezing with every breath, smoking a cigarette, a quart bottle of peppermint schnapps between his legs. Fire inspectors—most of them wearing masks against the smell—are picking through the place. Outside, a small crowd is pressing into the restraining ropes the fire department has strung across the front of the building.

There isn't much to see, and the crowd is smaller now than it was earlier in the morning; the firemen have told the television reporters there are no bodies.

Which is not completely true.

The dogs are rolled inside two towels at the foot of Jimmy Measles's chair, one of them pressed against his slipper. Jimmy's eyes are bloodshot and watery.

"They should of let the dogs out," he says.

"Maybe they wouldn't leave." Peter trying to find something to save.

Jimmy Measles drinks from the bottle of schnapps then leans forward and puts his hand across one of the blankets. "Why would they burn up a couple little dogs?"

"If you want, I could take care of them now," Peter says. "You could go talk things over with Grace."

Jimmy Measles takes the atomizer out of his robe pocket, moves the cigarette away from his lips long enough to use it. "She's asleep," he says. "Her mother called a doctor, in two minutes he was over to the house and gave her something that was in the Valium family."

Peter surveys the room, broken glass everywhere, the smell of burned dogs and burned wood and gasoline. Something sweet— Southern Comfort.

Looking to the front, he can see the fumes in the light from the street. It seems to him that Jimmy Measles cared about the dogs in a different way than he cared about the rest of the place. The dogs were just dogs, they weren't part of the show.

A policeman comes in, a saggy-faced man in a coat and loafers, stepping over what was left of the front door. He hesitates a moment, taking the room in, then makes his way to the back. "Mr. Katz?" he says.

Jimmy Measles looks up, does not answer. "Mr. Katz," the policeman says, "I wonder if you mind I ask you a couple questions."

Jimmy looks at himself and then at the ceiling. There is a

chandelier up there, hanging from its cords. He smiles in a familiar way that isn't a smile. The cop stays where he is, waiting until Jimmy is ready.

"What I wanted to ask you," he says, "do you know a reason somebody'd want to fuck with you like this?"

Jimmy looks into the barrel of the bottle. The cop squats until he is sitting on his heels, putting himself in front of Jimmy's face. "What I mean is, could you have a problem with the neighbors, or maybe you threw somebody out of here, they left mad and come back?"

Jimmy bends into his lap and breathes from his atomizer. He shakes his head.

"Were you experiencing business problems of another kind?"

"Wait a minute," Peter says, and the cop looks up at him, waiting. Peter speaks to Jimmy. "The next thing he's going to ask, are you insured."

The policeman comes up off his haunches slowly, as if it hurts him to stand up. "I don't remember asking you nothing," he says.

"He's lost his place," Peter says. "He can't tell you a thing sitting here in his slippers that he can't tell you the same thing later, when he's had a chance to calm down."

The policeman has another look at the room. "You insured, Mr. Katz?" he says.

Jimmy doesn't answer.

"I don't mean to put myself in your business," Peter says to the policeman, "but he's upset. He lost his place and he lost his dogs . . ."

The policeman considers Jimmy a different way. "Is that right, Mr. Katz?" he says. "You lost your dogs?"

The policeman notices the towels rolled up at Jimmy Measles's feet. "You know, there's some people, Mr. Katz, would burn up their own dogs."

Jimmy Measles gets out of the chair and heads for the front door. He takes the bottle; he leaves the two rolled packages there on the floor. At the doorway between the bar and the restaurant he stops, dropping the cigarette on the floor and then carefully grinding it out with his slipper. Then he goes outside.

The cop kicks at a piece of the ceiling, and underneath is one of the small glass bowls Jimmy put on the tables. The carnation inside it still looks as if it just came out of the florist's.

"Those dogs were really his pets?" the policeman says to Peter.

"Yeah," Peter says, "those were his pets."

The next time Peter sees him, Jimmy Measles is standing on the corner of Ninth and Catherine in his underpants, soaking wet, swinging at a parking meter with a softball bat. It is five-thirty in the afternoon, and his wife is watching from the living room window.

What looks like half of South Philadelphia is in the street with him, rooting him on.

As Peter comes through the crowd, Jimmy stops banging the meter long enough to pick up his atomizer, which he has placed on his front steps next to a fresh bottle of schnapps, and holds it in his mouth while he pumps the trigger.

It reminds Peter somehow of the old Phillies, back before the players used golf gloves, when they'd step out of the batter's box for a handful of dirt.

"Blood for blood," Jimmy Measles says to the crowd, and moves back to the meter. "There's going to be Guinea blood on the streets."

The next swing he takes misses the parking meter—more memories of the old Phillies—and he splays across the sidewalk. He lies still, gathering his resources, and then, using the bat to lift himself off the sidewalk, he gets back to his feet.

He sees Peter then. "Hey, Pally. Tell Michael for me that we got something to do."

An announcement.

He tries another swing, but he is exhausted and the bat hits the pole and falls out of his hands.

Peter says, "Jimmy, where's your pants?"

"Blood for blood," he says. "We're gonna wash the streets with Guinea blood."

Peter picks up the bat, hands it to Jimmy Measles, and steers him inside. Jimmy Measles steps in the glass from the parking meter and limps to the step. He sits down, drinks from the bottle of schnapps, and then touches his foot, which is bleeding. He inspects the blood on the finger, and then holds it over his head for everyone to see. "Blood for blood," he says, and the crowd cheers.

Peter tries the door but she has it locked. In a moment he hears her working the chain on the other side.

Jimmy Measles walks into his living room to polite applause, trailing the bat, dirt and little rocks falling off his back, and sits heavily in a black leather chair. Peter looks at his wife.

"Guinea blood," he says again.

Peter sits down himself. "Jimmy, you don't mind, that's the Italian Market outside."

"Blood for blood," he says, and then he smiles his worst smile and closes his eyes.

Ｓhe asks him to help her get Jimmy upstairs. "He'll wake up if there isn't a television on," she says, "and he's going to want his pills."

Peter looks at Jimmy Measles, who is spreading out over the couch like a stain, and considers carrying him upstairs.

"Pills on a load like this?"

"He'll be awake in half an hour," she says. "The only thing that gets him back to sleep is his pills."

"Jimmy isn't that strong," he says, "to be taking pills and drinking the same time. He's better off awake."

"He isn't better off awake today," she says. She stares at her husband, lying on the couch. "He was over there," she says.

He looks at her, not understanding.

"When it happened."

It takes him a moment.

"He thought he heard the dogs," she says.

Peter pulls him by the wrists up off the couch. His skin lets go of the leather an inch at a time, it reminds him of peeling a Band-Aid. He puts his head underneath Jimmy's arm and moves him across his shoulder, balancing the load, and then stands up. Jimmy Measles smells like the fire. His skin is hot in back, where it was pressed into the couch, and cold and damp against Peter's cheek.

Peter carries him up the stairs, feeling an unfamiliar panic— something about the weight of the cold skin pressing into his face.

She walks ahead of him and opens the bedroom door. All the furniture upstairs is white. He takes Jimmy Measles to the bed and bends until the weight rolls off him. He covers him with a sheet, and he kicks it off.

Jimmy settles into his pillow and then slowly curls away from the light, his hands buried between his legs. His wife pulls the blinds and the room is dark. Peter has a sudden, transitory thought that he and Grace have finished a bedtime story and the baby has fallen asleep. She is careful closing the door, not to make any noise.

"Can you stay a little while?" she says downstairs.

He is halfway to the front door, she is in the kitchen.

"These guys don't want him," he says, thinking she is afraid, "and if they did, they wouldn't come into his house." He sits down on the couch, brushing some of the dirt onto the floor.

She comes out of the kitchen with two drinks. He notices the ring Jimmy Measles gave her. There must have been a scramble in the diamond mine the day they found the stone.

She sits so close to him that he can feel the heat off her arms. Her hair is black, and she has pulled it away from her face. He looks at his watch.

"Just a few minutes," she says, "to make sure Jimmy doesn't get up and go back outside with the bat."

They are on the couch twenty minutes when the noises start

upstairs. There is a bump and another bump, and then a bump that shakes the ceiling. Jimmy begins to yell.

Peter sets his drink on the floor and slowly stands up.

Jimmy Measles is standing on the edge of the bed when Peter opens the door. He holds out the flat of his hand to warn him not to come any closer, as if it were a suicide.

Peter says, "Jimmy, I refuse to talk you down off a bed."

He dives from the bed to the floor then—dives without arc, the way timid children dive into swimming pools, leaning forward and down to meet the water—and lands on his stomach. The clock falls off the night table. He lies still a minute, as if trying to remember where he is.

Peter sits down on the floor next to him. "The hell, Jimmy," he says, "you didn't say you were over there when they did it."

Jimmy Measles gets slowly to his hands and knees and crawls back to the edge of the bed. He has scraped the skin off his elbows, and one of them is beginning to bleed.

"They wouldn't let me get the dogs," he says, pulling himself up. He crawls onto the bed and then, unsteadily, he stands.

"I said to them, 'I don't care what you do, let me get my dogs out of here first.' "

He dives again, and this time Peter thinks he has knocked himself out. Jimmy Measles lies dead still half a minute, his nose pressed into the carpet, and when he looks up again there are rug burns on his chin and his forehead.

"You turn yourself into a human scab, you keep this up," Peter says.

Jimmy drops his face back onto the floor, and his words still seem to be inside his body, something Peter overhears. "I asked him, the guy at the door, could I please have the dogs. He wouldn't answer. I can hear them in the back, barking at the one in the basement, but the guy at the door wouldn't let me in."

His face comes up off the rug, and he is fighting for his breath. The atomizer is on the floor near the night table, and Peter reaches it and hands it to him. Jimmy Measles puts it in his mouth and pumps the trigger with every breath he takes for half a minute, until it seems to settle him down.

"I said to them, 'It isn't my business what you're doing, just lemme get my dogs out of your way.' "

The room is quiet while Jimmy Measles remembers it. "He wouldn't answer," he says. "I didn't want to go in. If I walk in there, I'm dead, and it's not even my business."

He pushes himself up again and takes as deep a breath as he can. His chest and stomach rise and fall, his face looks sunburned. "The one at the door said to go back across the street and call Michael, tell him what's happening to his place," he says. "I told him it's my place, it isn't Michael's. But he just says I better go back across the street."

Peter sits still and Jimmy begins working in the direction of the bed.

"I called Michael," he says, "but Leonard says he's asleep. And then, while I'm still on the phone, I hear a noise, it sounds like somebody blowing out a candle, and it shakes the house. And when I looked out the window, the inside of the place is already orange."

It is quiet again, he is remembering the dogs. Remembering that he walked across the street and left them.

Peter thinks of something Nick said once about dying. That the nuns had it wrong, you have to be grateful. Peter knows that means something here, but it is just out of his reach.

"A fire like that, they were dead in five seconds," he says finally.

Peter sits still and Jimmy Measles lowers his face until it is resting again on the floor. He has tried to call Michael, he's beaten up a parking meter and thrown himself off the bed; and none of it has made any difference.

He goes to sleep.

Peter takes the blanket off the bed and covers him, but before he leaves the room, Jimmy kicks it off and curls toward the far wall, away from the light.

Early in the morning, Michael comes about the money.

He and Leonard Crawley duck under the police barrier across the front of the club, Peter following a few steps behind, and they walk into the burned-out doorway, stopping when Michael is hidden in the shadows.

He sends Leonard across the street to knock on the door. Monk has parked the car and is walking slowly in the direction of the club, checking the parked cars and doorways for the Italians.

Michael stands still, dripping sweat inside his silk shirt, but it is not the old men in the raincoats he is afraid to see.

He watches Leonard push the bell, half a dozen times. The door opens a few inches, and he sees half her face, her hair falling over the shoulder of her robe as she hugs the door to listen to what he says.

She shifts her eyes and searches the building Michael is standing in. Michael backs deeper inside and her eyes do not fix on the movement.

Peter goes into the cooler and finds himself a warm Coke. Half a minute later, Leonard makes his way back through the bar, kicking pieces of burned furniture, breaking glass. Peter watches him come.

His cousin stands in a puddle of black water under the chandelier in the restaurant, still staring at the house across the street.

He trembles, wanting to hurt her.

"He's comin'," Leonard says. "His old lady said he's in bed, she'll get him up."

Leonard notices a chair that the fire has missed. He picks it up, brushing off the dust, and sets it behind Michael. "Take a load off," he says. "He ain't here in three minutes, I'll go back and get him out the fuckin' bed myself."

Michael sits down and crosses his legs, and a few minutes later

Jimmy Measles walks into the club. Monk comes in behind him, looks at Michael and shrugs.

Jimmy Measles moves through the place slowly, looking every-where at once, as if this were the first time he'd seen the damage. His eyes are red, he has not shaved in two days and there is a vague peppermint shading to the smell of alcohol he is giving off. There are scabs on his forehead and chin.

"You're shit-faced, right?" Michael says.

Jimmy Measles smiles, looking at the room. Michael looks only at Jimmy Measles.

"Lenny said you called the night before last."

"When they killed my dogs."

Michael nods, as if he understands. "I heard that. Pally told me that. Told me I ought to come over, see what I could do. He's been tellin' me what to do all the time lately, did you notice that?"

Peter feels Leonard Crawley's eyes settle on him.

Jimmy Measles reaches into his pocket for the atomizer, and uses it twice. He has tucked his pajama tops into his pants and a corner is stuck in his zipper. He is still wearing his slippers.

"What is that fuckin' thing, anyway?" Michael says.

"It's so I can breathe, when I got asthma."

Michael takes a deep breath of his own, lets it go. He shrugs. "So," he says, "what're we gonna do, keep you breathin'?"

Jimmy Measles cannot bring himself to meet Michael's eyes. "That's what I called you for," he says, looking at a section of collapsed flooring, "to see what we could do."

"You insured?"

Jimmy Measles smiles. "I wouldn't call you the middle of the night about insurance, I called on account of the dogs. . . ."

"The money don't matter to you, is that what you're tellin' me?"

"It's complicated," Jimmy Measles says. "The insurance likes to make it complicated."

Michael shakes his head. "What's complicated, Jimmy, you owe me fifty-five thousand."

It is quiet a moment and then a sparrow flies onto one of the window ledges, and then into the room. Leonard picks up a piece of burnt floor and begins to follow it.

Michael says, "Let me ask you again, you insured or what?"

"I got insurance," Jimmy Measles says, "but the insurance guys, they're going to try to say I did my own place. It can take a long time."

The bird lands and then moves as Leonard gets close. He corners it in a pile of soaked carpet near the kitchen, and swings as it flies over his head. The wood falls apart in his hands, the heavy end crosses the room spinning and hits the wall.

Michael is talking to Jimmy again. "If what you're tryin' to tell me here, that it can take a long time to get paid, I got to tell you that a long time don't do me no fuckin' good, Jimmy. Just so there's no confusion on that, a long time ain't good for anybody."

Jimmy Measles says, "I thought maybe, you know, because it was part of your problems with the Italians that I got burned down . . ."

"My problems are my problems," he says, coming out of the chair, "your problems are yours. . . ."

Jimmy Measles opens his mouth to say something, Michael stops him. ". . . and the only problem we got together is the fifty-five thousand."

Leonard Crawley wanders the room, picking up pieces of things that fall apart in his hands. He finds a scorched beer bottle and tosses it through a small window, one that the fire department missed.

"What the fuck you doin' in there?" Michael says.

Leonard comes back into the restaurant, crosses his arms and leans against the wall.

Michael stands over Jimmy Measles. "You want some help," he says, "I understand that. I'm comin' to you like a friend, and I'm tellin' you to get the fifty-five thousand. You fight some insurance prick a year to get your money, by the time he pays, you owe it all anyway, a point a week—I'm talkin' about business here—plus, you got the whole year to worry about it. So as a friend, I'd tell the insurance prick let's do something here gets us both off the hook."

He looks at his cousin. "Am I right, Pally?"

Peter stands completely still.

"All of a sudden, he quits telling me what to do," Michael says. He turns back to Jimmy Measles. "Maybe your wife's got something she could let you have."

Jimmy Measles shakes his head and Michael shakes his head with him, imitating the motion.

"It was me, I'd shake her till the change falls out her pussy. This ain't a game, Jimmy. What's happened, she ought to appreciate you're in a spot."

Jimmy Measles shakes his head but he is thinking it over. "You could ask her," Michael says. "What harm does it do to ask?"

Leonard nods, agreeing with that. The wires holding his jaw in place shine in the wet cave behind his lips. Peter watches him, thinking of the old man tied to his water heater in the basement.

"See what you do," Michael is saying, "you take care of the fifty-five, I'll get you a couple new dogs."

Jimmy Measles lights a cigarette, then puts his hands in his pockets, ashamed at their shaking. He walks past Leonard Crawley on the way out, and then, before he leaves the room, he looks quickly at Peter, and smiles.

Jimmy Measles is sitting on the bed in his underwear. He is holding a drink in one hand, a cigarette in the other. His atomizer is on the night table.

His wife is packing her clothes. There are four full suitcases already crowded near the door, as if they were waiting in line to get out, and her closet looks as full to him as when she started.

She is doing shoes now, a suitcase full of shoes. She takes them out of the closet two pairs at a time and holds them a moment, making calculations he doesn't understand. Some she puts in the suitcase, some she throws into the corner.

Watching from the bed, Jimmy Measles can't see much difference between what she keeps and what she tosses out, but he knows that once she decides, she isn't going to go back through the pile for another look.

There are sweaters in the corner too, and half a dozen dresses of the wrong length to be in fashion. Fashion. One day he notices more of her legs under her skirt, and by the end of the week every woman he sees in the street is wading the same depth. It has occurred to him that she controls it.

He finishes the drink in his hand and reaches for the bottle on the floor. Vodka. He loses his balance but catches himself just as he begins to fall off the bed.

He sits up and pours. He fills the glass, covering a tiny, festive umbrella on the bottom that floats slowly up and then hangs suspended halfway to the top. All the ice is gone, it is half an hour since he had ice. He hates the taste of warm liquor, but he cannot bring himself to leave the room, even for the two minutes it would take to go to the kitchen.

He has a vague feeling of holding on to her now, and that leaving the room he would be letting go. He puts the glass against his lips, and then, without drinking, trades it for the cigarette.

An ash falls onto his chest, rolls half a foot down and is caught in the folds of his lime-colored shorts. All of Jimmy Measles's underwear is the color of fruit.

She was working on her eyes when he asked her. "Listen, I don't like to mention it, but we got a problem with the club . . ."

Her hair was still wet from the shower, he'd made himself a gimlet in the kitchen.

She watched him in the mirror, still holding the mascara pencil in her hand. Still scared from the fire.

"The thing is, there's some loans I took to do the remodeling, they got to be paid back."

"Your friend Michael," she said.

"I was thinking maybe your father could help us out, maybe put us together with an attorney that sues insurance companies or something, dig us out of the hole on the loan, and then we pay it back when we get the insurance."

Slowly, she shook her head no.

"Fifty-five thousand," he said. "We do it right now, it's only fifty-five thousand."

And she stood up, went into the closet and came out with a suitcase. And a few minutes later he got the bottle, and settled into a spot on the bed to watch.

"You know," he says now, "it looks disloyal, you walking after I get burned out. . . ."

She is holding a pair of red shoes as he speaks, and for a moment she seems to lose her purpose. She stands still, surrounded by the suitcases and the evidence of what she is doing, and she thinks it over.

And in the end, she decides to keep the red shoes.

She finishes packing and Jimmy follows her downstairs.

"There's other ways I can get the money," he says.

She stares out the window, waiting for her sister. The suitcases are all over the living room, he has no idea how many there are. She is sitting on one of them.

The sister is younger than Grace and lives in Cherry Hill, just across the Delaware River in New Jersey. He allows for traffic and thinks he might have another fifteen minutes, and then she is gone.

"It seemed like the least complicated thing, asking your father," he says, "but there's other ways."

Her makeup is done now, her hair is brushed and shines; she took care of that before she called. He hears the words: "Bring the station wagon."

He is drawn to her appearance, even now. Looking at her, he reminds himself that it isn't just anybody who has a woman like this to lose. It establishes a standard, he thinks; anyone who has ever seen them together knows his standard.

Even as she is on the way out the door, Jimmy Measles sees himself in her reflection.

"I could borrow the money," he says. "I just thought of a guy."

She keeps her eyes on the street, watching for the station wagon. It's a Volvo—the sister also has a Mercedes, one child and no husband. Her father keeps her in cars and in the house in Cherry Hill. Jimmy Measles remembers the father, taking him aside at the wedding reception. *You ever raise your hand against my daughter, I'll have somebody to cut it off.*

He smiles, everybody's a gangster.

"And what's this guy you thought of going to do when you can't pay *him*?" Grace says.

He does not answer.

"He's going to send some fucking monster to the door to tell me to get your ass out of bed, only this time maybe you aren't home."

He sees that happen as she says it; and he is lost in remorse.

The bottle is on the floor near his chair. He picks it up, holding it at eye level, and pours until the glass is half full. The umbrella lies at the bottom, barely stirring under the wash of new vodka.

"Sometimes you're in the wrong place at the wrong time," he says finally. "Sometimes that's the way things happen."

A horn sounds outside, and Grace stands up without saying another word. She squares her shoulders under the weight of the first two suitcases, and steps out the door, leaving him there like someone she'd met while she was waiting for her plane.

He goes into the kitchen, drops some ice into his glass, and sits at the table until she is gone.

Even with the sister helping, it takes a long time to get all her luggage out of the house.

They are somewhere in Delaware when Michael turns the conversation from horses to fighters, and then to Nick and Harry.

"What I'd like to do," Leonard Crawley says, "is have the little motherfucker in the street, see how he does there."

Leonard looks in the rearview mirror to see if Peter is listening. He senses Peter sliding away from Michael's protection; he senses that Peter feels it too.

Most of the people Leonard Crawley has known, he has hurt. Until he hurts them, there is something to settle. Some fear to quiet. He has never reflected on whose fear it is.

He locks on Peter's eyes, half a second, feeling it, and then looks back at the road. "All that shit with rules," he says, shaking his head, "useless in the street."

They are out on I-95 South again, on the way back to Maryland. Michael's man has found him another horse.

Peter tries to remember the things Michael has bought in the last year that he doesn't need. The limo, a condominium in Atlantic City, a fur coat and now a horse.

He looks in the mirror and sees Leonard Crawley watching him again. Leonard smiles.

Peter leans forward until he can see Leonard's face, the wires holding it together. "Lemme ask you something, Leonard," he says, "you think Nick's kid ate breakfast this morning through a straw?"

"That wasn't the street," he says. "What I said, I'd like to have him in the street."

Peter lets go of the front seat and drops back into his spot next to Michael. His cousin is smiling, seeing Leonard has bothered him. Peter looks out the window. It frightens him to hear them talk about Harry and Nick.

"So tell me something," Michael says a little later, "what harm does it do, the kid makes a few dollars while he can?"

"You don't understand the way they live," Peter says.

"What, they don't like money?"

It is quiet a moment, and Peter says, "They like things the way they are."

Michael smiles at that, Leonard's face appears in the rearview mirror, and he is smiling too.

Peter turns to stare at his cousin. "You think Nick doesn't know his kid can fight?" he says. "He taught him. He's been where that kid would go, and it's not worth it. They got enough right where they are, not to throw it away doing something they don't want to do."

"The kid don't like to fight."

Peter closes his eyes. "He likes to fight," he says slowly, "he just doesn't want to sell it."

"You ever thought," Michael says a little later, "maybe it isn't the kid that don't want to sell it? Maybe it's just the old man, afraid he'll lose him."

Leonard Crawley smiles in the rearview mirror. Peter sits forward again, his hand on the front seat. "I been wondering about something, Leonard," he says. "You figured out yet how to suck dicks through those wires or what?"

The horse's name is Helen's Dream, and he is a monster. Peter has never seen a horse this size before, but he is sure that nothing this heavy can run.

Michael stands in front of the stable half a minute, his mouth cocked into a smile, and then takes a roll of bills out of his pants pocket.

"Eight thousand," he says. "Right?"

Mornings, they visit the horse.

A wasted, clubfooted trainer named Carlos meets them at the stall and reports on the animal's legs, which are always sore, or his chest, which is always congested, or—on days that he has worked out—that he has bled from the nose.

In spite of the bad news, the horse affords Peter a certain relief. Michael does not seem as interested now in the boxing career of Harry DiMaggio.

Michael touches the animal while Carlos offers his reports. He runs his hands up its neck and then down the slope of its nose, carefully, as if he is feeling for something, and then when the report is finished, when the clubfooted trainer has told him again that the horse isn't ready to run, Michael backs away from the animal smiling, taking him in, and he says, "Lookit the size of this motherfucker, would you?"

Some days, Michael goes to the track by himself. He feels safe there, believing that something in the old Italians' rules won't let them shoot up a stable and kill innocent horses.

Some days Peter goes with him, and some days they pick up Jimmy Measles, who comes out of his house now as if he were coming out of a coma. Somewhere time is missing.

Jimmy settles into a seat, carrying a bag usually—apples or carrots for the horse—and begins one of his stories, and sometimes for a little while, crossing the bridge into New Jersey, things are the way they were before the club burned.

At the track, Michael sends him for coffee or Danish or to find the trainer.

Peter watches them touch, Jimmy and Michael, he sees the skin blister, day by day.

Jimmy Measles will not move away from him, though. He feels safest when he is close to the source of his trouble, getting Michael to laugh at his jokes, reminding him of the food he sent to the hospital, of the way he took care of him at the club.

Sometimes Peter walks off and wanders through the stables, unable to watch. Nick has a word for the feeling, *skeeved*.

He looks at other horses, stopping to rub their noses—they all seem to be the wrong size after Helen's Dream—thinking of a way he can tell Jimmy Measles he is wasting his time.

Michael sticks a cigar in his mouth and stares out over the infield—the two ovals of the track, dirt and grass, and inside them the pond. It is late afternoon, and beneath him an old couple poses for pictures in the winner's circle with their horse and jockey.

Jimmy is on one side of Michael, Leonard is on the other. Peter is sitting two rows higher in the private box, alone, drinking a beer, his shoes on the seat in front of him.

"What I'm wondering, Jimmy," Michael says, looking straight ahead, "is when I'm going to see some of my fuckin' cash."

He is sitting with twelve hundred dollars' worth of bad tickets in his pocket, the program crushed in his hands, his pulse visible in his jaw. Even Leonard Crawley knows better than to say anything now.

Jimmy Measles swallows what is left in his cup and begins to explain his problems with the insurance.

Michael stops him. "I don't want to hear nothing about some prick at the insurance company. I want to hear when I'm going to see the cash."

"The minute I get paid, you got the cash."

Michael nods, still looking out over the infield, thinking that over. "I hope that's soon enough," he says.

And then, before he lets go of the view of the track and un-wrinkles the program to begin looking for a big horse, before he sends Jimmy Measles back to the window to place his bets for the next race, he says, "You understand what I'm saying here, that this is business."

And Jimmy Measles turns to look at Peter, and he smiles.

His face goes gray, as if the smiling itself drains his blood.

No one wishes Michael more luck with the ponies than Jimmy Measles.

Jimmy Measles calls Peter at six in the morning to ask if he is driving to the track or going over with Michael.

Peter picks him up in the Buick.

In the car he asks, "How long is it before I got a problem with Michael?"

Peter closes his eyes. The traffic is coming into the city from Jersey on four lanes of the Ben Franklin Bridge. He hears horns, and thinks of driving like this, with his eyes shut, until something outside the car stops him.

He opens his eyes, finds that he is still in his own traffic lane. He takes a deep breath and lets it seep out, a slow leak.

"The thing with your cousin," Jimmy says, "with all due respect, he never says I got a month or a week or five minutes to come up with the cash, he just says time's running out. It makes you more worried than just knowing it was here. . . ."

Peter drives the car.

Jimmy says, "I think this guy at the insurance company, he's ready to come across with something."

Peter nods, staring into the traffic.

"It isn't the same guy," Jimmy Measles says. "They took the other guy off it, and this one, he said he wants to get me off his desk."

Peter pulls into the far right lane, gives the man in the tollbooth a dollar.

"What I was wondering," Jimmy Measles says, "could you talk to Michael about it. I bring it up, it only reminds him he's pissed off."

Peter drives away from the city, passing the topless clubs along Admiral Wilson Boulevard. He remembers that Michael owns one of them; something he bought and turned over to someone on this side of the river to look after.

"Pally?"

Peter takes the ramp to Highway 70, and follows it to the track. Jimmy Measles stares at his hands, waiting for Peter to tell him what to do.

They stop at the gate in back and Peter shows the guard an owner's pass. They drive slowly through the stable area.

"The way I see it," Jimmy says, looking out the window, "the insurance guy worries a while, and then he gets tired of the whole fucking thing and makes everybody happy."

Peter stops the car near the stables. "That isn't what those guys do," he says, "make people happy."

Jimmy Measles takes the atomizer out of his coat pocket and puts it deep into his mouth, as if he wants to swallow it.

A little later Jimmy says, "Michael isn't going to do his own friends for, what is it now, sixty-five thousand?" He considers what he's said, agrees with the logic of it again. "Sixty-five thousand, he's lost that in an afternoon."

"You shouldn't count on being friends with Michael," Peter says.

"I've seen him with that much in his pocket, he doesn't even know it's there," Jimmy Measles says.

Peter says, "Michael doesn't know anything about business. He's got strangers telling him what it costs to do shit he didn't know he wanted to do it. But where he tuned in, is sixty-five thousand dollars. He knows it's something that's his, and somebody else has got it."

"The insurance guy . . . ."

"The insurance is just something else Michael doesn't understand," Peter says. "What he understands, you've got something that's his and he wants it back. You don't hand it over, to him you're stealing."

Jimmy Measles reaches for the atomizer.

They see the clubfooted trainer then, leading Helen's Dream in the direction of his stable. All the horse's legs are bandaged today, and he is favoring the one on the left side in back badly.

"Oh, shit," Jimmy Measles says, more to himself than to Peter.

Peter watches the horse until he has disappeared behind the line of stables. "What I think," he says, "it might be a good idea if I drive you over to the High Speed Line, you took the train back to town before Michael shows up."

But then he looks in his rearview mirror and sees the limo coming through the gate behind him. Leonard at the wheel. The early morning sun catches his glasses as he gets out to open the door for Michael.

S uch things happen," the trainer says.

Michael is standing just outside the stall, his hands at his sides, staring at the horse. He does not give the impression he is listening. There is a pitchfork in the corner, some blinders hanging from a nail.

"We take him for the gallop this morning," the trainer says, "try to make everyone happy, get him into shape so he can race like you said, a nice easy gallop and he pulls hisself lame in the back leg. I have the vet to take a picture, and he's broke a bone. Not too bad, it ain't much of a break, but the truth is, you know, this ain't really a sound horse."

He steals a look at Michael. "I'm tellin' you the truth, Mr. Flood. Such things happen."

Michael moves his gaze from the horse to the trainer. Leonard picks up the pitchfork, feeling its weight.

"What you're saying, this horse ain't really a racehorse."

The trainer shrugs. "He used to could run," he says. "It ain't that he couldn't used to run. But a horse's legs is a delicate thing

228

and something happen. Maybe his breeding ain't right; maybe, you know, he's just too fucking big."

Michael turns away from the trainer and seems to notice Jimmy Measles for the first time that morning. "The horse is too fuckin' big," he says.

"Might be that," the trainer said. "Might be his father and mother."

"Might be," Michael says, looking back at the trainer, "he's been around you so fuckin' long, he thinks that's how he's s'posed to walk."

The trainer shrugs, Peter turns to look at the horse.

Its nose is wet and a muscle flutters down it's back, a minnow under the coat.

Leonard is playing with the pitchfork, lifting it and dropping it so the prongs stab the dirt on either side of the toe of his loafer. Michael reaches into his waistband and comes out with a pistol. The trainer freezes.

"You're supposed to shoot these fuckin' things, right?" he says.

Leonard smiles, everyone else stands dead still.

"You can't shoot your horse," Peter says. Leonard holds the pitchfork, poised over his alligator shoes, and watches Peter slide farther away from Michael's protection.

"I own the fuckin' thing," Michael says.

Peter shakes his head. "All the time you been out here, you seen anybody else shooting their horse?"

"I ain't seen nobody else out here got a horse that isn't a horse."

"There's a lot of broke-down horses, Mr. Flood," the trainer says.

"You already talked, told me the horse is too big," Michael says. "My cousin's talking now, telling me I can't shoot the motherfucker. When he's through tellin' me what I can do, then it's your turn again."

"They inject them," Peter says.

Michael thinks it over, the gun still in his hand, the horse still dripping from the nose. Michael looks at the trainer. "A needle?" he says.

The trainer nods, watching the gun.

"Go get it."

The trainer shrugs and heads off in the direction of the barn; Michael puts the gun back inside his pants. The horse blows and twitches, Jimmy Measles uses his atomizer. Leonard throws the pitchfork into a bale of hay, trying to get it to stick.

The sun breaks the line of stables and touches the top of the stall. Peter studies Michael's mood, waiting for the time to talk him out of killing the horse. He doesn't want an argument; if Michael thinks there is an argument, he will shoot the horse to settle it.

Another trainer walks past, leading another horse. Michael's attention drifts, following the awkward, unsteady motion of the animal's rear legs; they walk as if they are on high heels.

"You know," Peter says, "there's no reason we got to do something right now. We could ship him back to Maryland, have them take a look there."

"Look at what?" Michael says. "The assholes stupid enough to buy him?"

"He isn't a bad horse," Peter says. He notices Jimmy Measles then, standing at the corner of the stall, watching him negotiate for the animal's life. Jimmy Measles doesn't seem to be breathing. The horse nuzzles Jimmy's coat for a carrot.

"We take him back, maybe they fix him so he can run around the meadow," Peter says, "maybe let him fuck little horses once in a while, that way the colts come out, they're the right size."

Michael looks at Helen's Dream, thinking.

"I didn't buy him to run around the meadow and fuck other horses," he says finally.

The veterinarian is wearing tennis shoes and a stained shirt, and looks at his watch as if he has someplace else to go. His hair is pulled into a ponytail and he squints through rimless glasses, looking over the four men gathered at the stall in an impatient way.

He reminds Michael of a kid named Butchie he used to chase home from school.

The veterinarian sees Michael watching him. "You the owner?" he says.

Michael nods, noticing the tone of his voice. He thinks it has been too long since somebody chased Butchie home.

The veterinarian opens his bag and comes out with a piece of paper. "Owner's signature," he says.

Michael takes the paper and signs it against the door of the stall. The veterinarian takes it back and turns it over to the trainer, who signs it too.

The veterinarian puts the paper into his shirt pocket and stretches a pair of rubber gloves over his hands. He goes back into the bag again, this time for the syringe.

There is something so sudden in the gesture that even Michael feels it, a coldness. Jimmy Measles turns away; he does not like needles.

The veterinarian studies the animal's neck. "Hold him," he says, and the trainer wraps his arms around the horse's face.

The horse accepts the embrace.

The veterinarian runs his fingers along the neck, finding the spot. He holds the syringe with his other hand, pointed down and away from himself; a single, clear drop of liquid hangs from the tip of the needle, and then drops.

He puts the needle in twelve inches beneath the head, pointed in the direction of the brain. His hand stretches under the rubber to accommodate the size of the syringe, and then he squeezes his thumb and his fingers together.

The needle comes out and the veterinarian takes a step back. The trainer holds on a moment longer. The horse begins to blow, and then, as if there is something he's forgotten, he suddenly stops, and shudders, and drops.

The ground moves under Peter's feet.

The horse lies still, his nose protruding a foot out of the stall, his tongue a few inches beyond that, coated with dirt.

The veterinarian peels off his gloves and makes out his bill. His fingertips are stained yellow and there is grime under his nails. Two hundred and forty dollars.

Michael hands the bill to Peter; Jimmy Measles has gone white.

Peter pays the veterinarian out of his pocket, peeling off the bills without looking at the man who is taking them. Leonard sits down on a wooden fruit box near the animal, holding the pitchfork between his legs.

"You want me to have somebody come get this?" the veterinarian says.

The trainer looks at Michael, who does not answer.

"Yo," the vet says. "You want me to take care of this, you want to have it done yourself?"

Michael examines him then, up and down, and in that moment the veterinarian changes, as if he has spilled a little of what he gave to the horse on himself.

"The thing is," Michael says, still watching him, "I changed my mind."

Leonard stands up, showing the veterinarian the wires in his mouth. He takes off his sunglasses and hangs them outside the pocket of his shirt.

The veterinarian looks at the trainer, and then, seeing there is no help, back at Michael.

"You hear what I said?" Michael says. "I changed my mind."

The veterinarian starts to smile, tries it and then lets it go. "You said you . . ."

Peter steps between Michael and the veterinarian, cutting off the line of sight. "Michael . . ."

Michael moves around him where he can see the veterinarian again. "Leonard," he says, "gimme that fuckin' bag."

Leonard takes the bag away from the veterinarian and hands it to Michael. He opens it, looking over what is inside, and takes out a syringe that is similar to the one the veterinarian put into the horse's neck.

"Give him his bag," Peter says. "You told him put the horse down, he put the horse down."

"He's a big shot," Michael says.

"So now you scared him, he isn't a big shot anymore," Peter says. "Let him have his bag."

Michael cocks his head. "Tell me something," he says. "Since when do you decide? This ain't your horse, and it ain't your business."

There is a noise then, Jimmy Measles behind the stall, choking. His stomach empties and the noise keeps coming, like an engine that won't start.

The sun moves deeper into the stall. Peter takes a quick glance at the horse. The flies have settled on him now, in the eyes and nose, making electric noises as they touch each other and move furiously into the air.

And then resettle, glistening green.

Michael is staring at the kid veterinarian. Suddenly he smiles. "Tell you what," he says, pointing to the horse. "Why don't youse kiss and make up?"

The noise from behind the stall stops as suddenly as it begins, and a moment later Jimmy Measles reappears, red-eyed, his mouth and chin glistening spit. "I haven't been feeling too good," he says.

"How you feeling, Doc?" Michael says to the veterinarian.

The vet takes half a step backwards and bumps into Leonard. He says, "It's Mr. Flood, right?"

Michael nods.

"Be careful with that shit, Mr. Flood," he says, pointing at the syringe in Michael's hand. "You got a cut or something and that gets in it, it doesn't take much."

Michael holds the syringe up for a closer look. "Like one drop of this . . ." he says.

"It gets in your bloodstream," the veterinarian says, "yeah." Peter can see the veterinarian beginning to feel more comfortable, moving on to a subject which is not kissing the horse.

Michael says, "And so you put this into a person . . ."

"They'd be dead before you could get it half in," he says.

Michael nods, looking at the syringe. "How much of this you got?" he says.

"How much you need?"

Michael drops the syringe to his side and turns to Peter. "See? I like this guy better already."

The veterinarian nods, a small nod, and tries to step backwards again, and bumps again into Leonard Crawley.

"I can have this one right here?" Michael says.

"All you want," he says.

"And you don't mind I take this."

The veterinarian shakes his head. "No sir."

Michael hands the bag to Leonard, who returns it to the veterinarian. "Now," Michael says, "was there something you was going to ask me?"

"Just about taking care of your horse," the veterinarian says. "If you wanted me to take care of him for you."

Michael nods. "I would appreciate that very much."

"No problem," he says. "I'll do it right now."

"In a minute," Michael says. "First, what do you say let's kiss him good-bye."

Peter walks back to the limo to wait.

Jimmy Measles tries to go with him, but Michael stops him with a look.

Peter climbs into the front seat of the car and closes his eyes. Ten minutes later a door opens and Michael gets in next to him, still carrying the syringe. The limo barely moves under his weight. Leonard and Jimmy Measles climb into the back.

There is a smell that comes in with them, part Jimmy Measles, part Leonard.

Leonard says, "Michael, man, that was fucking *sick*." A compliment from the heart.

There is no answer and the men sit in silence another ten minutes, Michael wanting to see for himself that someone takes care of the horse.

The tractor is an old John Deere diesel, and the man driving could be a jockey, except he has no quickness at all. Michael watches him, thinking he is maybe a jockey who got kicked in the head.

He backs the tractor to a spot a few feet in front of the stall, and turns it off. The engine shakes and black smoke coughs out of the exhaust pipe. He climbs down awkwardly, stumbling as his feet hit the ground. He takes off his cap and scratches his head, as if he cannot remember what he is there to do. He looks at the horse then, and seems to remember.

He unwraps the chain from the winch in back and loops the end around the animal's neck and then, using the winch, drags Helen's Dream out of the stall, digging a wide, shallow track in the dirt. When the animal has cleared the stall, the man takes the chain off the neck and ties it to the hind feet.

He climbs back on the tractor and forces it into gear. He looks back once as he starts, and then, satisfied, hits the throttle and pulls his load off in the direction of the large green barn at the far end of the stables.

The men in the limousine watch the horse go, its huge head bouncing on bumps in the ground. They watch until the tractor turns a wide corner at the end of the line of stalls and disappears, and the horse follows it out of sight.

Peter opens the door and steps out of the car. In the back, Jimmy Measles opens his door too.

Leonard stops him, pinning his throat to the seat. Michael turns in his seat, showing him the needle.

"I can't breathe," he says.

"Never mind you can breathe," Michael says. "You think about what you just seen."

Jimmy Measles nods as much as Leonard's hand will let him.

"I'm not fucking with you now," Michael says. "I will put this motherfucker into your neck, you understand what I'm saying? I give you the same dose they gave the horse, the same place, and then I'm done with you the same way I'm done with him. One way or the other, it's settled, and I don't have you around anymore to remind me."

He looks at Leonard. "Leave him go," he says.

Jimmy Measles's neck is white in the places where Leonard held him, and then the places begin to glow. He reaches into his pocket for his atomizer. Leonard leans across his lap and pushes the door to the limo open.

As soon as Jimmy has his feet on the ground, Leonard shuts the door, and a few seconds later, spitting dirt, the limo makes a U-turn and heads out the gate.

Peter sits in the Buick and watches Jimmy Measles coming toward him, walking now in the smooth path the horse left in the ground, between the tire marks of the John Deere tractor.

He is holding his neck and sweating, but he isn't hurt. He stops for a moment, sticks the atomizer in his mouth and pumps half a dozen times, and then, after he has put the thing back in his pocket, he looks up and catches Peter watching him.

Peter closes his eyes, not to see him smile.

I got to see my wife," Jimmy says.

"You don't mind my saying so, it wouldn't hurt, you know, you brushed your teeth and changed clothes first."

They are crossing lanes on Race Track Circle, headed back into the city. "You smell like they scared you inside out," Peter says.

He sees Jimmy wrap his fingers around the door handle; he is thinking of jumping from the car. Peter knows there are people who will jump from a car as a gesture, and he knows Jimmy Measles is one of them. "Which way is it?" he says.

Grace's sister lives in a 200-acre development of new two-story homes in Cherry Hill. The houses have small yards with newly planted grass and frail, dead-looking trees held in place with wires attached to stakes in the ground.

There are signs on the street warning thieves that the neighborhood participates in Community Watch, and signs warning drivers of deaf children. Jimmy Measles reads the street signs out loud, and the names—Valley Hollow, Meadowview, Pineview— take on an eerie quality coming out of his mouth.

The street they want is called Charity Lane. They see Prayer Circle and Hope Street, so they are in the right area. "What do these places go for, anyway?" Peter says. "A couple of hundred?"

Jimmy Measles stares at the street signs, looking grim and serious. It is the only time Peter can remember when he's wanted to hear him talk, and he won't.

"People pay a couple of hundred to get out of the city," Peter says, "they get a tree they got to hold up with ropes. What's the point?"

Jimmy Measles spots the house across the street. "There," he says. There is a Volvo station wagon parked in the driveway, and a tiny bicycle with training wheels wedged behind it against the back tire.

"Two kids, right?" Peter says. "The big one puts the little one's bicycle underneath the car, and the mother runs over it and the little one gets blamed."

The car stops. Jimmy sits still, looking across the street. He shakes his head. "There's only one kid," he says.

"He does that to his own stuff?"

Jimmy Measles's voice is a monotone. "They got him going to a child psychologist. . . ."

Without another word, he gets out of the car and crosses the street. He knocks on the door, and a long time later it opens, Grace herself. Peter sees her from the car, sees her robe take the shape of her hip and thigh as she leans forward to hold open the door.

They speak and then Jimmy walks in; the door closes. Peter settles into his seat to wait, and, to get Jimmy's wife off his mind, he thinks of Michael making the kid veterinarian at the track kiss a dead horse on the mouth.

It is getting out of hand.

Jimmy Measles is inside the house half an hour.

When he comes out his head is tucked into his shoulders, as if he were walking into a cold wind, and his hands are rolled into fists. As if they might be cold too. He crosses the lawn and the street without looking up.

Peter follows him all the way to the car door, trying to see how it has gone, and then, as the door opens, he notices Grace.

She is standing in the front window watching the yard, like somebody's mother. She moves away as the door opens and Jimmy ducks into the car, back into the room behind the glass, and then the curtains close and she is gone.

Jimmy sticks the atomizer into his mouth and pumps. Peter backs out of Charity Lane, taking one last look at the bicycle behind the Volvo's tire. He wouldn't mind being here to see Grace's sister back over it.

He picks his way back to Route 70, turning into half a dozen cul-de-sacs and dead ends before he finds it. Jimmy stares out the window without offering directions, and sucks at his atomizer.

"Tell me something, Pally," he says when they are finally on the way back to the city, "how long's Michael been fucking my wife?"

"Michael isn't fucking your wife," he says.

"All right, how long *was* he fucking my wife?"

Peter looks away, Jimmy Measles stares at him across the seat. "The first thing you got to ask yourself," Peter says, "why would she tell you something like that?"

"The first thing I ask myself, how long was it going on?"

"He's fucking her, but she isn't fucking him. . . ."

"That morning they shot him walking across the street, he was coming from the house."

"And you were coming from Atlantic City, where you got blown twice. So he gets blown, you get blown, and then he gets shot in the whang. How much justice you think there is in this world?"

They are back on the bridge before Jimmy Measles says anything else. "I think of all that fucking food I had Otto fix him and bring to the hospital."

Peter drives the car.

"All those nights we went to the fights," Jimmy Measles says, "you know Michael was with her then?"

Peter doesn't answer.

There is a small park on the other side of the bridge with a large, modern sculpture in the middle of it, welcoming tourists to Philadelphia. To natives, it looks like something the city council might have built itself.

"Let me out."

Peter pulls the car to the curb and waits. Jimmy sits with his hands folded over his atomizer.

Peter sees him building to something reckless now, probably to make up for whatever he did in front of his wife.

"Listen," Peter says, "the truth is, I thought maybe you knew it too. Maybe you and Grace had one of those understandings."

He turns off the car and waits, wishing he'd never taken him to see her.

"I treated you both like friends," Jimmy says.

Peter takes his time. "The only way Michael knows something isn't his, Jimmy," he says, "he don't want it anymore."

Jimmy sits with one foot inside the car, one foot out. He seems to be looking into the tops of the trees in the park, or perhaps at the sculpture, deciding what to do. Peter doesn't hurry him.

"I ought to send him a fucking bill," he says finally. "All the food I sent him at the hospital, all the drinks I gave him at my place. I ought to send him a bill for all the fucking carrots I bought for his horse. . . ."

He gets out then without shutting the door, and sets out across the park.

Peter waits a few minutes, until he sees him on the sidewalk on the other side, walking up Vine Street toward center city. Then he starts the car and drives himself home and goes to bed thinking of the horse, of the unnatural stretch of its hind legs as it followed the chain and the tractor in the direction of the barn.

There is a call that afternoon from the Italians, the ones who own the streets.

Peter puts the phone against his ear and listens.

"We hear a story today," the man says, "comes from the Cherry Hill police, something which occurred at the track."

Peter waits.

"A veterinarian, one Dr. Walter Craddock, D.V.M., has filed a complaint against your brother."

"My cousin," Peter says. "He's my cousin."

"Right, your cousin. He forced a track veterinarian to kiss a deceased horse."

The line is quiet; Peter hears his own breath against the receiver.

"What does that tell you about your business?" the man says. "How much time you got before this thing you have falls apart, somebody takes it away from you?"

Peter doesn't answer.

"You there?" the man says.

"Yeah."

"You want some help, saving what you got, maybe we can work something out," he says. "One way or the other, though, Michael ain't long for where he is."

And then he hangs up.

An hour later, the phone rings again. Peter hears the wheeze before he hears the voice.

"You seen Michael?"

The sound of the atomizer.

"You tell him what I said about him and my wife?"

Peter says, "Jimmy, I left you off, I came home and took a nap. This is when I sleep."

"I called before, the phone was busy."

"That was some guy didn't have anything to do with you," he says.

"What guy?"

"Somebody you don't know."

There is a pause on the line, then, "Don't tell him I know what he did, Pally."

Peter sits up in bed and puts his feet on the floor.

"Pally?"

"I wasn't going to," he says.

Jimmy Measles is quiet.

Peter waits him out, waits for him half a minute, and then he hears the sound of the atomizer and the phone goes dead.

Two days later, Jimmy Measles is sitting in a cab outside Peter's house. He hasn't shaved or slept. His hair is collected in damp, oily clumps, and pieces of it fall across his forehead.

As Peter comes out, Jimmy opens the door and his shoes drop one at a time on the street beneath it. Loafers, no socks. He stands up slowly and turns to the driver, handing him everything in his pocket.

The driver accepts what Jimmy has given him, sorts it, turning the bills so they all face the same way, and then offers some of it back.

"Keep it," Jimmy says.

"I don't want your fucking driver's license," the driver says, but Jimmy doesn't seem to hear him. He crosses the street without checking for traffic.

"How long you been waitin' out here?" Peter says. "You should of come up."

Jimmy Measles looks up and down the street. "I got to talk to you," he says.

Peter starts up the street, toward his car. "You didn't have to wait outside," he says.

Jimmy takes a cigarette out of his shirt pocket, lights it, and then lets it hang from the corner of his mouth. They walk slowly, Peter with his hands in his pockets, Jimmy Measles falling in next to him.

He feels safer now that he is walking.

"I thought of something, takes care of this problem I got with Michael," he says, looking at the street.

Peter rubs his eyes.

"The thing is, I got an aunt left me a piece of property."

Peter stops walking.

"Three acres in the middle of San Jose, California."

It is quiet a moment. He looks up at Peter. "You ever been in San Jose?"

"Yeah, and I got to tell you Jimmy, somebody stole your land. There aren't three acres of anything there."

"It's there," he says. "Some kind of a trust I couldn't break until I was forty-five years old. I forgot I had it."

Peter begins to walk again; Jimmy Measles follows him, squinting through a line of smoke.

"So what do you think?" Jimmy says.

"You mean about the trust from your aunt that you just remembered?"

They look at each other.

Jimmy says, "Let Michael know for me the money's coming for me . . ."

Peter shakes his head. "You're going to run, Jimmy," he says, "don't tell him ahead of time."

"I swear to God . . ."

Peter walks to his car, Jimmy Measles right behind him. He stops when Peter stops, and waits while Peter finds the key to the door. Peter gets in the car, and Jimmy leans close to the window until their faces, separated by glass, are half a foot apart. Peter rolls down the window.

"You want a ride?"

"Talk to Michael for me, Pally?"

"Get in the fucking car, let me take you home."

Jimmy Measles sits with his head against the cushion of the seat, the cigarette still hanging from his bottom lip, staring at the ceiling of the Buick. He is sweating, and he works for his breath.

"What if it turns out the San Jose thing is real?" he says. He is still looking at the ceiling, dreaming.

Peter turns north on Broad Street, headed in the direction of center city.

"I got another one," Jimmy Measles says a few minutes later. "What if Michael wasn't the only one fucking my wife?" He turns his head without moving it off the cushion and looks at Peter.

There is a blur in the corner of Peter's vision, and then a small, weightless fist crosses the front seat of the car and hits him in the cheek. And then, a long moment later, another one. It takes

243

Peter two punches to understand what Jimmy Measles is doing.

Peter pulls the car to the curb and stops. Jimmy Measles sits studying his right hand. The knuckle is scraped, probably from the overhead light. His chest rises and falls, fighting for breath.

The car is quiet.

"You all right now?" Peter says.

Jimmy Measles stares at his fist. Peter runs his hands over his face and stares at South Broad Street, and before long he notices the street staring back. Twelve-, thirteen-year-old kids with hard eyes; everybody's got a comb in their hair this year.

Jimmy Measles takes another cigarette out of his pocket, lights it, and tosses the match on the floor.

"What did she tell you?" Peter says. "She said I did it, is that what she said?"

"*Almost* did it."

"How do you almost do somebody?"

He realizes that is a question with too many answers. He thinks of the girls who had changed their minds at the last minute, the times he'd changed his mind about at the last minute. He thinks of the ones who drank too much and got sick, the times the telephone rang at the wrong time—he would have to be doing someone three times a day for the rest of his life to catch up with the ones he almost did.

"You start to and then you don't," Jimmy Measles says.

It is quiet again and the kids come by in their new sneakers and their eyeballs, and Peter sits in his seat wishing she'd told him something else. Thinking there had to be a different way to get rid of him.

He starts the car. "You all right now?" he says.

Jimmy Measles is silent and Peter pulls back onto the street. They are almost to Catherine and Ninth before he looks at Jimmy again.

"Listen," he says, "I'll see what I can do."

Jimmy Measles gets out of the car as soon as it stops rolling. The blood from his knuckle blots against the upholstery behind the door handle. He walks to his front door and opens it without using a key.

The place looks as black inside as a cave, and Jimmy walks into it, slow and tired, and disappears.

A moment later the door swings shut, as if by itself.

One of the Italians is lying in the bedroom with broken legs. Not one of the old men from Constantine's time, but a younger man, a lawyer.

He has been there almost two days.

He'd shown up at the house in the afternoon, when Michael was out, and Leonard and two of his people, who do not know one Italian from another, took turns breaking his legs in the living room.

It fed them that he was a lawyer, and not used to being frightened or hurt.

He is in the bedroom now, waiting. The air conditioner comes on, shaking the floor, and he screams.

Leonard and his people are on the couch in the living room, Peter can see them from the kitchen. They look at each other—*how-were-we-supposed-to-know?*—waiting for Michael to forgive them.

"I don't believe this happened," Michael says.

He smiles. Peter hasn't seen him afraid in this way since they were children.

"How come they send somebody over without calling first?" he says. "Tell me that."

"What did they want?" Peter says.

Michael looks into the living room. "Who knows?" he says. Then he stands up and walks to the refrigerator, takes out a tray of ice, empties it into the sink, and fills it with water. He leaves the ice tray on the counter and sits down again at the table.

"I can't let the guy out of here," he says quietly. "I got no choice about that. The way they did him, he's crippled. Even if I pay for all the medicine and doctor bills, it still don't change what happened. They find out about this, they're going to think we're out of control here."

Peter waits while that settles.

Michael stands up again and walks a few steps toward the living room, then comes back. It is as if he wants something in there, but cannot decide to take it.

"What kind of a fucking mothball they got for a brain, they don't know the difference between a bunch of old long-nose guys from Constantine's time and a guy in a nice suit?" Michael says. "How do you make a mistake like that?"

The air conditioning goes off; the man in the next room moans.

"You ought to get him something for that," Peter says. "Call a doctor to give him a shot."

Michael is not listening. "Maybe the guy just disappears," he says.

Peter waits. "You think they don't know they sent him?"

"We say he never got here."

Peter gives Michael time to think that through from the other end, how it would sound if someone told it to him.

The lawyer moans again. "At least turn the thermostat up," Peter says, "it isn't rattling the house every five minutes."

"You want to take a look?" Michael says.

Peter shakes his head.

"I don't believe this happened," Michael says again, and it is quiet between them a long time.

"You want to know what I think," Peter says finally, "you pick up the telephone, call them and tell them what happened. That three of your people got excited and broke the guy's pins when he came to the door."

He looks at Peter, blinks.

"They got stupid Italians too," Peter says. "They'd see how it happened. And then you tell them, they want the ones that did it, here they are. Break their legs, set them on fire, anything they want."

Michael looks into the living room again, considering it.

"You think so?" he says.

Peter shrugs. "Who knows with these guys?" he says. He pauses, looking at his cousin. "Now I got something to ask you," he says.

"What's that?"

"Let Jimmy Measles slide a little on this money."

It is quiet again. "You seen him walking around the street," Michael says, "that means he already got his slide. Now he's got to come up with it."

Peter waits.

"He's into me sixty-five," Michael says. "That's one thing when he's got a club, it's another thing he's a bum. It's the same thing now as he couldn't stay off the tables in Atlantic City, that's how much I like him walkin' around owing me money."

"It isn't his fault, what happened at the club."

Michael shrugs, his shoulders looking as big as Leonard's. "What's that mean, *his fault?*" he says.

The air conditioning comes on again, and a long, hollow wail comes from the next room. Weaker than before.

Peter fixes on his cousin, trying to distance himself from the sound in the next room, to find a place farther away to watch the things. Far enough away so that the man in the room becomes temporary—stalled here a few moments, a passing tremor in the long settling of this house.

Far enough away so the lawyer's sounds do not mingle with his own.

The noise suddenly stops and Michael leans across the table. He smiles, the way he always does when he's asking for something Peter doesn't want to give up.

"You want to look at him for me, Pally?"

Peter doesn't move.

"Lookit," he says. "I need another opinion here. . . ."

Peter looks across the table. "Give Jimmy some slack," he says, "I'll go in and have a look."

Michael stares at him, beginning to get worked up. Then something changes.

"Fuck it," he says. "Tell Jimmy to relax."

From half a block away, Peter sees the front door is open. It is eleven o'clock in the morning, the sun is reflecting at him off flattened cans and pieces of glass in the street, from the windows of the stores and houses, from everywhere but Jimmy Measles's open door.

The thought of burglars never enters his mind.

He parks the Buick on the sidewalk, a few feet from the steps, and sits behind the wheel. He can't imagine going into the house and seeing what is there; he can't imagine not going in. He opens the car door and steps out.

He doesn't bother to knock. He steps into the place and hears a sound upstairs, someone running a shower. He stands still, listening to the water, making himself stay. He finds a light switch, but the electricity is off.

The place smells damp.

Beyond the light switch are the drapes. Jimmy mentioned once what his wife spent for drapes, Peter can't remember the number. He pulls one a few inches open and holds it in place with a chair, and looks at the staircase. He knows that is the direction.

All the doors are closed upstairs, and he opens them as he moves toward the noise, lighting the hallway.

The door to the bathroom opens half an inch and stops. There is a hook-and-eye lock, he thinks perhaps it was put there to keep the dogs out. He pushes through. An easy push, the sound of the hook hitting the tile floor, the sudden coolness of the room. A half-empty bottle of Beefeaters gin is standing next to the tub, a few inches from Jimmy Measles's hand. Beside it is a martini glass and the atomizer.

The pill bottles are in a line across the sink, all empty. The tops have been dropped on the floor. Jimmy Measles is sitting under the shower, his head resting against the back of the tub, the cold water splashing off the swell of his stomach. He is still in his underwear, a pastel shade of blue today which sticks to him like another skin.

Along the line where his weight presses into the porcelain, his blood has settled and the color is darker.

Peter turns off the faucets and sits down on the edge of the tub, Jimmy Measles's hand almost touching him. For a moment he believes he is lying on the cold porcelain too.

He would leave the room now if there were someplace else to go.

The water drains out of the tub, out of Jimmy Measles's shorts. Peter picks up the Beefeaters and empties it.

It's a better gesture, finishing the bottle.

He thinks dying must have come up on Jimmy quietly or he would have done it himself.

Grace is waiting for him outside a Presbyterian church in Cherry Hill. She smiles as he walks through the heavy wooden doors, relieved.

"How you doing?" he says.

"I don't know yet," she says.

He understands that she cares about what has happened to Jimmy Measles—they have been calling him James Katz for the last half hour; he still can't think of him with that name—but she keeps more of herself back than she gives away, even now, to Jimmy or anyone else.

He finds nothing in that to resent or regret because she has never pretended it was some other way.

"Are you going somewhere?" she says.

The church empties. Only eleven people have come for the service, including Grace's sister and her son. Halfway through the service, the child began to cry, and the sister took him outside to wait in the car.

Nine mourners.

Peter is reminded of the club, Jimmy Measles and all his friends.

"I wouldn't mind," he says.

A familiar smell is in the air around her. It teases the edge of the things he remembers, just beyond his reach. They walk away from the church toward a Mercedes parked up the street.

He stops before they get to the car and looks at the sky—a clear, cloudless day, with the moon hanging just over the line of the church roof—and when he begins to move again he is a step behind her. He finds himself staring at the small of her back, fastened to that spot where she is in perfect balance—where all her movements come together, and cancel each other, and leave her, in that place, completely still.

They are at the car.

She opens the door, and drops her head inside. He hears her say, "You go on, I'll catch a ride." She closes the door and they walk to the Buick.

She doesn't ask where he is going, even when he enters the Garden State Parkway outside of Atlantic City and turns south. She puts her hand on his leg, as light as a glove, and leaves it there all the way south to the end of the peninsula, where New Jersey stops at the ocean.

"Cape May," she says, looking around.

He drives to the house and takes her inside, leading her by the hand through the door. The doors and windows have been closed a month. He takes her upstairs and then to the bedroom where he sleeps. She sits down on the bed.

He lifts her skirt to her waist and peels the stockings off her legs, stopping at the bottom to take off her shoes.

He kneels on the floor, feeling her watching him. He reaches behind her and finds the small of her back, and pulls her into him, the soft cushion of hair beneath her panties pushing into his mouth and nose. He holds her there until he feels her hands on his head, touching his ears, the back of his neck, asking him for something more. He moves the panties aside, tearing them, hearing her breathing now.

His hand presses into the small of her back, and he feels it there first. Even before the shaking is in his mouth, his hand senses it coming, from the distant parts of her body, and as it narrows it surfaces.

She wraps her legs around his head and shakes—a hooked fish coming to the top, to that other place, and then she breaks the surface gasping for breath, gasping in the new light.

She is lying on her stomach, her face resting against the back of her hands. A piece of her hair falls across her eyes, and she stares at him through it. "You're nothing like Michael, are you?"

He does not want to think about himself and Michael. He gets up to open the window. There is a breeze off the ocean and it fills the thin white curtains and pushes them into his face. The tide is coming in, and he can hear the sound of the water and the sound of the wind. He crosses behind the bed, out of her line of sight, and then covers her carefully with his own body, fitting himself against the cool rise of her bottom, and then puts himself inside her.

Her face is still resting against the back of her hands, and when he is fully in she closes her eyes. They lie still for half a minute, the only movement in the room is the rise and fall of their breathing, and then slowly he feels her tighten, squeezing him a long time, letting go, milking.

Her bottom moves, and she takes him slowly along the edge

of a circle inside her, no more than an inch around, and it seems to him now that she knows what he is feeling. And that thought, more than the feeling itself, finally pulls him away from Jimmy Measles lying in a spray of cold water, and fills him with an old stillness that lifts him in the direction of the surface.

Is this where you bring girls?" she says.

He shakes his head. "This is where I come to sleep."

She sits up and looks around the room, the sheet falling into her lap. The sun has set and the sky outside his window is deep and black. He senses them falling—this house, the woman, himself. The stillness returns.

"Jimmy couldn't sleep," she says, the first mention of his name since the church. "He had doctors all over the city, none of them knew about each other. They all gave him prescriptions."

"I saw the bottles," he says.

It is quiet for a moment. He notices the fine hairs at the base of her back.

"He had to have the television on," she says.

Peter stares at the wall behind her. Then at the ceiling. Everything is exactly where it was, but everything is changed. Jimmy Measles is fresh in the room.

"What did you think, when you saw him?" she says.

He shakes his head.

He feels her watching him, waiting for him. He is reminded that she asks for more than she gives.

"He was cold," he says. "I turned off the water and sat down, and the coldness just came off him. I didn't touch him but I felt it, and it made me cold too."

"He looked the same?" she says.

It takes him a moment to remember. "There wasn't a lot of

light in there," he says. "They'd cut off the electric." He takes a deep breath, trying to get it out of his head. "I've seen him looking worse."

She puts her hand on his leg again, the way she had in the car. The room seems to breathe, the curtains rise and fall.

"I'm glad it was you that found him," she says.

She moves over him then, climbs over his chest and sits on him. She pulls his penis from beneath her and lays it on his stomach in such a way that it might belong to either of them. She traces a line up the underside with her fingernail.

She raises herself off him, and then guides his hand underneath. "Just one finger," she says. "Close your eyes and put one finger inside."

He does, and she squeezes it.

She rides his finger, and he is wet to the wrist.

"Pretend," she says, and he feels the weight of his penis change on his stomach, heavier at first, and then suddenly light as it fills and lifts itself off.

And then he is inside her again, but the newness of it has washed off, and beneath it is the purpose.

He can't bring her with him this time, and when he has gone to the surface and come back, he looks at her in the half dark of the room, and sees that she is crying.

And he knows that for a little while Jimmy Measles has his wife back.

Peter returns to the gym, the first time since he washed Leonard Crawley's blood off the ring floor. It is Friday, five weeks to the day.

Nick is sitting in a chair by the window, still in his work clothes, his elbows resting on his knees, bending into an open newspaper as if he were sitting on a toilet. Harry is jumping rope. It is a few minutes past six o'clock; the place is always empty on Fridays in the summer.

Nick sees him as he clears the staircase, and drops the paper on the floor. "Peter," he says, getting up, "where you been?"

Peter looks around the room, everything familiar. The ring, the pictures on the wall, the towel lying under the bench, the hand wraps hanging from the chinning bar. It feels as if he has been gone a year.

Nick crosses the gym, smiling. "Hey, how you been? This place, it's like a fucking museum here the last couple of weeks." He puts an arm around Peter, smelling of gasoline, and pats his back.

Peter is washed in relief.

The buzzer sounds and Harry quits jumping rope. There are welts across his back and shoulders where the rope has hit him. He is soaked in sweat. "You got time to move a couple rounds?" Peter says.

Nick ties and tapes his gloves, and then twenty minutes later he unties them.

Peter sits on the bench, trying to even his breathing. He closes his eyes and rests his head against the wall. Harry thanks him for the work and crosses the room to hit the heavy bag. Nick tugs at the gloves. "You going to live?" he says.

The question terrifies him.

He smiles and rolls his head against the wall. "It was up to me," he says, "no."

The gloves come off, and his hands feel cool and light, and he stands up and walks into the shower.

He stays under the water a long time, letting it run into his mouth. When he comes out Harry is still hitting the bags.

He sits down with Nick and they watch his son work. "He looks like he just got up from a nap," Peter says. The punches have a heavy sound, interrupted now and then by a sharp crack—an air pocket created between the glove and the leather bag.

"That was bad news about Jimmy Measles," Nick says after a while.

Peter checks his side, where some of the skin has scraped off against the ropes. He takes a deep breath to see if anything hurts. "He got into something," he says, "he couldn't get out."

Nick thinks of him up here, talking to four people at once over by the lockers. "He always seemed like he could get out of anything," he says.

Peter wipes fresh sweat off his head.

"I liked havin' him around," Nick says later. "He was a character."

Peter says, "His only trouble, he was ashamed of himself. I think about it now, it seems like everything he did was to hide what he was."

"That guy could make you laugh," Nick says.

"Yeah, he could."

Peter tried to remember when Jimmy Measles had made him laugh.

"Where you been?" Nick says, a different question than what he asked before, when he came in.

Peter shakes his head. "You know, Michael brought the guy up here and got you upset."

Nick nods at that. "Something's different, you don't know how to act." He looks at Peter and smiles. "Maybe three times in your life something new happens and you know the right thing to do. The rest of the time . . ." He shrugs.

Peter falls quiet, looks around the gym.

"Anyway," Nick says, "nobody got hurt. It wasn't anything but his jaw was broke, right?"

Peter nods. "Still wired," he says. "I think maybe he likes it, makes him look scary."

"He ain't eating, he must of lost some of them muscles by now."

Peter thinks about it, picturing Leonard Crawley. "No," he says, "everything he likes, he takes it through the nose anyway."

Nick is picturing Leonard Crawley too, and he begins to smile. "What it reminded me of, you know at the start of a fight you look across the ring, and you're always thinkin' there's gotta be some mistake? That this guy ain't the same weight, you ain't sure he can even talk? The guy with Michael was what you always imagined was across the ring, and it turns out he can't fight anyway. So what's the harm in that?"

"They come up here like everything was theirs."

Nick shrugs, looks around the room. "They didn't take nothing out but what they brought in."

The limo is parked outside Peter's apartment when he gets back from the gym. The engine is running and a shallow pool of water collects underneath it, and spills over into little streams that run from there to the curb, condensation from the air conditioner.

Peter gets out of his Buick, exhausted and calm. The bag with his cup and his shoes and his wet clothes hangs from his hand, dead weight. He stares at the limo and waits.

The dark back window hums and stops, the sun picking up the blues in the tint. Above it, one third of his cousin's face stares out.

"You're gettin' harder to find all the time," Michael says.

Peter walks to the car; the door opens. "Lemme throw this shit in the trunk, we don't smell it," he says.

"The trunk's full."

Michael slides across the back seat, making room, and Peter takes the spot where he had been.

Leonard is behind the steering wheel, a man Peter has never seen before is sitting next to him. Another weight lifter.

Peter shuts the door and the limo pulls into the street. They drive out of town on Broad Street, past the stadiums and get on I-95.

"You popped the lawyer," Peter says. It is quiet a moment. "They'll be coming for us now."

Michael smiles. "Maybe not," he says.

Peter looks at him, waiting.

"They still want to do business," Michael says. "We still got something they want."

Peter doesn't say a word.

"He was gettin' infected," Michael says. "He goes delirious at night, making so much noise I can't sleep in my own house, what am I supposed to do?"

Peter leans back into the cushioned seat and positions his legs, one at a time, on the seat in front of him, beginning to feel stiff. He tries not to picture the man in the trunk, and in the trying he sees him, lying on the cot in the house. The man's eyes are closed, and then, when Peter speaks to him, he looks up. He says, *"Are you the one that kills me?"*

"There's no reason we have to take care of this ourselves," Peter says to Michael.

Michael says, "The reason is, I want to make sure it's done right. I know the place to do this."

"What place?"

"A place Phil showed me."

And it is quiet again before Michael says, "What we're saying, if it comes up, the guy was fine when he left the house."

"If it comes up," Peter says.

It is quiet in the car.

"You did it in the house?"

Michael shrugs. "Him screaming like that, I couldn't see moving him someplace else. . . ."

The car passes the airport and begins to accelerate. Peter watches the man sitting next to Leonard, wondering if he was swinging one of the bats too.

"You haven't heard from his people?" Peter says.

"There's some guys come around a few places, asking. That's all."

The limo brakes, coming up behind a van, and Leonard straightens his whole body against the horn. The van moves to the shoulder of the road, and the limo goes past. The pitch of the tires climbs an octave and levels.

"Tell him to slow down," Peter says.

Leonard looks in the rearview mirror; Michael shrugs. Leonard changes the angle of the mirror to glance at Peter, then puts it back. The new man watches him, memorizing everything he does.

Michael says, "See, there was a problem with what you said, for us to explain to them how it happened."

Peter waits for Michael to tell him the problem.

"Time," he says. "The longer we waited, the worse it looked. The afternoon you come over, it was already a day, a day and a half. If I turn him over then, it looks like I decided to do one thing and got scared, tried to do something else. It makes us look weak."

Peter sits up and looks over Leonard's shoulder at the speedometer. Eighty-five.

"He gets a body in back, he thinks he's an ambulance," Peter says.

Michael looks into the front seat and says, "Lenny," and the car begins to slow. They ride for a while in silence, into Delaware, the sun low and wide in the west.

"You know," Michael says, a long time later, "we got a situation here, Pally, and it don't feel like you want your part of it."

Peter doesn't answer.

"Pally?"

Slowly, Peter nods. "That's it," he says, "I don't want my part."

And it is quiet again. There is a glow in the sky where the sun has gone down. The state could be on fire. Without wanting to, he thinks again of the man in the trunk, lying in the dark with his broken legs, shaking as if he were cold as the tires vibrate against the road.

Michael directs them off the freeway and then down a dirt road to a spot behind some trees. "Right here," he says, and Leonard stops the car.

Peter steps out and looks around. There is enough moonlight to cast shadows. Leonard opens the trunk and finds a shovel, and hands it to the man who has been riding with him in the front seat.

The new man digs as if this were a job he wanted to keep. Dirt flies in front of him, over his shoulder, left and right. Leonard backs out of range, until he is standing at the car with Michael and Peter. He crosses his arms over his chest and watches. Once in a while he disappears into the trees and returns with a runny nose.

It is a quiet place. The kid grunts, Leonard sniffs, somewhere a long ways off there is a noise that might be a fire alarm. Except for that, they could all be in the ground themselves.

The quiet grows and the sound of the sniffing grates on Michael's nerves. He looks at Leonard and says, "How many shovels you brought?"

"Two or three, I threw some in there."

Michael stares at him until he understands, and goes back to the trunk and gets a shovel for himself, jerking it from the trunk when it catches on something inside. A little piece of the plastic they used to wrap the man inside comes out with it.

Leonard takes off his shirt and lays it carefully across the hood of the car before he steps into the shallow hole. The kid takes off his shirt too; chains dangle in the moonlight.

Peter watches a little longer and then climbs back in the car and closes his eyes. Time passes, and he hears Leonard's voice. "Michael, how deep you want this fuckin' hole anyway?"

"Deep enough, the next time you break some guy's legs in my house, you know you fucked up without me sayin' it."

Later, he hears Leonard again. "Michael, you mind I ask you a personal question . . . Michael?"

"What?"

"What I want to ask you, I think maybe you used this hole before. All of a sudden, we're diggin' up bones and shit like that."

Peter sits up in the back seat of the car. Leonard and the kid are standing chest-high in their hole, Michael is leaning over them, getting edgy now. "Get out of there," he says, "that's deep enough."

Peter stares at his cousin, suspended for a moment in the thought that his own father could be in the ground here too.

259

The men climb out, shaking the dirt out of their pants, and go back to the trunk. There are bumping noises behind Peter's seat. The car drops and lifts, and then he sees them carrying the lawyer, encased in a clear plastic mattress cover, to the hole. The new man walks backwards, and seems to have the heavy end.

They walk in short, uneven steps; the mattress cover sags, the man inside sways as if he were in a hammock.

Michael steps aside, giving them room. The new man stops, his arms shaking under the weight, waiting for some signal to let go. Leonard drops his end without ceremony, pulling the new man off balance.

There is no noise at all as the body hits bottom.

The new man hangs at the edge of the grave, motionless in that long second between falling and finding his balance—a tight-rope walker—and then, recovering himself, he is suddenly staring into the hole.

Leonard goes back to the trunk for the lime. The new man is still looking into the hole when he comes back carrying the sack. He sets it down heavily and tears off the top. Then, as he lifts it shoulder-high to pour, Peter hears the new man's voice, so timid it barely carries to the car, even in the quiet.

"He's in there crooked."

They are back on the interstate to Philadelphia when he thinks of the bones. In the seat next to him, Michael has made himself a drink.

"I think we're gonna be all right," Michael says. "What do you think?"

He looks at Peter, waiting.

"What do you think?" he says.

"I'm out of it," Peter says.

Two weeks pass, and in that time Peter answers his phone only once.

The Italians again.

"You understand something's got to happen now, right?" the man says.

Peter finds himself nodding.

"You still got time," he says, "you could save yourself. Your brother and the rest of them—today they're here, tomorrow they're not. It's settled, except you got a chance to be here when they're gone. We're going to need somebody, you understand? We can't just walk in and announce the unions are under new management."

It is quiet a moment.

"Wait, he ain't your brother," the man says, "he's your cousin. Makes it that much easier, right?"

Peter hangs up.

After the call, he spends every night at the house in Cape May, and comes into the city only in the afternoon to go to the gym. He fights as many rounds as Harry and Nick will give him.

He does not see or talk to Michael.

He barely talks to Nick. Even after they have boxed, he finds himself unable to speak more than a few sentences at once. The relief that comes with exhaustion is gone.

On the way back to Cape May, he calls Grace at her sister's house from a pay phone outside a bar on Admiral Wilson. One night he says to her, "I can't make up my mind, you like having me around or not."

She doesn't answer.

Another night she asks him to masturbate while they talk.

"Not in a phone booth," he says.

But he does.

The next time he calls, her sister picks up the phone. "She isn't home at the present time," she says. "She's got a date or something. May I take a message?"

He goes back to the house in Cape May and thinks of other women. Women who have said they loved him and would search his face after he had fucked them for things that were familiar or simple—as if once they saw the stains, they could clean them.

In the end, they couldn't imagine his stains, and there was nothing they could give him.

His business is with Grace.

Michael appears again in the gym at six o'clock on a Monday afternoon. Peter has not seen him since the night they buried the lawyer.

He makes no noise coming into the room. Leonard Crawley is with him, and Monk, and a black man named Eddie Bone, who was once a promising fighter.

Peter remembers Eddie Bone, a true Philadelphia middleweight. He terrified the whole division, and then, before fighting could make him famous or rich, he killed his girlfriend and her mother and went away to Graterford.

Eddie Bone looks around the small gym now and smiles.

Peter thinks, *It's always the ones who smile at the wrong time.*

Nick looks up from his chair. He is sitting in bare feet and long pants, reading the newspaper. His son is shadowboxing in the ring.

Michael crosses the wooden floor, leaving the others at the stairway. "Nick," he says, "I got a guy here used to fight a little, I was thinking maybe Harry could work with him a couple of rounds, see if he's got anything left."

Nick looks at Michael a moment, then at Eddie Bone. He folds the paper and puts it on the floor next to a cup of coffee. "We ain't going to train today," he says.

Michael smiles. "Nothing serious," he says, "just a couple rounds."

On the other side of the gym, Eddie Bone pulls his shirt over his head. A thick, raised scar runs on a diagonal from his shoulder down his chest and stomach. Peter stares at it, imagining the opening itself, the feeling of being opened. For a moment, the scar seems translucent.

Eddie Bone steps out of his pants, smiling. The timer goes off and Harry ducks between the ropes and out of the ring. "Harry," Michael says, "how you doin'?"

Harry doesn't say a word.

"I was askin' your father here could you give my man Tyrone a couple of rounds."

Harry looks at his father, neither of them speaks. Leonard Crawley has crossed the floor now, and is standing over Nick. An odor comes off his skin and he is breathing through his mouth.

On the other side of the ring Eddie Bone laces his shoes. Nick turns once to look at Peter, and there is almost a happiness in the look that it takes Peter a moment to understand.

He sits where he is, pressed from both sides.

Nick stands up, smiling an unnatural smile. "Lookit," he says, nodding toward Eddie Bone, "we know who that is."

Leonard Crawley cocks his head to put his face near Nick's. Michael smiles too.

Peter hears Nick talking again.

"You want to come in here and work out," he says, "bring whoever you want. But that guy there"—he nods across the room—"he ain't here to work out."

Michael turns and looks at Eddie Bone. Eddie is tying one of his hand wraps with his teeth, and smiles without letting go of the ribbon of cloth.

"Harry ain't ready yet for somebody can fight?" Michael says.

Nick puts a cigarette in his mouth and lights it. His hands are slow and steady. "What I'm sayin', this ain't the place for somebody like that."

"It's a gym, right? He's a fighter."

"It's my gym," Nick says. "I built it myself, from my own idea, and bringing guys like that around . . ."—he points at Eddie Bone, then at Leonard—"and guys like this, wanting to see them hurt somebody, that ain't what I built it for."

Leonard Crawley moves half a step closer to Nick, his head still cocked.

Harry stands to one side, knowing something is happening, waiting to see where it will go.

Monk leans against the wall, his arms crossed and his head down, embarrassed.

Michael shrugs, as if it's over. "You don't want Harry to fight, he don't have to fight," he says.

Nick nods, holding the cigarette between his teeth, ignoring Leonard Crawley.

Michael looks at the ceiling and the walls. "I just thought maybe you'd want to do me a favor."

There is something in the way he surveys the room . . .

"I'll do you a favor," Nick says.

Michael turns, surprised. He begins to smile, and in that moment Nick's open hand crosses the space between them. The slap turns Michael's head halfway around, and he stumbles backwards, his heels catching on the base of the ring, and he falls, sitting down hard just outside the ropes. His cheeks bounce as he lands, one of them already carrying the print of Nick's hand.

The slap hangs in the air, numbing the room, and what follows is dreamlike and slow. Leonard reaching for Nick's throat, Harry suddenly between his arms, his right hand coming in overhead, finding the edge of Leonard's jaw.

Leonard drops to the floor as if someone had cut all the strings. Michael's hand covers the side of his face, tears collect in his eyes.

And everyone in the room—even Eddie Bone—knows that Nick is dead.

Nick and Michael stare at one another in a curious way, each of them realizing what has happened. Peter sits in the window, afraid to move. Afraid to leave this moment, as if by holding on he is holding back everything to follow.

Michael gets to his feet, careful to maintain a distance between himself and Nick; he heads for the stairs. Eddie Bone waits for him, holding his pants and his shoes in his hand. Monk pulls Leonard up off the floor and they follow Michael out.

Peter sits still, and what seems like a long time later he hears his cousin from the bottom of the stairs. "Peter, you comin'?"

Nick and his son watch him push himself up. Peter thinks of their living room, the smell of food. Nick's wife.

"You comin' with us or not?" his cousin says.

Peter walks between Nick and his son, close enough to touch either one of them.

A moment is lost, and then the next; it comes to him it is all lost. He is heading down the stairs.

Drifting, he thinks of the living room again; he looks back up at the gym.

It occurs to him that Nick has built the things in his life, he didn't just show up and try to take them from someone else.

They are closed into a small room in the basement of a row house near Veteran's Stadium.

Leonard Crawley is lying openmouthed on a cot, lost in the drug he is rubbing onto his gums. He holds his jaw in place with one hand and feeds himself the white powder with the other, his finger going from his mouth to the open plastic bag on his chest, back and forth, waiting for Michael to take him to the hospital.

The house belongs to an old roofer who once did jobs for Michael's father. He is upstairs with his cat, listening to the radio. He didn't ask what they wanted in his basement, he simply saw who it was, opened the door and turned on the lights.

Peter is sitting across a card table from his cousin. It is cool in the cellar, and the water condenses on the pipes over their heads and drips on the cement floor. The light from the street swings in the spiderwebs covering the windows.

Michael's face is bloodless. The slap has faded off his cheek, leaving him with only a swollen lip. He dabs at the lip with the back of his hand.

They have been in the basement over an hour, Peter has not spoken. There is no way to frame the argument against this; there is no argument.

"We do them in the morning," Michael says, testing the way it sounds.

Peter looks at him, waiting. He has changed his mind—morning to night—half a dozen times. Both times leave something unsatisfied.

Michael puts his hands behind his neck and stares at the sweating pipes, reconsidering the timing. "What I wish," he says, "there was a perfect moment, you know? When what's gonna happen is right there with what already happened, where Nick sees it all at once, the cause and the result. . . ."

He thinks, then shakes his head and looks at Peter. "Tell me how to do it," he says.

Peter doesn't say anything.

"What I wish," Michael says, "we could do them more than once." He sits looking at Peter. Peter trembles, and something in that satisfies Michael, gives him back what is his. He looks at the pipes.

"We park a car in front of his garage door in the morning," he says, trying it out. "And when they stop, the kid gets out to open the door, we do him bang, on the sidewalk, in front of the old man where he can see it. I want to make sure he sees it, before we do him."

He looks down from the ceiling again, his fingers still laced behind his neck. Peter sits still. Nothing has changed, and that satisfies Michael, and gives him back what is his too.

There is a noise on the cot, Leonard Crawley sneezes, then breathes deeply through his nose. He moans softly, "Fuck me," and puts his finger back into the envelope.

"In the morning," Michael says to Peter. "You and Monk do it in the morning. I don't care who does who, but do the kid first."

It is quiet a moment and then Michael suddenly pushes himself up, the table unsteady under his weight, and climbs the wooden stairs into the old man's kitchen. A moment later Peter follows him up.

The old man is sitting in a straight-back chair, holding the cat in his lap, looking out the window.

"What do you got for me, Frank?" Michael says.

"What you need?" the old man says.

"Something sawed," he says. "Pump, double-barrel, it don't make no difference."

The old man shakes his head. "I ain't got nothing like that," he says.

Michael sits down and stares at the old man; the old man stares out the window.

"I ain't got time for this," Michael says.

The old man shrugs. "You got other places you can go."

"I need them right now."

"You need everything since you were ten years old right now," the old man says. "Get yourself a cat, Michael. They teach you it don't get you nowhere to be in such a hurry."

His hand strokes the animal's head. An old hand with sunken, spotted skin. Peter sees the bones all the way to the wrist.

"Let's see what you got," Michael says.

The old man looks out the window.

Michael closes his eyes, then notices Peter standing at the door-way. He winks. "I got to go upstairs and tear the place apart?" he says. "That's what I'm gonna do, Frank, you don't put the fuckin' cat down and show me what I want."

The old man turns in his chair to look at Michael, and then at Peter, and then, without another word, he puts the cat on the floor and stands up.

Michael follows him upstairs into a small bedroom and Peter follows Michael. There are pictures all over the walls—ancient, formal portraits of his family on the steps of a large white house. His father and mother, six children arranged by height in front of them. Two girls, four boys. Peter wonders which one of the children is the old man.

The old man opens the closet door and pulls the string cord to the light. The closet is half full of women's clothing. Peter tries to remember when the old man's wife died. He thinks it must be fifteen years.

The shotguns are on the floor farther back, and Michael chooses two of them, both double-barreled, both sawed at eighteen inches. Oiled and cleaned. He breaks them open and closes them.

The old man finds a box of shells and turns off the light. "How much I owe you?" Michael says.

The cat appears in the doorway, then wraps itself around the old man's trousers. He bends slowly at the waist and picks it up, and then sits on the edge of the bed and strokes its head.

"Seven hundred," he says.

Michael goes back through the kitchen to the basement stairs, holding a shotgun in each hand. Peter follows him.

They are exactly where he left them, Leonard on the cot, Monk standing over by the wall. Peter sits down at the table.

Michael sets the guns in front of him. "You ain't going to try to talk me out of this?" he says.

Peter doesn't answer. He looks at the shotguns, accepting them as part of what has happened, and what will happen next.

Michael drops the box of shells on the table between the shotguns. Peter stares at them; he does not move.

"Take what you need," he says.

Peter blinks, looking slow and tired, and then his hand reaches across the table and picks up one of the open weapons. He looks at the gun, he looks at his cousin. Michael sees there is no argument in him. He sees everything is settled.

"Remember," he says, "the kid first, then the old man. He's got to see it happen."

Monk picks up the other shotgun and drops half a dozen shells into his coat pocket. He pushes the box across the table to Peter, who takes only two. Tired and slow.

Peter puts the shells into the chambers and closes the breech.

"There ain't nothing to talk about, right?" Michael says. He watches Monk shake his head; his cousin is looking at the gun in his hands. Michael smiles.

"I was just thinkin'," he says, "it might be best you did the old man yourself, Pally. Keep it in the family. . . ."

And he watches his cousin slowly nod, as if he had expected that, and then slowly lift his eyes.

And then, just as slowly, he lifts the shotgun until its barrels are eyes too.

One of them blinks, and it is the last thing Michael Flood sees in his life.

He feels his arm jump, and Michael is blown backwards toward the stairway. Peter stares at the shotgun, deaf or numb from the noise, he doesn't know which, trying to understand what has happened.

Not the act itself, but the things it changes.

Leonard Crawley is scrambling up out of the cot, Monk reaches into his pocket, looking confused, the broken shotgun awkward in his hands.

Peter watches it happen from a long ways off, watches himself stand up, knocking over the chair, and put the mouth of the gun in the middle of Leonard's throat. His arm jumps again, and the noise fills the room, and overfills it, and he is insulated in silence. A certain feeling settles, and it seems to him it is snowing.

Monk closes the breech of the gun in his hands and brings it up even with Peter's chest. He stops, not knowing what to do. He looks from the stairway to the cot. He whispers, "The fuck did you do?"

The two men stare at each other, and small noises return to the room, and the place fills with the smell of cordite.

269

"Peter," he says again, "the fuck did you do?"

When they walk upstairs, the old man is back in his chair by the window, holding his cat. "Something's happened," Peter says.

The old man nods and stares out the window. He does not turn to the voice. Peter sees he is waiting for something, and understands what it is. He touches the old man's shoulder, to let him know this isn't his time, and the old man jumps at the touch.

"Everything's over," Peter says. "I ain't going to hurt you."

The old man nods and stares out the window, waiting to be shot.

She comes out of her sister's house carrying a package. The box is long and narrow, wrapped in black paper. A single pink ribbon is wound once around the top.

She puts it between them on the seat of the Buick as he starts the car. "Where have you been?" she says.

He backs out of the driveway. His cousin is dead less than an hour; he wonders if the old man has called the police. The smell of the basement is all over him. She leans across the seat, across the package, and touches his neck with her lips.

"I brought you something," she says, so close to his ear he can feel her breath. He thinks of the concussive noise as the gun jumped. Her hand runs the length of his thigh and then is gone.

She straightens to her own side of the seat and picks up the black package.

"What is it?" he says.

She shakes her head. "Wait," she says. He turns onto Route 70 and heads for the expressway. She moves in her seat, hiking her skirt up her thighs. He reaches to hold her hand, to begin to find a way to tell her what has happened, but she stops him.

"You've got to wait for everything," she says.

And he sees that is true, and he waits for her to see something has happened.

She picks up the present and taps it lightly against her lips, and leaves it there a moment to consider him. Her lip swells and creases against the edge and he sees the pink inside the crease.

She lays the package across his lap. "You have to be undressed when you open it," she says.

He looks at the package, the tiny wet spot where it touched her mouth. "That's the only way," she says, "I can tell if you like it or not."

The next time he looks across the seat, she is taking off her underwear. They are on the Atlantic City Expressway. She slides her panties off, her hands between the fabric and her legs all the way to her shoes. She drapes them across the seat back, near his shoulder.

Something happened with my cousin," he says.

"I don't want to hear anything about your cousin."

They have turned south on the Garden State Parkway, headed toward Cape May. The heel of her hand moves up and down his leg, dragging her fingernails an inch or two behind. He looks out the window; a heron rises out of the tall grass.

"You ought to get away from him," she says.

He parks the car on the street in front of the house. He sits quietly a moment, staring at the place, trying to tell her. The words aren't there; the thought itself is blurred. He wants something that doesn't have a name.

She puts her lips against his ear and kisses him. "Let's go open your present," she says.

He steps out of the car; his ear is wet and feels cold in the breeze from the ocean.

He opens the front door with a key that is as old as the house. The familiar, dark living room waits on the other side, its air cool and ancient. He steps into it and feels her behind him, close enough to touch.

"Come on," she says.

He follows her up the stairs and into the bedroom. He opens the windows and smells the ocean. When he turns back into the room, she puts the present in his hand. The box is heavier than it felt in his lap, the wrapping paper is slick under his fingers.

She steps closer and he feels her hand on his zipper. It will not open for her at first, and she holds the top to pull it down. Her hand comes inside, sliding under the elastic of his shorts until she finds his penis. It is soft in her hand, and she smiles.

"Stay just like this," she says. "Take off your clothes but think of something, don't let it get hard."

He sits on the bed, still holding the gift. He wonders if there are television cameras outside the old man's house, waiting to take pictures of Michael as he is brought out in a bag.

He leans forward and unties his shoes. She watches him, he watches himself. He takes off his shirt and then his socks. He thinks of the feel of the sheets, the drop of the bed. He is tired.

She watches him take off his pants. The present sits beside him on the bedspread, and he is naked.

"I didn't think you could do it," she says, looking at his penis.

He is still lost in what has happened. He sees this room and he sees the other room, with Michael lying on the floor.

Her hands go to the waist of her skirt, and a moment later it drops around her shoes. She stands still, the line of her blouse falling even with her pubic hair; the curtain rises and falls, a shadow as soft as stockings wraps her legs, again and again.

He looks at the box, then back at Grace. The room and everything in it is balanced so carefully he is afraid to move.

"Michael's dead," he says. He cannot hold still forever. "I did Michael."

Something is put into motion then that he cannot stop. She stands in the middle of the room, in the middle of her skirt. And then she bends at the waist. Her bottom shines, and when she stands up again she brings the skirt with her. She turns, checking herself in the mirror. There is a certain familiarity to being in the bedroom when she looks at herself in the mirror, but that is gone even before she is.

She picks her purse off the chair and steps toward the door.

"The car keys are downstairs," he says. "You can leave it at your sister's."

He hears her on the stairs, then opening the front door. He stands up and walks to the window and watches her get into his car. He sits down in the chair, the wood is cold against his skin, and she drives to the end of the street and then turns left, headed for Cherry Hill.

Her present lies in black paper, unopened on the bed.

He is still sitting in the chair when the car with Pennsylvania plates stops across the street. An hour has passed, perhaps more. He watches the car a moment—three men inside it, talking—and then goes back to the bed and begins to dress.

He waits until he hears them knock downstairs, and then opens the window that faces east to the water and fits himself into the frame.

They knock once, wait a moment, and then come in. He hears them in the kitchen and the closets downstairs, opening doors, and then they are on the stairway.

A breeze comes in off the salt water, a smell as old as the world. He thinks of Nick, wondering what he will make of this. He remembers something he said, *gratitude* . . .

The door opens and the Italians walk into the room, holding their guns. The last one closes the door behind him, and then looks at Peter; a glint of recognition. As if he has caught him at something, as if they know each other's thoughts.

There is a white dog in that look and it freezes his heart.

He sees the dog, and then the child, bundled in her snow suit against the cold, floating toward him through the air. The ground shudders as she lands.

Distinctly shudders.

And then he is floating too, breathless, the familiar stillness of falling fills his chest in an unfamiliar way, and he is watching himself from an unfamiliar place.

And in the moment he hits the ground in the back yard, he sees himself in perfect focus; he sees that he is forgiven.

March 22, 1991
Useless Bay

About the Author

PETE DEXTER lives on Puget Sound with his wife and daughter, a dog, two cats and a bird called Parrot Trout.